FORT COVENANT

Chronicles of a Legionary Officer:
Book One: **Stiger's Tigers**
Book Two: **The Tiger**
Book Three: **The Tiger's Fate**
Book Four: **The Tiger's Time** (Coming 2018)

Tales of the Seventh:
Part One: **Stiger**
Part Two: **Fort Covenant**
Part Three: **Eli** (Coming 2019)

The Karus Saga:
Book One: **Lost Legio IX**
Book Two: **To Be Named** (Coming 2018)

FORT COVENANT

Tales of the Seventh: Part Two

MARC ALAN EDELHEIT

This book is a work of fiction. Names, characters, places, and incidents are either the product of the author's imagination or are used fictitiously. Any resemblance to actual persons, living or dead, or to actual events or locales is entirely coincidental.

Fort Covenant: Tales of the Seventh Part Two

First Edition

I wish to thank my agent, Andrea Hurst, for her invaluable support and assistance. I would also like to thank my beta readers, who suffered through several early drafts. My betas: Barrett McKinney, Jon Cockes, Norman Stiteler, Nicolas Weiss, Stephan Kobert, Matthew Ashley, Melinda Vallem, Jon Quast, Donavan Laskey, Paul Klebaur, Russ Wert, James Doak, David Cheever, Bruce Heaven, Erin Penny, Jonas Ortega Rodriguez, April Faas, Rodney Gigone, Brandon Purcell, Steve Sibert, Tim Adams, and Brett Smith. I would also like to take a moment to thank my loving wife who sacrificed many an evening and weekends to allow me to work on my writing.

Editing Assistance by Hannah Streetman, Audrey Mackaman

Cover Art by Piero Mng (Gianpiero Mangialardi)

Cover Formatting by Telemachus Press

Agented by Andrea Hurst & Associates

http://maenovels.com/

*To my loyal and amazing fans who have made
my writing so successful.
From the bottom of my heart, thank you!*

Author's note:

This story takes place after *Stiger, Tales of the Seventh Part One*. You may wish to pick up that tale first. It is available on Amazon Kindle and in Print.

Fort Covenant began as an experiment... a way to give fans more Stiger while they waited for *The Tiger's Time* as I worked on another project. Released one chapter at a time for free on my website under the title of *The Interludes*, it was meant only to be a novella, but quickly grew into a full-blown novel. It was an instant hit, with fans messaging me on Facebook and emailing questions and thoughts on what would happen next. (Please note: This final version is slightly different than the original and more polished.)

Writing *Fort Covenant* has been a labor of love and a joy. You may wish to sign up to my newsletter to get the latest updates, especially considering that I expect to do this again and release a new book one chapter at a time for free on my website.

http://maenovels.com/

Reviews keep me motivated and also help to drive sales. I make a point to read each and every one, so please continue to post them.

I hope you enjoy *Fort Covenant* and would like to offer a sincere thank you for your purchase and support.

Best regards,

Marc Alan Edelheit, author and your tour guide to the worlds of Tannis and Istros

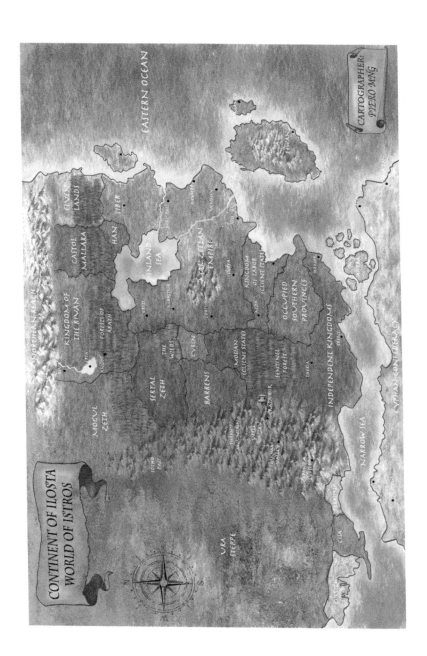

CHAPTER ONE

"What do you think?" Stiger glanced over to Sergeant Tiro.

The two men were crouched down behind a small stone wall. Stiger laid a hand on the moss-covered stone. Beyond the wall was a wide-open field, which had once been pastureland. A handful of rotten posts were all that was still visible of the fencing that had hemmed in the field of waist-high grass and weeds. The saplings scattered across the field were a sure sign that the forest to their backs desired nothing more than to reclaim the land it had lost.

Tiro scratched his jaw, squinting his eyes as he surveyed the field. "We could just go around."

"We could." Stiger turned back to the field. The tree line on the opposite side was perhaps a mile away. "That would just eat up time, which, I might add, we likely don't have."

"True," the sergeant said and took a deep breath. "I really don't feel like crossing out in the open like that, even if it does save us an hour or two. My recommendation would be to stick to the trees and work our way 'round, careful-like. Safer, I think."

"Still nervous about cavalry?" Stiger asked.

"Do you really expect me to answer that?" The sergeant glanced behind him into the trees. The rest of Seventh

1

Company waited several yards back, mostly concealed by the undergrowth, which grew thick on the border of the field.

Stiger followed the sergeant's gaze. The men, all eighty-two of them, had taken a knee to avoid inadvertently being spotted. After the hard pace and exertions of the last few hours, they were taking advantage of the unexpected halt. Corporal Varus was checking on each man, likely making sure they had not dipped into their haversacks for the last of their precooked rations.

Looking over the men, Stiger felt a sudden fondness for them. They were his men, and he was their lieutenant and commanding officer. After the recent action against the Rivan, the Seventh had suffered terribly. They were a shadow of their former strength, less than the equivalent of a light company.

Stiger turned back to the grizzled old sergeant and gave him a wry grin. "I'm still nervous, too."

"Then let's go 'round and be safe about it." Tiro gestured off to their left, swinging his arm about to demonstrate the movement around the field. "Those tracks we crossed on that trail a couple of hours back tell me enemy cavalry is active in this area."

Stiger rubbed his jaw as he considered his options. Sweat freely ran down his forehead. The heat of the unusually late summer day was broiling them all, even in the shade of the trees. Stiger couldn't wait until the heat passed over to cold weather, but then he was sure he would long for the warmth of summer. He let out a long, slow breath.

"We go around."

"Excellent decision, sir," Tiro said cheerfully. "I whole-heartedly approve."

"Right, let's get back to the men."

They worked their way back through the brush and deeper into the trees, careful to keep low. A few weary heads came up with knowing looks. The respite, however brief, was about to come to an end.

Stiger caught the eye of Corporal Varus and gestured the man over. Varus was the last surviving corporal in the Seventh. With only eighty-two men remaining to his command, Stiger had not thought to promote another.

Stiger glanced around at his men. On direct orders from the general, he had led his company southeast into the wilderness. They were headed to an old backwater garrison in the Cora'Tol Valley far east of the main routes north that led deep into Rivan territory. Stiger rubbed his eyes. It was supposed to have been a quick and easy march out and back, taking two weeks at most.

"What's the word, sir?" Varus asked. The corporal carried his helmet under an arm. He mopped his brow with a small, dirty wool rag, which he likely used to clean his kit. Varus's shield rested against a tree a couple of feet away, along with Stiger's, both still nestled comfortably in their canvas covers like the rest of the company's.

"We," Stiger said, "are going to skirt around the field and stick to the trees."

"No more encounters with cavalry," Tiro said firmly.

"Amen to that," Varus said.

Stiger pointed in the direction they would be going. "Send one of our scouts forward. I want him to have a look ahead." He glanced quickly around again at his tired men. "We will give him a five-minute head start."

"Yes, sir." Varus stepped away, heading in the direction of Legionary Milos Bren, one of the company's best scouts. Bren was sitting and speaking with several of the men next to the trunk of a large tree to Stiger's left. Bren had been a poacher before being caught and sentenced to the legions. A few moments later, Varus was back and the scout was clambering to his feet, gathering his kit.

"Let's get the men up," Stiger said. "Tiro, take the roll. Kindly make sure we are not missing anyone."

"Yes, sir."

Tiro and Varus began moving amongst the men, quietly passing out orders as Bren set off, disappearing into the trees.

The men fell in, forming two loose lines. Tiro began taking roll, walking down the marching column and checking off names from a tattered pad with a charcoal pencil. Stiger waited patiently as the count was taken.

Tiro returned to Stiger's side.

"All present and accounted for, Lieutenant."

"Thank you, Sergeant."

Tiro looked off into the woods, in the direction they had just come. He shifted his stance, and Stiger suspected the old veteran's thoughts were unsettled.

"What?" Stiger asked.

"Do you think they are still following us?" Tiro asked as the company formed up for march.

Stiger nodded.

"I think so too," Tiro said. "Let's just hope we can make it to Cora'Tol before they catch up to us."

"If they do," Stiger said with a glance back into the woods, "we will fight."

"Might I make another recommendation, sir?"

Stiger nodded for the sergeant to continue.

"Next time..." A hint of a smile appeared on Tiro's face. "It might not be a bad idea to scout the surrounding area before we decide to take out an isolated file of Rivan infantry, even if they are distracted ransacking a farm."

Though Tiro had said it as a jest, Stiger sensed a reproving look in the man's eyes. It had come as quite a surprise to discover an entire enemy company had been hiding nearby. The Seventh had been lucky to escape, but the cost had been a spirited pursuit over many miles. Stiger had hoped to give the enemy the slip, but so far he had been unable to do so. Had they not been outnumbered, Stiger would have turned and offered battle.

"Next time," Stiger said, "how about giving such sage advice in advance?"

"Trust me," Tiro said, "I will endeavor to do so, sir."

"All set, sir," Varus said, approaching.

Stiger looked over his men as he picked up his own shield and marching yoke. Settling the yoke and shield comfortably in one arm, he waved a hand forward, and the Seventh started moving, armor chinking. Stiger almost winced. They made one heck of a racket, though he recognized it was not as loud as his imagination made it. Sound carried poorly in the forest. He just hoped none of the enemy were near enough to hear.

The trees they marched under were tall hardwoods. They had an ancient feel, and every so often Stiger found himself glancing upward. So high up was the thick canopy of green that the undergrowth through which the company marched was nearly nonexistent. The Seventh moved at a good pace, treading over soft beds of moss and last year's fall leaves, hobnailed sandals crunching with every step. Despite the heat, the smell of dampness and decay was sharp.

Closer to the field, just a few yards away, the underbrush thickened considerably. Stiger reckoned that they were well-screened from view as they skirted around the edge of the field. Periodically he moved toward the brush line and surveyed the sunlit field. There had been no sign of the enemy.

As Stiger marched with the men, he shifted his yoke back over to his shield arm and reached up to touch the puckered scar on his cheek. Though it had mostly healed, the skin was still fresh and tender. Stiger found it an effort to refrain from scratching. The surgeon warned him if he gave in, the subsequent scratching could reopen the wound. Infection might set in.

The traitorous Sergeant Geta had given him that little memento, just moments before Stiger had killed him. In a way, the wound that marred his features was a parting gift, a reminder to be ever watchful.

Stiger pulled his hand away from his face and shifted his yoke again. He did this more to keep his hands busy than anything else. He glanced around. Everything was in order.

Stiger had taken to marching in the middle of the column. Tiro was at the head, Varus at the rear to make sure no one straggled and got left behind.

The company made it almost all the way around the field when word was passed back for Stiger to come forward. The column ahead had not halted, so it wasn't something critical. Stiger increased his pace, sweating under the oppressive heat, and made his way to the front of the march.

"Sir," Tiro said when Stiger fell in alongside, "Bren's returned."

Stiger saw the scout and motioned him over. Bren saluted smartly as they continued to march, the men of the company at their backs.

"Report." Stiger returned the salute.

"Sir," he said, and then pointed in the direction the company was marching. "There is a dirt road deep with wagon ruts about a quarter of a mile ahead. I saw fresh tracks. At least several files of men, moving northward along the road. The tracks were no more than a day old."

"Rivan, you think?"

The scout shrugged, as if to say he could not tell.

Stiger felt himself frown. Not only were they being pursued, but there was a force of enemy cavalry roaming about, and now the possibility of more of the enemy somewhere in the direction of Cora'Tol, their objective.

"That sounds like the road we are looking for," Tiro said with an unhappy tone.

"It does," Stiger agreed and reached into his cloak pocket, removing the small map that General Treim had given him. It was a simple camp copy made by a scribe. He held it up as they walked so that Tiro could see, and then touched the line that indicated the road they were looking for. "If I am correct, when we hit the road, we should be about here."

"That seems right." Tiro nodded. "Looks to be around ten miles to the Cora'Tol garrison then, with that village there in the middle."

"We could be at Cora'Tol within a few hours then," Stiger said.

"If we take the road." Tiro shared a long look with Stiger.

"You are thinking we might blunder into an enemy formation."

"It's very possible," Tiro said. "Who would have guessed that the enemy would be this far southeast?"

"If the general had known," Stiger said, "he would have sent at least a full company, perhaps more, and we'd be cooling our heels back in camp."

Stiger turned to the scout, who had been following their conversation. "Get on ahead to the road and keep an eye out."

"Yes, sir." The scout saluted and broke into a jog. In moments, he was out of view, lost amongst the trees.

"There should be no enemy in these parts," Stiger said with some frustration. "They should be way up northwest and across the river where the legions are."

"And yet, here they are, sir," Tiro said.

Stiger was incredibly frustrated and kicked at a fallen branch as they walked.

"Feel better?" Tiro asked.

"A little."

"So, what are we going to do? Take the road or stick to the forest?"

Stiger expelled a slow breath. He had been surprised at the strength of the enemy operating in this area. It was possible that the garrison at Cora'Tol was besieged. For all he knew, it might have even fallen.

He glanced behind him at the marching column. His men had enough rations for at least one last meal. Then they would go hungry. To make matters worse, he was being pursued by at least a full company of enemy infantry. Should he play it safe? Should he stick to the woods and take the longer route? Or should he take the risk and push right on to the garrison, hoping to make it before the enemy caught up with him? Was the garrison still there?

Stiger shifted his yoke again and rubbed the back of his neck. These questions and more worried at him terribly. Worse, he was the one who had to make the ultimate decision. No one would make it for him.

"I am thinking we stick with what is working and play it safe," Stiger said finally. "We stay to the woods, even if it takes us longer."

CHAPTER TWO

"**D**own," Tiro hissed and shoved Stiger roughly into the dirt.

Lying prone amidst the brush growing alongside the road, Stiger froze. He waited a moment but heard nothing. He turned his head to Tiro, an eyebrow raised. Tiro held up a hand and showed five fingers twice, pointed two at his eyes and then in the direction they had just come.

Stiger nodded his understanding. There were at least ten men coming up from behind them.

Stiger glanced at Bren to Tiro's left, also prone. The scout slowly pulled out his short sword, never taking his eyes from the road. Stiger took the hint and drew steel as well. He looked over at Tiro, whose attention was also directed onto the road, mere feet away. Stiger scanned what he could of the road but saw nothing. He strained his ears, listening.

Birds happily chirped away. Hunting for a good meal, a woodpecker hammered in spirited bouts at a tree somewhere off in the distance. Stiger heard nothing out of the ordinary, then—

It was an unmistakable sound. Stiger had heard it many times before, the tread of many sandaled feet. Stiger held his breath as a file of soldiers appeared, marching in the direction of Cora'Tol, all wearing the blue cloaks of the Rivan.

The enemy were heavy infantry, uniformly armed and armored with chainmail shirts, small round shields, and short swords. Unlike Mal'Zeelan legionaries, the enemy wore long gray, woolen tunics under their armor that extended down to their calves. In the heat, Stiger wondered how they managed to stay cool. Instead of being worn, helmets hung from their necks by ties. It was easier on the neck that way. Stiger, like Tiro and Bren, had left his back with the rest of the company. Infantry helmets tended to be a pain in the neck.

The enemy file had prisoners. Four Mal'Zeelan auxiliaries, light infantry from the looks of them. All were likely from the garrison. Heads hanging, eyes on the ground, hands bound securely behind their backs, they plodded along miserably with their captors. All four looked like they had been given some rough treatment.

Damn.

Stiger held himself still until the enemy file had passed them by. Even then, he waited to make sure they were out of earshot. He pulled himself slowly up to his knees, scanning the road in both directions to look for any hint of movement. Tiro and Bren did the same. Stiger stood and brushed the dirt from his face, chest, legs, and finally his hands.

"That was close," Tiro said in a near whisper.

"Too close." Stiger glanced up at the darkening sky. In another hour it would be dusk. "Bren, how far to Cora'Tol?"

"Less than a mile, sir," the scout replied. "Just over that little ridge, the other side of which is a valley. The garrison's fort is set in the valley, next to the town."

"And they've burned both?" Stiger could smell the faint trace of smoke on the air.

"Yes," Bren confirmed. "Perhaps the day before last."

"Are you certain you want to continue, sir?" Tiro asked.

"Yes," Stiger said. "I need to see it."

"Why, sir?" Tiro looked like he thought this a bad idea. "Cora'Tol is gone. There's no longer any point in continuing our mission."

"I can't return without having laid eyes on our objective," Stiger explained. "The general will want a detailed report, and he is likely to question me closely."

Tiro hesitated a moment. "Let's keep off the road then. That's the second group we've nearly blundered into."

"Agreed." Stiger turned to Bren, sheathing his sword. "Lead the way."

"Yes, sir," Bren said and set off. The scout quickly led them deeper into the forest and farther away from the road. Stiger was impressed with Bren's ability to move near-silently through the trees. Every so often, the scout stopped to listen, and Stiger did his best to not make any noise.

Within twenty minutes Stiger found himself prone again, this time peering through the brush down into the valley. Tiro was to his left and Bren his right.

"Well," Tiro said with a heavy breath, "the garrison is most definitely gone. Can we go now?"

Stiger said nothing as he studied the valley. He was sure it had once had a peaceful look to it, with a large town near the center. A stream meandered its way past. Neatly cultivated farm fields spread outward from the town, which was now nothing more than a smoldering wreck. Only the charred stumps of timber and stone foundations remained. Just beyond the town was the fort. Oddly, the wooden-staked palisade still stood, yet the interior of the fort had burned.

"I don't see any breaches in the fort's walls," Stiger said.

"Looks like they just opened the gate and let the enemy in." Tiro pointed.

The gate stood open and seemed to show no evidence of being forced.

"There may be something we can't see," Stiger said. "We're over a half mile away."

"Could be as you say, sir," Tiro said. "But I've been through more than my fair share of sieges and assaults. There should be more damage if the enemy forced their way in."

Stiger nodded. Tiro's experience had served him well so far. Stiger had learned to listen to the old veteran's advice.

"Look there, a lot of bodies just outside of the town, sir," Bren said and pointed. "In that field. Some spread out like they was running, others grouped about, probably executed. Townsfolk, I would hazard, sir."

Stiger looked, following Bren's finger. He sucked in a breath.

Carrion birds circled the valley above the spot. More were grouped around those who had fallen, feeding hungrily. The sight sickened Stiger. It also angered him, for the large group of bodies seemed clustered too close together to be the remains of the fallen from a fight. They were, as Bren said, likely civilians from the town. Either they had been executed there or their bodies had been dragged to that point and left to rot. Stiger leaned toward the former explanation, as it seemed too much effort to drag them, especially if you weren't going to bury or burn the bodies.

He shifted his gaze beyond the town. A small camp had been erected away from the ruins on the other side. Stiger squinted to see better. He counted tents, twenty-eight in total. A number of mules were tethered to stakes in neat rows next to the camp. There were also two horses, likely officers' mounts. Stiger counted five sentries slowly walking the boundaries of the camp. Unlike a legionary marching camp, there were no defensive structures, such as a wall.

He chewed his lip as an idea occurred to him. He knew Tiro would not like it.

"Looks like at least a full company's tents," Stiger said.

"Maybe two hundred men minimum," Tiro said. "But I don't see many of them down there, unless they are sleeping off the heat of the day, sir."

"There was an auxiliary cohort stationed here." Stiger found his anger building. He slapped the ground. "I don't see how a single company could overwhelm the defenses of the fort. That's a solid-looking wall."

"Must have been surprised, sir," Tiro said. "This valley is well away from the front lines. Command likely stationed a third-rate cohort here. I've seen it before. They got lazy, and paid for it."

"Perhaps." Stiger tapped his fingers on the ground as he thought it through aloud. "We don't know exactly how the fort fell. We've already crossed paths with at least two files of men, and each was hauling along prisoners. Is it possible the cohort was ambushed and broken outside of the valley? They could be out hunting down survivors."

"That is a possibility," Tiro said. "Slaves fetch good money."

"Well, whatever occurred, the general will not be happy about this," Stiger said. "We know that there are more Rivan forces in the area. Counting the ones pursuing us, that makes at least two companies of heavy infantry and a contingent of cavalry. Seems an odd force to send so deep into enemy territory for the purposes of raiding."

"How so?" Tiro looked over at Stiger. "Two companies of heavies and some cavalry is a pretty formidable force, sir."

"Light infantry would be better suited for this kind of work," Stiger said. "With the legions up north pursuing the Rivan army, it seems damn odd to send heavy infantry all the way down here just to raid. Besides, it's kind of out of the way, don't you think?"

"I think," Tiro said slowly, "that I don't like them being here, sir, whether they be heavy or light infantry."

Stiger chuckled softly.

"We have to get word back that the enemy has sacked Cora'Tol," Tiro said. "What is the nearest garrison?"

"Cora'Mal," Stiger said, "twenty or so miles to the east."

"We should warn them," Tiro said.

"Our map doesn't go that far." Stiger rubbed his chin. He did not much like the idea of moving farther away from the legion than they already were. "Traveling through the forest instead of the roads might see us lose our way."

"We should warn them," Tiro said again.

"We do that and it takes us farther away from the Third."

"We need food, sir," Tiro pressed. "Cora'Mal is the only option."

"What if Cora'Mal has been sacked as well?" Stiger turned back to studying the enemy camp, the idea growing into a plan of action. It had hit him moments before, but looking over the enemy's mule train solidified what he wanted to do. "As it is, the company is going nowhere."

"What do you mean, sir?"

"We're out of food," Stiger said. "Without it, we can't travel very far. If we move to Cora'Mal and that garrison is gone too, we will be in real trouble."

"I am almost afraid to ask." Tiro's eyes narrowed. "What do you have in mind, sir?"

"I am thinking..." Stiger expelled a long breath. "That tonight we attack the enemy's camp."

"Are you serious, sir?"

"I am."

"Attack an entire company?" Tiro rolled onto his side to better look at Stiger, an incredulous expression upon his face. "Whatever for?"

Stiger returned the sergeant's look. "We're out of food, and they have it. I intend to take what we need, including all those fine mules. Maybe even the horses, if we can." Stiger grinned at Tiro. "There is good money in that, too."

Tiro blinked, but said nothing.

"Do you see any defenses down there, or patrols for that matter?" Stiger said.

Tiro turned and scanned the valley.

"No," Tiro said after a moment. "I only see their camp sentries. Bren, do you see anything out of the ordinary?"

"No, Sergeant," Bren said. "I do not."

"Looks like they've gotten lazy," Tiro said. "Must be thinking they eliminated any threat for miles around. It is possible they've not yet gotten word from the company pursuing us that we're around."

"We've run into two files of men outside the valley," Stiger said. "Each file had taken prisoners. There may be more ranging farther afield. It could mean the company down there might be a few files light when we strike."

"I guess that is possible," Tiro said grudgingly. "I think we might be able to do it. That is, if we can silence those sentries without too much fuss first and catch the rest sleeping. Varus, Bren, Aronus, and I have some experience handling such things, sir."

Tiro drew a slow finger across his throat to underscore the point.

"Later, when it is good and dark, we bring up the entire company, sneak up on their camp, silence their sentries, and attack. With luck, we will have the element of surprise on our side."

"What about the other Rivan forces in the area?" Tiro squinted as he returned to studying the enemy camp. "I would not want to be caught in the valley come dawn to find enemy reinforcements arriving or that company that's been snapping at our heels showing up."

"We make tracks well before dawn then," Stiger said. "We move south and then dogleg it back west toward the Third."

"What about getting word to Cora'Mal?"

"I am hesitant to take the entire company that way," Stiger said. "Better that we return and report. We can send one of our scouts."

Tiro scratched an itch on his neck, clearly considering Stiger's proposal.

"This could all go horribly wrong."

"Yes, it could," Stiger conceded, "but if we are to go anywhere, we need their food. It's well over seventy-five miles back to the Third."

"I can't believe I am actually considering this madness with only eighty-two men." Tiro shook his head. "Are you set on this path, sir? We could always try to forage."

"We are being pursued," Stiger said flatly. "We may not be allowed time to forage properly. Besides, I kind of like the idea of the enemy doing us the courtesy of feeding us."

"Excuse me, sir?"

Stiger looked over at the scout, who had been intently studying the enemy's camp.

"Go ahead," Stiger said.

"Looks like there are some men under guard down there, about a dozen." Bren pointed off to the side of the enemy camp.

corporal was wearing only his service tunic. There was a large dark stain on his chest, nearly dead center.

"All set, sir," Varus said between heavy breaths. "We've taken out all of the sentries. Lazy bastards were not even doing their duty proper-like. Bren and Aronus are on their way to alert Sergeant Tiro."

"Good work." Stiger clapped the corporal on the shoulder. "Now get your kit on. Follow just as soon as you are able."

"Yes, sir." Varus stepped over toward where the assault line was waiting, hidden amongst the wheat, as Stiger turned to the fire party.

"It's time," Stiger said. "Good fortune."

The three men came to their feet. Careful to not make too much sound, they began moving toward the camp. Each carried an unlit makeshift torch, the end of which was thick with dried grass that had been tightly interwoven.

Stiger watched them for a fraction of a second, then moved back to his assault force and retrieved his shield from where he had left it.

"On your feet," Stiger called, just loud enough to carry to his men and no farther. As if rising from the dead, the men stood, appearing where moments before nothing had been visible. They quickly dressed themselves upon one another, a task that was more difficult in the near darkness than it sounded. In short order, they were formed up into an assault line two ranks deep.

"Draw swords."

The swords came out with a mass hiss. Stiger drew steel. He flexed his hand, finding a comfortable grip. Without verbalizing the command, he simply pointed toward the enemy camp and began walking. The two ranks followed. The sound of their footfalls was muffled by the wheat that, nearly ready for harvest, grew thick, tall, and golden brown.

There was an abrupt clatter as two shields banged loudly together. Stiger felt himself frown. He turned to look, seeking out the careless culprits. A dog somewhere in the sacked town to his right began to bark, harsh and loud, drawing Stiger's attention.

Another dog joined the first. Stiger cursed silently in frustration. Surely the banging of the shields and the dogs would alert someone in the camp. He ground his teeth as the distance steadily closed.

The dogs continued to bark.

Stiger took a deep breath and calmed himself. There was nothing he could do. He was committed now. Thoughts of the plan he had settled on, a two-pronged assault, worried at him.

Stiger ran everything through his mind again. He, with half of the company, would attack from one side of the camp, while Tiro, with the other half, would hit from the opposite side. They would meet somewhere in the middle. Two fire parties would strike as both assault forces pushed forward. With luck, Stiger hoped it would create a general panic as both prongs went in. Amidst the chaos, Stiger's picked men would make away with the enemy's mule train. Should things go poorly, both he and Tiro would break off the attack.

It was so simple, and yet Stiger knew that even the best of plans could go awry. Had he missed anything? He couldn't see that he had.

Everything hinged on catching the enemy by surprise.

Then he heard a loud, discordant sound. It took Stiger a moment to realize it was snoring, coming from the tents ahead. Stiger and his assault force were less than ten feet from the nearest tent. They were so close that, even if someone sounded the alarm, it would be too late for the enemy.

Stiger said a quick prayer to the High Father, asking for the assault to be successful. Before he could finish, fire sprouted from a tent to his left, leaping up into the air with a suddenness that was shocking. Another tent to the right flared into brilliance, weatherproofing oil burning furiously. A third blazed, flames leaping hungrily up into the air, then a fourth, before the screams and cries of alarm began. Men, dressed only in their gray service tunics, began pouring out of the communal tents.

"Chaaarge!" Stiger shouted and broke into a run. The assault force behind him gave a great shout, and the sound of pounding feet followed as he ran the last few feet into the camp.

Stiger felt the intense heat of a burning tent as it flashed by, then he was amongst the confused enemy spilling forth from another tent that was nearly fully engulfed. Stiger bashed his shield into a startled man, his momentum knocking the man back and into the burning tent, which collapsed over him. Stiger jabbed outward, stabbing at another who, unarmed, had turned to run. Stiger felt his blade punch deeply into the lower back, sword grating against bone. Screaming, the man fell forward to the ground and off the blade. Stiger stabbed downward, striking his enemy in the back of the neck, ensuring he would stay down.

A fraction of a second later, legionaries were rushing by, mercilessly stabbing and jabbing at the confused enemy. Stiger straightened back up and looked around. It was pure chaos. Tents were burning; men were screaming, yelling, calling out oaths. The sweet, sickly smell of blood was on the air, mingling with smoke and the stench of an open latrine.

The man Stiger had bashed into the burning tent pulled himself to his feet, his tunic ablaze. Horrified, Stiger watched as he ran screaming into the darkness and out into the field, leaving a trail of burning wheat in his wake.

A massed shout came from the far side of the camp as the other half of the assault went in. The clash of sword on sword dragged Stiger's attention to his left. A small group of men had emerged from a tent that had escaped the fire. Though not armored, they were armed. These were quickly set upon by Stiger's legionaries. The group fought desperately. It was an unequal contest, as they were badly outnumbered. Stiger's men used their shields to deflect as they advanced, steadily pushing the group back deeper into the camp.

Stiger stepped over the body of the man he had killed. The ground was slick with blood, and he almost slipped. Edging around to the side of the group of defenders, Stiger closed with the enemy, shield up.

A legionary to his left jabbed out and caught one of the enemy under an arm. It was a shallow strike, but all it took was two inches from a short sword to mortally wound. The man fell back, clutching his armpit. The legionary pressed forward.

Two more of the enemy joined the determined bunch, taking the wounded man's position and striking back at the legionary. Stiger saw what he took to be a sergeant standing behind the defenders' line, calling out orders in Rivan or perhaps even attempting to rally the enemy to him. Stiger did not speak their language but understood that he had to break this group before the enemy's defense became more organized.

"Push!" Stiger shouted as loud as he could, and the legionaries with him shoved forward.

There was a loud *thunk* as Stiger's shield boss was struck a powerful blow. He almost dropped the shield as the pain of the strike was communicated to his arm behind. Stiger's fingers tingled numbly.

Reaching around his shield, Stiger jabbed forward, his sword sliding into the belly of an enemy soldier, even as his shield was struck again with a solid-sounding *thump*. It was all he could do to simply hang onto the shield. Yelling incoherently, Stiger bashed his shield forward, throwing his shoulder into it, and felt a solid hit as it connected with a body. Suddenly there was no more resistance, as the man he had hit crashed backwards to the ground. A legionary was on the stunned enemy in a flash, stabbing viciously downward.

"Push!" Stiger shouted. The men with him shoved forward, and under intense pressure, the defenders fell back farther.

Stiger took a step forward, intent upon advancing with his men. He tripped and staggered to a knee, almost falling. Badly off balance, he planted the bottom of his shield in the ground to keep from tumbling forward. By the time he regained his feet, the fight around him was over and the group of defenders broken. The legionaries who had been with him just moments before had pushed forward, leaving their lieutenant behind. Stiger glanced down and saw that he had tripped over a tent's guide rope.

Chest heaving, Stiger took a moment to stop and check his surroundings. He remembered Tiro's advice a few weeks before about officers needing to keep their heads. He surveyed the scene around him.

The confused fighting had made its way deeper into the enemy's camp. Figures struggled in the darkness, broken only by the flickering sentry fire or the blazing of a tent. There were bodies seemingly everywhere, all wearing service tunics of the enemy and without armor. Most were still, but some writhed in agony. It was an astonishing sight. Stiger could see none of his legionaries down.

This wasn't a battle.

It was a slaughter, pure and simple.

For a moment, Stiger felt sympathy for those who had fallen before the blades of the Seventh. Then he remembered the razed town and the civilians' bodies out in the field, being feasted over by scavengers. His anger returned, and his heart hardened.

"Sir?"

Stiger turned to see Varus hustling into the firelight. He was securing his helmet one-handed. Stiger read concern in the corporal's eyes.

"Are you all right, sir?"

"I am."

Stiger turned back toward the action and made his way deeper into the camp. The sounds of the fighting and chaos were steadily dying off, though he could still hear some fighting on the other side of the camp. A number of dark forms were running into the darkness, fleeing before the vengeful legionaries.

Toward the center of the camp, the sound of serious fighting erupted. Stiger quickened his pace. As he neared, he saw around fifteen of the enemy struggling against a greater number of legionaries, with more joining the fray every second. All of the enemy were unarmored. An officer, judging by his fine tunic, was directing the efforts of those who stood firm with him. Fighting alongside his men, the officer cut a brave and fearless figure. For a moment, Stiger admired the man's courage.

There would be no escape for them, Stiger realized. They were nearly surrounded. Shields to the front, Stiger's legionaries were pressing tightly in on the defenders. Stiger stood back and watched the action. The enemy's defense was doomed. With each passing moment, their numbers dwindled as they fell to the unrelenting short swords that jabbed out from behind the protection of the shields. Then, under a flurry of strikes, the officer was brutally cut down.

"Hold," Stiger shouted as the last of the defenders threw down their weapons and raised their hands in surrender. A legionary caught up in the moment plunged his sword deep into the belly of one attempting to give up. The man gave an agonized scream before falling to the ground. The legionary stabbed downward. The scream abruptly cut off.

"Hold." Stiger shoved the legionary roughly with his shield to get the man's attention. "I said bloody hold!"

"Sorry, sir," the man said and stepped back.

"Corporal Varus," Stiger called. "Varus, where are you?"

"Here, sir." The corporal had been following.

"Secure those prisoners," Stiger ordered. There were four still on their feet. "They may have intelligence. And spread word to accept any further surrenders."

"Yes, sir." Varus began shouting orders and several legionaries stepped forward, swords held at the ready, closing in on the prisoners. Another sheathed his sword and began gathering up discarded weapons.

Stiger wondered how the fighting on Tiro's end of the camp was going, where the prisoners from the auxiliary cohort were being held. One of Tiro's objectives was to free them.

A massed cheer in the direction of the far side of the camp snapped Stiger's head around. He relaxed. The other prong of the assault had broken the last knot of resistance. A handful of the enemy were running into the darkness, just as fast as they could go. With that, all sounds of resistance ceased.

Stiger looked about him. At least ten tents were burning furiously enough that he could feel their heat from several yards away. The enemy's camp was in complete shambles, bodies lying everywhere. He took a deep breath and let it out slowly. The assault from beginning to end had taken less than ten minutes. In the process, thanks to his enemy's carelessness, he had wrecked an entire company, and with an inferior force. After days of being hotly pursued, it felt good to strike back. A grin snaked its way onto his face.

The enemy's camp, including the supplies he badly needed, was his.

would see the legions' supply line severed. Why else send heavy infantry so far from the front? It was the only explanation that made any sense to him.

"This could be the advance party of a more substantial force," Stiger said.

"You may be right, sir," Tiro said.

Varus spoke up, moving to the other side of the table. "Which could mean that we are in the path of whatever else is coming down the road intending to push south."

Stiger glanced up at the corporal and chewed his lip. "How many prisoners did we take?"

"Twelve," Varus said.

"Do any of them speak Common?"

"One that we know of," Varus said. "He was begging for his life to be spared. The others just jabbered at us. Couldn't make any sense of it."

Stiger nodded, thinking rapidly. "How many of our men did we free?"

"Seven auxiliaries," Tiro said unhappily. "The Rivan had taken more, but they were torturing our boys and then killing them off one at a time when they finished with their fun."

"Then," Stiger said slowly, "they were not taking prisoners for slaves?"

"It would seem not." Tiro cleared his throat. "They must have been looking for information."

"Right," Stiger said, turning to Varus. "Question that prisoner and find out what he knows."

"Yes, sir," Varus said. "I will get right on it."

The corporal ducked out of the tent, moving with a purpose. Stiger rubbed at his tired eyes, feeling a headache coming on.

"What else did you find, Asus?" Tiro asked.

"The company strongbox," the legionary said, pointing at the small locked chest in a corner. It appeared quite sturdy. Asus handed a key to Tiro. "The officer's purse is in that trunk, along with personal possessions and…" He lifted a small canvas bag off the floor and handed it over to Tiro, a sour expression on his face, as if he were parting with gold. "I found this, Sergeant."

Tiro took the bag and looked inside. He put his nose to it and breathed in deeply, before letting it out in a pleased breath. After a moment, he whistled. There was a smile on his face as he looked over.

"The good stuff." Tiro handed the bag to Stiger. "You will want to claim this for yourself, sir."

"What is it?" Stiger asked, peering in the bag. "Tobacco?"

"The good stuff," Tiro affirmed again. "Eastern tobacco, nothing finer."

"I don't smoke," Stiger said, wondering why Tiro was making such a big deal out of a bag of tobacco.

"Now, that is a crying shame," Tiro said seriously, then grinned. "Sir, I promise you on this count. We will fix that oversight later. There is nothing better to help one relax and think over his day than a fine pipe." The sergeant furrowed his brow and looked to the standard-bearer. "Say…Asus, did you find a pipe?"

"I did, sir," Asus said and opened the trunk that held personal possessions. He took out a bone pipe and handed it over to Stiger.

Stiger examined the pipe. An elephant was carved into one side and a fearsome-looking boar on the other. He recognized an expensive piece when he saw it. The officer who had owned it, and this tent, had clearly been a man of some means.

"You will want to keep that too, sir," Tiro said. "Trust me. It's too fine for the men."

Stiger set the pipe and bag down on the table. He gathered up the enemy's map and folded it carefully, then did the same with his own and placed both in a pocket.

"Sergeant," Stiger said, "see that the strongbox and purse make it onto the mule train. We will treat it as prize money."

"Yes, sir," Tiro said. "The men will like that very much, sir."

Stiger nodded and glanced around the tent. A large portion of the money would go to the legion, a more modest percentage to Stiger, Tiro, and Varus. The rest would be dispersed to the men's pensions and reserved for their retirement should they survive long enough to reach it. A small amount would be paid out in cash at the legion's quarterly salary payment, which in turn would likely be spent as rapidly as possible on wine and women.

"See that the tobacco and pipe are set aside for me," Stiger said to Asus.

"Yes, sir."

"We have a mule reserved for your things, sir," Tiro said. "It will be there later."

"Good." Stiger scanned the interior of the tent once more, nodded to himself with satisfaction, and then stepped back out into the night. The fire in the field had spread rapidly in the short time he had spent in the tent. With what he had just learned, Stiger cursed himself yet again. The burning wheat was lighting up much of the valley. He had inadvertently signaled his position, for the glow of the firelight surely reflected off the clouds above. Worse, he judged the blaze would soon spread throughout the rest of the valley.

He glanced over his newly acquired supply train. The legionaries were working frantically to load the twenty-plus mules they had captured.

There was a bright side, however. The fire meant that the ready-to-harvest wheat would be denied to the enemy. Stiger almost smiled at that comforting thought—almost.

Tiro emerged behind Stiger, looked over the fire, and then spat on the ground. "Wouldn't you know it, to get back to the Third we need to go west and now the only way open to us is east."

Stiger closed his eyes in frustration. The sergeant was right. They would have to move east, climb out of the valley, and then make their way south, skirting the valley, before turning northwest. It would take time ... which Stiger felt he did not have.

"Nothing about this mission has gone right," Stiger said with irritation. He reached into a pocket and pulled out his orders. With the garrison destroyed, and the man he had come to find likely dead, the orders were now moot. He walked over to the nearest fire and tossed them in. The paper caught, flaring brilliantly before folding in upon itself and blackening, edges curling back slowly.

"Don't you know yet, sir?" Tiro said, coming up behind him. "Nothing ever goes right for the infantry."

Stiger glanced over at the sergeant, his frustration warring with amusement.

"Sergeant," Stiger said, "since I've joined Seventh Company, I don't think much has gone right."

"Oh," Tiro said, "I'm not so sure about that, sir. Once you came along, plenty has gone right for the Seventh."

"Let's go see the prisoners," Stiger said, feeling uncomfortable with Tiro's praise. "I would look upon my enemy."

They walked over to the prisoners, who were sitting under a heavy guard. Across the camp, bodies lay where they had fallen, requiring Stiger and Tiro to step around and over the dead. The ground was slick and muddy with drying blood. The company would be pulling out shortly and Stiger saw no need to care for the enemy's fallen.

"How are our casualties coming?"

"I've ordered a litter rigged for Legionary Cavius," Tiro said. "He should survive, if that leg wound of his doesn't fester. Our other two are walking wounded with minor cuts only. Bren stitched them up. Shame we don't have a doctor or surgeon's mate to care for Cavius. I'd feel better about him if we did, sir."

Stiger nodded as they made their way up to the prisoners, who looked a miserable bunch. They were being kept on the western side of the camp, the burning wheat field only yards away. To attempt to make a dash for it and flee in that direction was certain death. They looked up fearfully as Stiger and Tiro approached, then avoided Stiger's gaze like he had the plague.

The guard detail straightened to attention. Stiger waved for them to relax.

"Are they giving you any trouble?" Stiger asked, wrinkling his nose against the stench of smoke, which was stronger on this side of the camp.

"No, sir," Legionary Carata said. "This bunch don't speak any Common, but they understand pointing and such. Meek as lambs, sir. All fight's gone out of them."

"I see," Stiger said, glancing the prisoners over. He was confident that armed and armored they had appeared intimidating enough. As prisoners, they seemed a wretched bunch.

An agonized scream from the other side of the camp caused the prisoners to flinch.

"Varus is doing his questioning of the prisoner who spoke Common, sir," Tiro said.

Stiger simply nodded, but noticed one of the prisoners' eyes flick toward Tiro. Stiger quickly glanced away.

Perhaps there was more than one prisoner who spoke Common. He thought on how he could best use this knowledge to his advantage as he looked over the growing fire just beyond the prisoners. It was spreading more rapidly than he had expected. Stiger understood it was nearly time to go, whether they had all of the supplies they needed or not.

"We will leave in ten minutes," Stiger told Tiro. "I don't think we can delay any further."

The sergeant nodded his agreement. "What about the prisoners?"

"What about them?" Stiger asked, eyes roving over the captives before casually settling on the prisoner whom he suspected of speaking Common.

"We should kill 'em," Tiro said bluntly.

The prisoner flinched.

"Why not take them with us?" Stiger said. "We could turn them over to the garrison at Cora'Mal. There is money in that."

"We're going to Cora'Mal?" Tiro said, with no little amount of surprise.

"It is the nearest garrison," Stiger said. Was it his imagination? Was the prisoner following their conversation? "We have to get word out about the Rivan operating in this area. Then we can return to the legion."

"I see," Tiro said with an unhappy air. "Taking this bunch along with us is dangerous, sir."

"How so?"

"The best they can hope for is slavery in a mine, where life is measured in weeks. They would be looking for any opportunity to escape," Tiro explained. "That could see one of our boys injured or worse. My recommendation would be to kill 'em and do it now."

Stiger took a deep breath and looked over the prisoners again. He noticed the prisoner he suspected of speaking Common watching them covertly. When Stiger's eyes touched his, the man quickly looked away. What Tiro said made sense. However, Stiger had other plans.

"There has been enough killing today. When we march," Stiger said, turning to face Tiro, "free them."

"What?" Tiro was clearly surprised.

"Sergeant, those are my orders," Stiger said firmly, almost harshly. "Now, let's examine the work detail and see if things can be moved along."

Stiger resisted the urge to see if the prisoner looked relieved at the news he and the others were to be spared, freed even.

"Yes, sir." Tiro's tone was stiff and correct.

The sergeant followed Stiger over to the mule train, where the work was moving along at a frantic pace. Most of the mules were loaded and waiting.

"You realize they will spread word of us?" Tiro said.

"That is what I am counting on," Stiger said, flashing a grin at the sergeant.

"So," Tiro said, eyes narrowing, "we are not going to Cora'Mal?"

"No," Stiger said. "We are going back to the Third. I am fairly certain one of the prisoners back there speaks Common."

"A false trail then," Tiro said, glancing back.

"With luck, a little misdirection, and this fire, we might be able to slip away." Stiger paused a moment. "We will march out to the east, more to avoid the fire than anything else, then turn south, skirt the valley, and then dogleg it northwest and back to the Third. Thanks to the enemy, we now have a good map and sufficient supply."

"No offense intended, sir," Tiro said, chuckling, "but for a junior lieutenant you are one devious bastard."

"None taken," Stiger said, recognizing the sergeant's words as high praise.

"Sir." Varus came up at a run. The corporal looked pale as a ghost.

"What?" Stiger asked, fearing the response.

"The prisoner who spoke Common," Varus said. "The one you had me question. He says there is an entire army, twenty thousand strong, just thirty miles up the road. The enemy has a great big bloody second army. This company was the vanguard, and they are coming this way, sir. He was very sure of that."

"We're just bad luck," Tiro said, glancing at Stiger.

"That settles it." Stiger felt his headache becoming worse. "The enemy is trying to flank the legions. We must report this as soon as possible."

"Sir," Tiro said, "the rest of the army is somewhere far to the northwest. Our legion is the only one near enough to respond, and when they do ... the enemy will greatly out-number what General Treim can put into the field."

"I know," Stiger said, blowing out a heavy breath. He glanced out at the fire again and then up at the darkened sky. The glow from the blaze against the low-hanging clouds would likely be seen for miles, and the enemy had cavalry. Stiger judged it only three or four hours 'til dawn. "But it's all we've got. Right, then, it's time to go. We need to get out of this valley and into the forest as soon as possible."

"What of the road to the south?" Tiro asked. "We would move faster on the road."

"We have to avoid it," Stiger said. "The enemy will clearly want to investigate this fire. They may even be on their way here now. Besides, we already know they have cavalry. We stand a better chance of slipping away in the forest."

Tiro and Varus glanced nervously out into the darkness.

"Form up for march," Stiger ordered curtly. "And free the prisoners."

"What of the one I interrogated?" Varus asked. "I think he knows more than he is telling."

"Bring him with us," Stiger ordered. "I want to know everything he knows. Now, let's move!"

CHAPTER FIVE

Stiger stifled a yawn with the back of his hand. His legs burned as he climbed with the company up the steep slope and out of the valley. Sweating from the effort, he rubbed at eyes, irritated not only from lack of sleep, but the choking smoke that seemed to be everywhere. With each step, his armor weighed upon him terribly, and the higher he climbed, the more effort it took just to place one foot in front of the other.

"Sergeant," Stiger called as he reached the top of the ridge, seeing Tiro ahead speaking to a legionary who had collapsed. Stiger took a step over the lip and was surprised as the smoke dissipated, almost as if an invisible force held it back, trapping it within the valley. Ash, however, still fell like snow. Sucking in the clean air in great gulps, his breathing labored from the exertion, Stiger felt vast relief at completing the climb. He bent over, resting his hands on his knees, working to catch his breath. "Sergeant Tiro."

"Sir." Tiro turned to look and saw Stiger. The old veteran stumped over to him.

"Once everyone's up, let's call a twenty-minute break." Stiger's throat was dry and irritated. He straightened and tried to cough out the residual smoke that stung his lungs. Tiro waited as Stiger glanced back through the trees and down the slope. His men, with mules interspersed amongst them, were struggling up the steep slope in a single-file line that disappeared into the early morning gloom made worse by the smoke that swirled amidst the trees. Stiger turned his gaze along the rim of the darkened ridge before returning to Tiro.

"A break you say, sir?"

"That was a fearsome climb," Stiger said. "Twenty minutes' rest." Focused on the task at hand, he paused. "I think we will move farther into the trees and parallel the valley traveling south a bit before swinging west and then north. At least the ground will be somewhat flat, and it should be easier going."

"Down yokes, rest easy," Tiro called to the nearest men before leaning over the edge and shouting down at those still climbing the moderately steep slope. "Twenty minutes' break once you reach the top."

Those nearest who had already crested the ridge gratefully dropped their yokes and shields and settled to the ground with a chorus of groans.

"Sir, we will have to cross that north-south road," Tiro said, turning back to Stiger.

Stiger looked through the trees back down into the eastern end of the valley. The sun would be up soon. The sky was already beginning to brighten, the first steaks of crimson lacing clouds high above. Since there was little wind, smoke from the fire hung heavily on the valley below like a burial shroud. Stiger could see an angry orange glow illuminating the smoke where the fire still burned.

A larger, brighter radiance farther out into the valley was likely the fort's wooden barricade fully engulfed. A gentle gust of wind parted the smoke momentarily to the west. Long tongues of flame licked up high into the air before smoke closed back in. Stiger wondered if this meant that the trees near the valley's base had begun to burn.

"What was that you said?" Stiger focused his attention back to the sergeant.

"Sir, that north-south road. We are going to need to cross it," Tiro said.

"Yes," Stiger said. He had a foul taste in his mouth. Unhooking his canteen from his harness, he unstopped it and took a swig of warm water. He stopped it and returned the canteen back to his harness in a smooth, practiced motion. "There is no avoiding it. The fire should keep the enemy out of the valley long enough for us to cross. We break for twenty minutes now, then push on. Once we are a few miles from the valley and deep into the forest farther to the west, we will take an extended stop."

"I believe the boys will appreciate that," Tiro said. His tone told Stiger the old sergeant disapproved. "Very thoughtful, sir."

Stiger felt his brows knit together. The sergeant looked back innocently. Despite his weariness, Stiger became thoroughly amused with the wily old veteran. He barked out a laugh, which turned into a hacking cough. Heads turned toward them.

"You think we should rest now," Stiger said when he had recovered, "I take it?"

"Aye, that I do," Tiro said. "You said it yourself. That fire down there is likely to burn for a few more hours. It will keep anyone out of the valley. Sir, the boys are worn. They need an hour, maybe more, a little bit of shut eye and some food before continuing on, sir."

There was almost a pleading note to Tiro's tone. Stiger glanced around. The men climbing the hill were clearly dragging. He could see it in their weary, ragged step. Those who reached the top stumbled forward a few paces and collapsed to the ground wherever there was room. He could even hear the first snores. Stiger rubbed at his jaw as he considered them, feeling the coarse layer of stubble threatening to become a beard.

"If we run into the enemy," Tiro continued, "our boys may prove too blown to put up much of a fight."

Stiger let out a long breath, not liking the idea of stopping for whatever reason. His sergeant's reasoning, however, was sound. "Very well. We rest here. Do you think an hour and a half will be sufficient?"

Tiro gave a curt nod. "Might I kindly make another suggestion?"

"Do I have a choice?" Stiger asked, and it came out almost as a groan.

"You are in command, sir," Tiro said with a straight face. "As an officer, you always have a choice. Remember, sir, you are in charge."

Stiger grunted, but inclined his head for the old sergeant to continue.

"Get some rest yourself, sir," Tiro said. "Sleep like a babe. I will see a watch is set."

Stiger nodded, feeling a wave of exhaustion threatening to overtake him. Until speaking to Tiro, he had not fully realized his own fatigue. Grit and determination were all that had kept him going. He glanced around, found a tree a few feet off that appeared suitable, and tromped over. Tortured and overstressed muscles protested vehemently as Stiger eased himself down amongst the brush and long grass. He placed his back comfortably against the trunk, letting out a soft sigh as the metal scraped slightly against the bark.

With a chuckle, Stiger recalled how unpleasant it had been when he had first started wearing his armor. Had that been only five to six months ago? The leather straps had chafed his skin raw, to the point where he bled. Now, just months later, the armor was like a second skin.

After a long, hard day, it was always a relief to shed the heavy deadweight of the armor. Once off, Stiger never tired of marveling at feeling light as a feather. Removing his helmet, Stiger smiled at that thought as he leaned his head back against the rough bark of the tree. It would be nice to remove his armor. Unfortunately, there was no time for that. Besides, he was too tired to even try. Tiro had said rest and so Stiger closed his eyes, welcoming sleep.

"Sir." A hand shook his shoulder.

Stiger blinked several times, attempting to focus. Varus was bent over him, peering into his face.

"Corporal?" Stiger cracked his neck as he straightened. It felt like he had just closed his eyes.

"It's been a little over an hour, sir," Varus said. There was a concerned note in his voice, which, despite Stiger's exhaustion, alerted him to possible trouble.

"Right," Stiger said and held out a hand.

Varus hauled him to his feet.

"Gods," Stiger moaned softly, "I am really sore. I feel worse than after I've practiced hand-to-hand with Tiro. Everything seems to ache."

The corporal gave Stiger a grim smile and held out a small bundle wrapped in a towel. Stiger took it and unwrapped it, revealing a hunk of bread and a slice of cheese. Despite his concern for potential trouble, his stomach rumbled at the sight.

"Thank you," Stiger said.

"Courtesy of the Rivan, sir," Varus said. "Our thanks should go to them."

A gust of cooler air from the hills blew into the valley, driving the thick, acrid smoke up, out, and through the trees. Stiger coughed, as did a number of others. In thirty heartbeats the wind slackened and the air cleared.

"I'd expected the fire to have died down a little," Stiger said, taking a bite of his bread and chewing slowly.

"About that," Varus said, with a strained look that caused Stiger to pause mid-chew before completing the motion and swallowing. "The wind has picked up considerably. I think a storm is comin', but, well, it's not here yet. The fire has spread to the forest and is climbing up the ridge, sir."

"What?" Stiger took several hasty steps and peered over the edge. He could see orange flames sixty yards down the slope, smoke roiling skyward. He had no doubt the fire was climbing the slope as Varus had said. Stiger's hands clenched into fists. "Well, isn't that just fantastic. Not only did I set the valley on fire, now I've started a forest fire."

Varus stepped up next to him and jerked his head toward the fire. "Your first time, sir?"

Stiger scrutinized his corporal, wondering if Varus was serious. The corporal did not look to be joking, so Stiger said nothing, unclenching his hands.

"In the Wilds, we started a few fires to flush our enemy out of the trees and bramble," Varus said as a fresh gust of wind carried thick, choking smoke their way. Stiger and Varus took a step back. "'Course, the trick is you have to watch which way the wind is blowing before starting the fires, sir."

"The wind is blowing our way," Stiger said unhappily.

"It is," Varus said. "We just need to move farther south is all before the flames catch up to us, sir. With how dry things are, that fire will climb the ridge and sweep over the top. We will be forced south and maybe a little to the east, judging by the wind."

"We need to go west." Stiger seethed with frustration. He kicked at a dried pile of leaves that had fallen on the forest floor, scattering them.

"Sometimes life gives you sour grapes, sir," Varus said. "It's what I think they make cheap wine with."

Stiger glared at Varus, then deflated as his anger left him in a rush. Stiger rubbed his eyes a moment, not quite believing his poor luck. Fortune was a fickle bitch and the gods were clearly toying with him today.

Stiger let go a breath. He had to work with the poor dice that had been handed to him. There was no point in raging further.

"Where is Tiro?"

"Sleeping, sir," Varus said, pointing to where the sergeant was slumped against a tree, surrounded by dozing legionaries. "I was about to wake him."

Stiger shot a quick glance around at his men. Nearly everyone was asleep. The heavily loaded mules had been secured to trees. Not liking the cloying stench of smoke, the mules fidgeted about, stamping their hooves and braying, but surprisingly did not pull at their ropes. Only Bren and Varus were awake and had clearly been standing watch. Stiger wrapped his bread and cheese back up in the towel before dropping the bundle into his empty haversack.

"Wake the company," Stiger ordered curtly. "Everyone gets some food. Then we set off. They can eat on the move."

"Yes, sir," Varus said.

Stiger moved over to Tiro and shook the veteran's shoulder.

"On your feet," Varus called out harshly from behind. "Up, you lovely bastards. Nap time's over. Come on. Get on your feet."

"Sir?" Tiro blinked several times, focusing on Stiger.

"I don't recall giving you permission to loaf all morning," Varus called, kicking at a legionary who had not moved. "You joined the infantry, not the bloody navy. Get on your feet before you make me angry."

Tiro reached out an arm and Stiger pulled him to his feet. All around them, groaning men were dragging themselves up.

"The fire is climbing up the ridge," Stiger said.

"That's not good," Tiro said, stretching. Another cloud of smoke blew around them. Both Tiro and Stiger coughed. It passed. They could now plainly hear the crackling fire.

"The wind has picked up," Stiger said. "It's helping to fan the flames our way. I don't think we will be able to skirt the valley like I planned and avoid the fire. We have thirty to forty minutes before the flames reach our position."

"Perhaps I was little hasty suggesting we rest, sir." Tiro cast a worried look in the direction of the valley.

"No," Stiger said. "You were right. The company was blown, and so was I. We had to stop."

"In the Wilds," Tiro said, "I've had the misfortune to be in the middle of a forest fire, and it ain't a good place to be. What do you want to do, sir?"

"How far do you reckon it is to the road?"

"A quarter mile to a half, maybe a little more." Tiro's forehead creased. "Are you thinking of taking it now?"

"I am," Stiger said. "If we continue south and stay in the forest, our pace will be slowed and the fire may catch up to us."

"You are hoping to reach the road," Tiro said, "then follow it and gain ground on the fire?"

"Once on the road, we should be able to outpace the fire," Stiger said. "We march hard on the road a dozen or more miles south, then cut west into the forest and move back towards the Third. That is, assuming we can outrace the fire."

"It makes sense to me, sir," Tiro said with a glance in the direction of the valley, where thick clouds of smoke driven by a gust of wind were billowing up into the brightening sky. A loud crash signified the falling of a tree somewhere down-slope. This was almost immediately followed by a roaring of flame, the tops of which they could see. "Perhaps we should get a move on."

"Bren." Stiger called the scout over. "Go along the ridge," he pointed, "find the road, and determine if the enemy is there. We are going to use the road to outpace the fire."

"If it is clear of the enemy, sir," Bren said, "do you want me to wait for you or continue south on the road?"

"Yes, wait for us," Stiger said. "Aronus can go forward after that."

"I can keep goin', sir," Bren protested, a pained expression on his craggy face.

"I am sure you can," Stiger said. "But I will need you later when we plunge back into the forest. Better to have you fresh, eh? Now, go on and get going. We don't have much time."

"Yes, sir," Bren said and started off, in moments disappearing into the trees.

"Form up!" Stiger shouted. Another tree cracked loudly as it went down. The roaring of the fire grew louder. "Form up!"

CHAPTER SIX

"How are you?" Stiger asked, kneeling next to the litter. He almost sighed with relief at being able to rest. His legs not only burned, but shook slightly.

"Tolerable, sir," Legionary Cavius said, sweat beading on his brow.

His armor had been removed and he wore only his tunic. Cavius was clearly in a lot of pain and struggled to conceal it from his superior. He trembled as if it were cold. The litter he rested upon was a makeshift affair, constructed using two tent poles and heavy weatherproofed canvas hastily cut from a tent. Cavius's litter had been dragged behind one of the mules.

Since the company had stopped for an extended break, the litter had been detached and laid on the ground, providing the wounded legionary a break from the uncomfortable jostling and bouncing that Stiger was sure had been an agonizing experience.

"Tiro says your wound was a clean cut," Stiger said, patting Cavius on the shoulder. A bandage was tied tightly around the left leg. Blood had seeped through to stain the outer side. "He assures me you should be back up and on your feet in no time."

"As soon as the sergeant lets me, sir," Cavius said. "Being hauled along like this is not all it's cracked up to be. But it sure beats being left behind."

"I'd not leave you, or anyone else," Stiger said.

"I appreciate that, sir. I saw what the enemy did to the prisoners," Cavius said. He nodded over to the left.

The seven freed auxiliaries were just a few feet away. Like everyone else, they were exhausted and run down. Bruises and black eyes were evidence of their time spent in captivity.

Stiger's gaze lingered upon the seven. After being liberated, each had retrieved his chainmail armor and an assortment of weapons. Four had armed themselves with bows and short swords. The other three carried only swords and small round shields.

Stiger's eyes roved along the road, where the company was strung out on both sides. Men had dropped to the ground. Most had fallen into an instant sleep. A few sat and ate, looking despondent with exhaustion. Corporal Varus was moving down from the front of the column, checking the mules to make sure the supplies were secure and the animals tethered. Sergeant Tiro was farther down the road, speaking with Bren. A moment later, Bren gave a firm nod and set off scouting ahead.

"All the more reason to leave no one behind," Stiger said, turning back to Cavius.

"Yes, sir."

"Focus on rest and healing," Stiger said.

Ash began to fall again like snow. Stiger coughed, throat dry and hoarse from the smoke. He had pushed his company hard trying to gain as much ground as possible on the blaze. At the pace he had set, Stiger figured they were now several miles from the fire. At least, he hoped so.

An ugly pall of smoke hung overhead, obscuring the sun and creating near-twilight conditions. Stiger looked off to the west and into the trees. Had he felt confident enough, he would have plunged into the forest. However, judging from the ash fall, the fire behind them was growing in scope and intensity. He felt a need to put some serious distance between himself and the blaze before turning west. The only way to accomplish that was to march hard along the road.

With luck, the enemy was behind them and not to the front.

"I want you to focus on getting better," Stiger said, making an effort to reinforce his earlier statement. "No pushing it. Just lie back and enjoy the ride. You will be marching along with the rest of us soon enough."

"Yes, sir," Cavius replied, as if Stiger had given him an order, which, in effect, he had.

Stiger squeezed Cavius on the shoulder before standing. His legs protested, and it took effort to keep from groaning.

Stiger strode over to where the auxiliaries were resting alongside the road, clustered about the trunk of an old oak. One saw him approaching and made to stand. Stiger waved him and the others back down.

"Do you men need anything?" Stiger asked the auxiliaries.

"No, sir," one of the men said as the others shook their heads. "We're just grateful you rescued us."

"What's your name?"

"Ubid," the man said.

"What unit were you with?"

"The Sixth Hannish Cohort," Ubid said. "We was light infantry, sir."

"I see," Stiger said. "I would appreciate you telling me what happened. How did you come into the hands of the enemy?"

Ubid glanced nervously around and swallowed before working up the nerve to speak. Stiger well understood the man's concern. An entire auxiliary cohort had been lost, complete with her standards. The punishment for losing a standard was severe and could result in the execution of any survivors. Before they had departed, Tiro had ordered a search of the enemy's camp. It had proven fruitless.

"We was captured, sir," Ubid said. "Farms were being raided by bandits about ten miles north of the garrison. A few families were burned out. The captain marched the cohort to chase them off. We thought nothin' of it at the time. Well, we was ambushed right good by the Rivan."

"Sir." One of the other auxiliaries stood. "There was no warning. They attacked us on the road in a heavily forested area. They hit from both sides at once. It was a slaughter. Our cohort never stood a chance, sir."

"What's your name?"

"Dergo, sir."

Stiger was silent a moment as he considered what they had told him.

"I am curious," Stiger said. "Can you tell me, how did the fort fall? Surely your captain left a reserve? He would not have taken the entire cohort with him when he marched, would he?"

"I don't know how the fort fell, sir," Dergo said. "Lieutenant Aggar was left behind with forty men as a garrison."

Stiger's eyes narrowed as he looked from face to face. Each shook his head in turn.

"Did you see Aggar being held prisoner?" Stiger said, eager to hear what they had to say on the subject. "Or his body?"

"No, sir," Dergo said.

Stiger felt himself frown. "How about any of the men who were left with him?"

Dergo glanced around at his companions and then back at Stiger. "No, sir. We didn't see them, nor even their bodies. Which is strange, now that you mention it."

"So," Stiger said, thinking it through aloud, "they may have escaped then?"

"It is possible, sir," Dergo said. "Though I doubt they would get far if they did hoof it."

"Why do you say that?"

"Well, a force of enemy cavalry rode through the valley the day you attacked and rescued us," Dergo said. "We were being held outside. I saw them as they rode by and counted. Around one hundred strong."

"You mean cavalry is ahead of us on this road?"

Dergo gave a nod.

"The scouts..." Stiger said, thinking back to Bren's report, "have seen no evidence of a large body of cavalry, or for that matter even infantry, using this road."

In fact, the more Stiger thought on it, if Aggar had abandoned his post and fled, he had not taken this road. Bren and Aronus would have seen evidence of their exodus. They must have gone elsewhere or been killed when the Rivan company had taken possession of the fort. It was possible that the rescued auxiliaries had simply not seen their bodies.

"They might have taken the road to the Becket Plantation," Ubid said.

"That could have been where they went." Dergo nodded in agreement.

"Where is that?" Stiger asked. He could not recall seeing any other roads on the map.

"A mile to that way." Dergo pointed and swung his arm around in an arc. "It starts at the western end of the valley and goes for five or six miles, then wraps around and connects to this here road farther up a ways. The Becket Plantation is off of it."

"I take it the plantation is a large one?"

"Aye, sir," Dergo said. "Largest in the region, with over two hundred slaves. Occasionally we are called upon to chase down those that up and run off."

Stiger was silent as he absorbed this, pleased with the information he had learned so far.

"Tell me about the enemy army."

"What army?" Dergo's forehead scrunched up.

"The Rivan army marching this way." Stiger was surprised they had not heard of it yet, even from his own men.

"We did not know," Dergo said, looking suddenly nervous. "The enemy didn't say anything to us, only asked us questions."

Stiger changed the subject. "Can you use those bows?" He gestured at one leaning against the trunk of the tree.

"Yes, sir." Dergo picked up the weapon as if it were an old friend. "These are our bows. The enemy took 'em when we were captured. You show me an enemy you want dead and I will shoot him for you."

Stiger turned at the crunch of footsteps behind him and saw Tiro. Stiger looked over the auxiliaries again and then at his men resting along both sides of the road. Thanks to the late Captain Cethegus, the Seventh was a shadow of her former strength.

"Sergeant," Stiger said to Tiro, "have these men entered into the company books."

"Yes, sir." Tiro turned to the auxiliaries, flashing a broad smile. "Welcome to the Seventh, you maggots."

"Truly?" Dergo seemed shocked, almost as if he had not heard correctly. "You're making us all legionaries?"

"No punishment, sir?" Ubid asked, a guarded yet hopeful expression crossing his face.

"No punishment," Stiger said. "When you complete your service, you will be entitled to Mal'Zeelan citizenship."

"Thank you, sir," Dergo said, which was immediately followed by an enthusiastic chorus from the others. "We won't let you down none."

"I expect not. Work hard and serve the empire to the best of your ability," Stiger said. "In return, I promise I will be fair with you in my dealings."

He gave them a parting nod and stepped away. Tiro followed.

"Being auxiliaries and all, they may not be up for it," Tiro said, once they were out of hearing. "Most auxiliary cohorts don't have our standards."

"Yes," Stiger said, stifling a yawn. "I know, but we're incredibly shorthanded. No replacements were available before we marched. I'd be foolish to pass up seven healthy, able-bodied men."

"Aye, sir," Tiro said. "Varus and I will whip them into shape, don't you doubt that."

"They said that cavalry passed through the valley yesterday." Stiger came to a stop. "Apparently there is another road to the west that connects with this one somewhere ahead. It leads to a large plantation. They may be ahead of us."

"Cavalry to the front and fire to the rear," Tiro said, expelling a breath. "Screwed if you do, even more screwed if you don't. How things have been going, that should be our motto, sir."

Stiger felt himself frown at that.

"The auxiliaries told me they were ambushed to the north of the valley and that a force was left behind at the fort under command of Lieutenant Aggar," Stiger said. "They saw no sign of him or his men as they were brought back as prisoners."

"Is that the same Aggar we were sent to fetch?"

"Yes," Stiger said. "Did you see an officer amongst the dead auxiliaries when you looked about?"

"Not that I could tell," Tiro said. "I'd recall if I saw an officer's tunic."

A strong gust of wind blew through the trees, bending limbs and rustling leaves. The falling ash and smoke swirled around them. In the distance, there was the distinct, low grumble of thunder.

"Well," Tiro said, brightening, "looks like rain might be coming. Perhaps it will slow the fire a bit, even put it out."

"If it does," Stiger said, "the enemy army may be on the move soon after."

"Always looking on the bright side of things, sir," Tiro said with a grin, "aren't you?"

"Weren't you just the one who said our new motto should be, 'Screwed if you do, even more screwed if you don't'?"

"Aye, sir," Tiro said. "That I did."

Stiger chuckled.

"Let's give the men another ten minutes," Stiger said, "then we push on and hope the rain holds off."

CHAPTER SEVEN

Lightning flashed across the sky, illuminating the rain-slashed night. The trees, cultivated fields, and three farm buildings were in view for a fraction of a moment and then gone. Stiger lay prone in the grass, the rain pouring down around him. Bren was to his right and Tiro to his left. Not only was Stiger exhausted, but he was thoroughly soaked through and utterly miserable.

"They are in that big barn there, sir." Bren pointed as a gust blew the rain nearly sideways. "The officer seems to have taken the house for himself."

Another flash of lightning illuminated the structure. The barn was large, though the accompanying farmhouse was surprisingly small, modest even. Stiger wiped rain from his face with a muddy hand and tried to make out their surroundings a little better. They were just over a mile off the road. The small farm was tucked neatly into the forest a ways beyond the road that led to the Becket Plantation, perhaps a couple of miles back.

"How long have you been watching?" Stiger had to raise his voice a little to be heard over the rain, wind, and thunder.

"About an hour," Bren said.

"Where are their sentries?" Tiro asked.

"Near as I can tell, there are none," Bren said. "It's so nasty out, I think they all went inside." Lightning flashed again.

Thunder followed shortly after. "I crept up to the house and peered in the window. Seems only an officer and a sergeant. The rest of the troop is in the barn stayin' dry and being lazy."

"Did you see the family that lives here?" Stiger hoped they still lived, but was fairly sure the Rivan cavalry troop had killed them, like they had done to the residents of Cora'Tol. The thought angered him.

"Sir," Tiro said, "we need to get the men out of the rain."

"I know." Stiger was silent a moment as he thought, before rolling to his side and facing Tiro. "Think the men have enough left in them for another fight?"

"Aye, sir," Tiro said. "They may be miserable, wet, and exhausted, but the bastards will fight if we tell them that barn there is the only place that's dry for miles around."

"Right then," Stiger said and turned back to Bren. "How many do you think are in the barn?"

"Twenty," Bren said, "at most."

"Okay." Stiger rubbed his chin. "That's not too bad. How many entrances to the barn?"

"Two large sliding doors on either end and a smaller door in the middle on this side." Bren pointed. In the darkness, Stiger could not make it out. He took the scout's word for it.

"It'll be nice to catch those cavalry bastards off their horses," Tiro said. "It's time we gave them a little payback for what was done to the captain and the rest of the boys."

Stiger nodded in agreement.

"The bulk of the company will assault the barn," Stiger said. "Tiro, you and Varus lead them. I will take five men and handle the farmhouse. I want that officer alive."

"Bren," Tiro said, "you stick with the lieutenant and make sure nothing happens to him or you answer to me. Got that?"

"Yes, Sergeant."

Stiger pulled himself to his feet. Hunched over, he worked his way back to the men, who waited a few yards away. Tiro and Bren followed. Orders were tersely passed about. The mules were left in the care of a handful of men, while the rest of the company moved forward.

The rain was coming down in sheets and much heavier than before as Stiger led his five men to the house. One of the men with him lost his footing and slipped, landing heavily in the mud. Stiger helped him up as lightning illuminated the area in another flash. The crash of thunder followed several heartbeats later. Stiger froze, glancing at the windows, just steps away, soft orange light emanating from within. He hoped no one was watching.

Stiger pulled his sword out. The others did the same. Hunched over, he crept up to the window. The glass was of poor quality, but he was able to peer through.

A solitary man sat at a table with his feet up, wearing only a service tunic. The man had his back to the window and appeared to be dozing. Stiger could not see where his armor was, nor his sword. A nice-sized fire was burning in the hearth off to the man's left. Stiger could see no one else, though there was a closed door that led to another room. He ducked down and moved up to the door.

Bren had his hand on the latch. Their eyes met. Stiger held up three fingers, prepared to count down silently.

Three.

Two.

One.

Bren lifted the latch and yanked open the door. Stiger moved rapidly through. The man at the table started and turned, eyes going wide. Stiger was across the room in a flash. His sword point hovered at the man's throat. Stiger's enemy had gone very still, eyes traveling from the sword up to Stiger's face.

Stiger flashed him a pleased grin and held a finger to his lips. The man nodded in understanding. Bren stepped forward and removed the enemy's sword, which lay upon the table.

From behind the door there came a strangled scream, then what sounded like a slap, followed by something said in a harsh tone. Stiger motioned to Bren to cover the man at the table and then stepped to the door. He threw it open. The hinges, badly in need of an oiling, creaked. He found himself in a bedroom. On the bed lay a naked man atop a woman.

The man looked up in anger, which rapidly turned to astonishment, then fear. He rolled off the woman and moved toward his sword, which rested in a scabbard in the corner.

"Go for it," Stiger said, stepping closer and lowering his sword to the man's chest. Anger coursed through his veins. "Go on, you bastard. Go for it. See what happens."

"I surrender," the naked man said in slightly accented Common. He held his hands up. "I surrender."

Stiger motioned with his sword for the man to move to the foot of the bed. He did as bid. One of Stiger's men came into the room, sword drawn.

"Get him out of here."

"Yes, sir." The legionary grabbed the naked man by the hair, eliciting a yelp of pain. He dragged him through the doorway and out into the other room.

Stiger turned to the woman, who had curled up into a ball on the bed. She shook violently as she warily eyed him. Stiger took a deep breath and lowered his sword. He cast about the room. A single oil lantern burned on a shelf.

Under it was a discarded dress. He stepped over and tossed it to her, but she made no move to grab it.

"It is all right," he said to her, sheathing his sword. "I am Lieutenant Stiger, Seventh Company, Third Legion. That bastard won't harm you again. I swear it."

She said nothing, just shivered on the bed. Stiger considered going to her and offering what comfort he could, but then changed his mind. He had to find out how the fight in the barn had gone.

"Bren," Stiger called.

"Sir." Bren stepped into the room. He eyed the terrified woman for a moment before sucking in a deep breath.

"Secure those bastards," Stiger said. "And care for her."

"Yes, sir."

Satisfied, Stiger made his way out of the house. He stepped out into the rain and to the barn. He encountered a legionary standing in the downpour, just before the door. He had clearly been posted there as a sentry.

By the man's relaxed stance, Stiger realized the assault was over. His men had won. He made his way into the barn, which was hot from the press of bodies, including animals. There were at least twenty horses inside and all were unsettled. One whinnied and kicked at the wall in a wild panic, while a legionary attempted to calm it.

The sweet, sickly smell of blood was on the air. Several legionaries stood aside as Stiger entered. He stopped and looked around, carefully surveying the interior of the barn. It was a scene of chaos and carnage. Bodies lay scattered across the straw-covered floor amidst the animal shit.

"Sir," Tiro said, coming up, "the barn is secure. How did it go in the house?"

"Two prisoners," Stiger said. "One woman rescued, though I fear her virtue is not intact."

Tiro got the message and his face hardened.

"Casualties?" Stiger asked.

"We got lucky," Tiro said. "Two light injuries. One shallow cut on an arm and the other across the cheek." Tiro paused and made a show of studying Stiger's face. "Not as glamorous as yours, sir."

"Prisoners?"

"Three." Tiro jerked a thumb at where three men knelt with their hands behind their heads. "We've already put the injured out of their misery."

"Those horses make this a nice catch," Stiger said, eyes roving the barn.

"They do, don't they? Some good prize money, I am sure."

"Sir." Varus came up. There was a hard look to his face. "You need to see this."

Stiger and Tiro followed Varus out of the barn and back into the rain. The corporal led them around the far side to three bodies. One man and two young boys. Stiger knelt before the man. Lightning flashed, illuminating the grisly scene. The man looked as if he had been thoroughly beaten before he was killed. The children appeared to have been tortured as well.

Stiger felt a deep sadness mixed with a weary exhaustion wash over him. When he had started out to join the legions he had naively imagined glorious charges and victorious battlefields, not this. These poor people had not deserved what fortune had thrown their way, nor had the people of Cora'Tol. He felt a surge of renewed rage.

War was far uglier than he had ever imagined.

Kneeling in the mud, he bowed his head and said a brief prayer to the High Father, commending these three souls into the great god's keeping. He spared a look at the two little boys. They could be no older than seven. Blowing out a long breath, he stood and turned to Tiro and Varus.

"See that they are buried," Stiger ordered, voice harsh and cold. "I will tell the mother that her children and husband are dead." He paused, his throat catching. "I don't want her seeing this."

"Aye, sir," Tiro said. "We will take care of it."

"What about the prisoners?" Varus asked.

Stiger was silent for a moment as he considered their fate. He glanced at the bodies and ground his teeth in frustration. "We question them, then put the bastards to death."

"Are you sure, sir?" Tiro asked.

"Yes," Stiger said. He turned to Varus. "Drag all of the bodies out of the barn. Bring the mule train inside. Set a watch well away from the barn and house. I don't want to be surprised like these fools were. The men can sleep 'til morning."

"Yes, sir," Varus said.

Stiger looked over at the bodies, eyes lingering upon the small, dark shapes of the children.

After a moment he stepped away, moving around the side of the barn. When he was fully around the corner and away from the others, he fell to his knees and retched, emptying the contents of his stomach. Tears pricked at his already wet face and he cried for the two children. When he had joined the legions, he never imagined such senseless horror.

Stiger felt a hand upon his shoulder. He stiffened and glanced back.

"Are you all right, sir?" Tiro asked, voice gruff.

Lightning flashed across the sky and Stiger could read the concern on the sergeant's face.

"Are you injured, sir?"

"No, I'm fine," Stiger said. "The children…"

"War ain't pretty," Tiro said. "Not for us soldiers, and especially not for civilians. Best to remember that, sir."

Tiro reached down and helped him to his feet. Stiger's legs shook from exhaustion and strain.

"I suppose it's not," Stiger said and sucked in a deep, shuddering breath. He wiped his mouth and stiffened his spine. "War is nothing like I thought it was."

"No," Tiro said. "War brings out the worst in people, but it also brings out the best. In comrades that is, sir."

Stiger held the sergeant's gaze for a prolonged moment, nodded, then turned away and started for the house. Tiro followed.

A legionary stood out in front on sentry duty, eyes watchful. Stiger stepped past him and entered.

The two prisoners sat at the table. Three legionaries stood around them, swords drawn. The naked man had been permitted to don his tunic.

"Name?" Stiger demanded as he entered. Tiro shut the door.

"Lieutenant Crief, Second Horse Regiment," the man Stiger had found in the bedroom announced. There was not a trace of fear in his tone, which infuriated Stiger. "And yours, sir?"

"Stiger."

"Stiger, hmmm," Crief said. "I know that name, ah yes. I do. Your father is a general I think. A bloody general if I recall, yes?"

"Who my father is matters not," Stiger said and took a step nearer the other officer. He was angered at Crief's relaxed manner. Stiger turned to the other seated at the table. This man looked back at him with wary eyes. "And what is your name?"

The other man said nothing, but instead glanced to Crief.

"He does not speak your Common Tongue," Crief said, a hint of disdain in his voice. "That is Sergeant Sig and he is as odious as his brain is small."

Stiger shared a glance with Tiro before turning back to Crief.

"Why are you here?"

Crief had the gall to bark out a laugh, which irritated Stiger further.

The legionary standing behind Crief cuffed the enemy officer on the back of the head. "The lieutenant asked you a question, scum."

"How dare you lay a hand on me?" Crief screamed at him in outrage. "You common lout, I will have you know I am the Lord General's son."

Stiger held up a hand to stop Crief from being struck again. The legionary took a step back.

"And who is this Lord General?" Stiger asked, though he suspected it was the commander of the enemy army.

"My father, of course," Crief said.

Stiger let out a long breath before turning to look upon the enemy sergeant and contemplating the man for a few heartbeats.

"Tiro, have Sergeant Sig here placed with the other prisoners."

"Yes, sir." Tiro nodded and gestured to two men. The sergeant was hauled to his feet and led out into the rain. When the door closed, Stiger turned back to Crief, who had placed his feet up on the table and was reclining his chair back. He seemed to be enjoying himself. The smug look on his face irritated Stiger immensely.

"Lieutenant Crief," Stiger said slowly as he untied the straps to his helmet. "You seem to be under the mistaken impression that your rank somehow protects you."

Stiger removed his helmet and placed it on the table as Crief's eyes narrowed.

"I can assure you it doesn't," Stiger said as he moved slowly around the table to stand next to Crief. The other's eyes followed him. Stiger could read a flicker of doubt in them.

"You wouldn't dare touch me," Crief said loftily, placing his hands behind his head as he leaned back farther on the chair. "My father—"

Stiger kicked the chair out from under him. Crief landed with a crash on the floor. Before he could recover, Stiger reached down and grabbed the front of Crief's tunic, hauled him up, and slammed his fist into the man's face. Stiger punched him again and felt the nose crunch under the blow.

"Do you still believe I won't touch you?" Stiger roared at him, thoroughly enraged. "Do you?"

"My father will—"

Stiger hit him again.

"Will what?" Stiger demanded. "Come on, tell me what your daddy will do to me."

Dazed, Crief's eyes rolled.

"Sir."

Thoroughly enraged, Stiger looked over at Tiro.

"If you continue to knock him senseless," Tiro said, "we won't be able to properly question him, now, will we?"

Stiger glanced over at his fist, which was raised and ready to continue the pummeling. He looked back on the bloodied face of his enemy. It had felt good to hit this arrogant fop. He took a deep breath that shuddered a little. Tiro was right. Stiger released Crief, who collapsed to the floor in a heap.

Stiger's rage left him. His hand began to hurt and he shook it a little before turning to the last remaining legionary. "Take this raping piece of shit from my sight."

"Aye, sir," the man said and dragged Crief bodily out into the rain.

Tiro untied the straps of his own helmet and placed it on the table next to Stiger's.

"Feel better?" Tiro asked, shutting the door.

"A little," Stiger said, suddenly feeling drained and worn out, like an old dishrag.

Tiro picked up the chair and set it back on its feet. Stiger watched as the old sergeant threw another log onto the fire.

"You need some sleep, sir," Tiro said. "You're exhausted."

"We all do," Stiger said and turned toward the door to the bedroom. He could hear whimpering coming from the other side.

"Varus and I will see to the men and the questioning," Tiro said. "Will the lieutenant do me a great favor and get some sleep?"

Stiger turned his weary gaze upon Tiro.

"I have one more task to complete before I can," Stiger said and started for the door, prepared to inform the young woman in the next room she was now a widow. Worse, he dreaded passing on the news about her children.

"What about Crief?" Tiro asked.

"What about him?"

"Do we kill him with the rest?"

Stiger wanted desperately to say yes, but then shook his head. General Treim would want Crief.

"If he is as important as he thinks he is," Stiger said, "he has value to the enemy. We will bring him back with

69

us. Question him thoroughly, but make sure you keep him alive."

"Yes, sir," Tiro said before his eyes traveled to the door. "I could tell the lady."

"No," Stiger said with a heavy breath. "I will do it."

Stiger opened the door and found the young woman in the corner of the room crying. She was still naked. Though he wanted to do anything but, Stiger steeled himself to give the most devastating news that anyone could possibly give another.

CHAPTER EIGHT

Stiger closed the door behind him. The ground out in front of the house was wet and muddy. A few scattered strands of grass littered the farmyard. The sentry standing just to the side of the door stiffened to attention and saluted.

"At ease," Stiger said, stretching out his back. "Did you get much sleep, Tig?"

"According to Sergeant Tiro, I got plenty, sir," Tig replied, relaxing a fraction. "When he woke me, he told me sleep is overrated."

"That sounds like Tiro," Stiger chuckled. "Well, I am sure you got enough then."

"If you say so, sir."

Stiger wore only his service tunic, and it felt good to have left his armor in the house. He gazed around the farmyard. The rain had slackened considerably an hour ago. Now it was coming down in a steady drizzle. The sky was thick with low-hanging cloud cover. Stiger glanced back at the house, which was well-constructed and maintained, but very modest.

The barn a few yards away was overly large, but also well-built. The farmer had obviously taken pride in his work, for everything appeared well-cared-for and orderly. Even the four cords of wood along the barn's wall were stacked neatly.

There was a small fenced-in pasture off to his left, enough for a handful of animals. A good-sized field with wheat ready for harvest was to the right. Part of the field had been given over to potatoes. A vegetable garden stretched out to the left of the house, in which Stiger could see tomatoes, lettuce, and melons. It looked like there were even beans.

Judging by what he saw, the farm would have been more than enough to sustain the family. Any excess would have likely been sold to those living in Cora'Tol, perhaps even to the garrison.

Tucked deep into the forest, the farm was a peaceful setting. The farmer had chosen a nice spot. It was almost perfect, but for the arrival of the Rivan.

Stiger let out a heavy breath.

The enemy had forever shattered the peace of this place. Mood darkening, he started off for the barn, careful to avoid the puddles as he made his way across the farmyard. There was work to be done.

A sentry stood in front of the barn and two others by the trail, which led into the forest and ultimately connected with the main road. Stiger was heartened by their presence and watchfulness. As he stepped through the door, he nodded to the sentry, who stiffened to attention.

The barn was surprisingly warm. The close proximity of so many of his legionaries, coupled with the animals, generated more heat than the fire had in the house. Stiger took a moment to survey the interior of the barn. Most of his men were still sleeping. Varus was up and about. Tiro was sleeping just a few feet away, snoring contentedly. The old sergeant looked almost peaceful, nothing like the hardened veteran Stiger knew him to be.

Stiger caught Varus's eye and motioned the man over.

"How are you feeling, sir?" Varus asked in a low tone so as not to disturb those sleeping.

"Well enough," Stiger said, stifling a yawn. "You?"

"Passable, sir."

"Thank you for letting me sleep," Stiger said. "I think I managed at least six hours. But truth be told, I'm still bone tired."

"You needed it, sir. We're all done in," Varus said. "A few days of catch-up is all we need. Then we will be right as rain."

Stiger nodded as he ran his eyes once more about. He had seen his men asleep dozens of times, and yet suddenly he felt moved. The men in this barn had become dear to him. He recognized that now. Though they were mostly uneducated and without culture, he had long since stopped seeing them as mere pawns to be used and discarded in the furtherance of his career. Tiro and Varus had helped show him that.

Stiger nodded to himself. These men had gone through terrible trials and tests with him, perhaps even for him. They would march where he asked them to go, even if death waited at day's end. They were his men and he was their officer. He had come to love Seventh Company. It made what he was about to ask of them more difficult than he had imagined possible.

"Sleep is one commodity I don't think we're going to get much of," Stiger said, throat catching slightly. He took a moment to clear it. "We need to get a move on. That rain likely extinguished the fire. The enemy will soon be on the move and I have no doubt they will be looking for us. Especially after all that we've done."

"Aye," Varus said with a slow nod. "When do you want to leave, sir?"

"Soon," Stiger said and then eyed Varus. "You questioned the prisoners?"

"Yes, sir," Varus said. "Just after Tiro had checked in with you. We did it away from the farm."

Tiro had woken Stiger just before dawn and suggested that they take advantage of the inclement weather to allow the men to sleep in for a few more hours. Stiger had agreed and gone back to sleep. While he had gotten in those last precious hours, Stiger now understood that Tiro and Varus had been working over the prisoners.

"I wish you had woken me for that."

"You needed the sleep more than most, sir," Varus said. "You've been pushing yourself hard, sir. Besides, that's no job for a proper officer."

Stiger did not like that they had tried to shield him.

"Next time," Stiger said, adding a firm undertone, "you will make sure I am there. Understand my meaning?"

"Aye, sir," Varus said. "I do."

"Good," Stiger said. "Learn anything?"

"Yes, sir," Varus said. "We did."

Stiger saw Tiro stir. The sergeant opened his eyes and looked in their direction. Tiro stretched and then pulled himself to his feet. He walked stiffly over toward the two of them, cracking his neck as he came.

"Good morning, sir," Tiro said cheerfully.

"More like early afternoon," Stiger said, suspecting that the sergeant already knew this.

"Really?" Tiro said and made a show of glancing out the open door behind Stiger. "I would never have guessed, sir. Must'a overslept."

Stiger tired of the game. "Varus here was telling me that you got something from the prisoners?"

"Yes, sir." Tiro scratched at his jaw and grew serious. "Well, it's certain now and confirmed. The enemy definitely has a second army. It's up north, perhaps thirty to forty miles off. No idea on the actual size of said army, other than it's quite large." Tiro paused and let out a long breath. "And as we had thought, the troop of cavalry that we caught here is part of the regiment camping over at the Becket Plantation. We learned they sacked the plantation and murdered those that lived there, including the slaves. Great, bloody, murderous bastards, aren't they?" Tiro paused and glanced at the captured horses. "Lieutenant Crief's troop was to patrol south a few miles. The rain caught them on the road before they could return. Though they smelled smoke from the fire in the valley, they apparently knew nothing about it. It seems Crief decided to hole up and wait for the rain to pass. Our good fortune and his bad luck, and the bad luck of the family that lived here."

"So," Stiger said, thinking through what the sergeant told him, "this regiment likely doesn't know where the troop spent the night? Do I have that right?"

"You know," Varus drawled, with a slight trace of a grin, "I asked Lieutenant Crief that very same question. After a bit of persuasion, he became very cooperative and insisted he didn't get around to dispatching a messenger. One of the other prisoners who spoke Common confirmed this. Said the lieutenant was a lazy officer, sir."

"Well, that's a bit of luck, isn't it?" Stiger said. "What of the cavalry regiment's plans? Did he say anything?"

"All he knows is that they were to sit tight," Varus said. "At least long enough for that infantry company to finish up their business in the valley and move up. That would be the one we attacked and slaughtered, sir."

Tiro suddenly grinned. "With luck, they will be waiting for a good long time."

"Then what?" Stiger asked. "Do we know what their plans were?"

"Well," Tiro said, "we think they were going to move up to the next fort along this road and try to lure the garrison out from behind the walls."

"Like they did with Cora'Tol's garrison," Varus said. "That's what we are guessing."

"You are not sure on that?" Stiger looked from Varus to Tiro for confirmation.

"No, sir," Tiro said. "Only that the infantry and cavalry were to deal with the next fort before the army moved up."

"I see," Stiger said. His eyes once again swept the interior of the barn. He felt a sudden sadness again for what he must ask of his men. Though he loved the Seventh, there was service to the empire and duty to consider. Stiger gave an unconscious nod. He sucked in a breath and turned back to Tiro and Varus. "Both of you. Come with me."

Stiger led them from the barn back to the farmhouse. On the table he had left the map they had taken from the Rivan encampment, small stones holding its corners down. Tiro closed the door and moved over to the table. A good fire crackled in the hearth, and the smell of smoke was strong in the small room. The door to the bedroom was closed, but Stiger could still hear weeping. His anger welled with the heartbreaking sound, and it only strengthened his resolve.

"I am tired of running," Stiger said without any preamble, and he meant it. "I don't fancy being chased all the way back to the Third."

"What are you thinking, sir?" Tiro's tone was careful.

"Catching this Rivan cavalry troop here was fortunate. We now have multiple horses. I am going to send a couple of men with remounts back to the Third. Pushing themselves, they should be able to make it through the forest in a couple of days, three at the most. If we take the entire

company...well, on foot it will take us all much longer."
Stiger paused. "I would appreciate your thoughts on this."

Varus looked to Tiro.

"Sending two men back to the legion is a sound plan,
sir," Tiro said, eyeing Stiger. "Where are you thinking of taking the rest of us?"

Stiger had expected the question.

"Here." Stiger pointed down at the map, where a fort had
been circled in charcoal pencil. He tapped the fort again
for emphasis. Stiger moved his finger farther north. "If I
am correct, we are here, just twenty miles distant. Though
I don't know for sure, with luck there is an auxiliary cohort
stationed there."

Tiro and Varus said nothing.

"My thinking is this," Stiger continued. "We march to
this fort and alert the garrison as to what is coming. I will
strongly encourage the prefect to make the correct decision
and march south with us. We take the garrison to the next
fort, and I will also encourage that prefect to march with us,
until we come to this one here."

Stiger pointed at the last fort on the chain, before the
map's drawn arrow turned sharply west toward the north-
south road that Third Legion had marched north on just
a few weeks before. Stiger took this to mean this was the
enemy's planned route of advance. He glanced up at Tiro
and Varus before looking back down at the map.

"We hold here." Stiger tapped his finger on the last fort
again. "As long as Fortuna is on our side, we should have
three garrison cohorts and our company to defend the fort.
That should give us close to fifteen hundred men. We hold,
delay the enemy's advance, and we wait for the Third to
arrive and relieve us."

Tiro drew in a breath and spared a glance with Varus.

"A lot of shoulds in there, sir," Tiro said. "Fortuna is known to be fickle."

"Yes," Stiger agreed. "It could go badly for us, particularly if the Third can't reach us in time."

"I am pleased the lieutenant recognizes that," Tiro said.

"We hold until General Treim arrives," Stiger said. "That is the key to my plan. By holding this fort, we can block the enemy's advance."

"And..." Varus said slowly, "if he doesn't come?"

"Then we are in the shit," Stiger said. "As long as our boys make it, the general will have no choice but to come." Stiger pointed at the map. "The enemy army is marching down this road, well away from the main fighting. Truly, it is a brilliant plan. Uncontested, they will sweep south far behind our army, neatly cutting off communications. General Treim will not—no, let me correct that. He *cannot* allow that to happen." Stiger nodded, feeling almost as if he were convincing himself. "Yes, he will come. As long as our messengers make it to him, he will come. Our problem will be holding. And hold we must, at least long enough for the Third to arrive, relieve us, and check the enemy's advance."

"What if the enemy just bypasses us?" Varus asked. "They might march around the fort and ignore us."

"They can't afford to leave us behind their advance," Stiger said. "We will be a threat to their communications and supply. No, they will most assuredly assault the fort."

A silence followed that.

"I don't think those prefects will be too keen on the idea of giving up their forts," Tiro said.

"What if they don't agree to come with us?" Varus asked.

"Then we march without them," Stiger said and ran a hand through his short-cropped hair. "In our diminished state, we won't make much difference stopping to hold with a single auxiliary cohort. Our only hope is to concentrate the cohorts and together hold the last fort.

"This is the only road south within easy reach." Stiger paused, eyes roving over the map. After a moment, he looked back up. "We are surrounded by forest. If we don't do this, the enemy could very well get behind the Third and cut off supply to our army. I think we can all imagine how much of a disaster that would be. I hope you both understand, I cannot allow that to happen. This is a risk I feel we must take, even if it means the destruction of the company."

Tiro and Varus were silent as they considered Stiger's plan.

"All that said..." Stiger sucked in a breath and let it out slowly. "I will not embark upon this plan without your support. Should you both disagree with me, I will take the company through the forest and back to the Third, while sending messengers ahead with word of what I believe to be the enemy's intentions."

Tiro rubbed the back of his neck and returned his gaze back to the map before looking meaningfully at Varus. After a moment, the sergeant looked over at Stiger.

"What's life without a little risk, eh?" Tiro said.

"There is a lot of risk with this plan," Stiger said. "I ask for your full support in this endeavor."

A few weeks ago, Stiger would never have dreamed of asking for anything from a ranker. A lot had changed in such a short time.

"It's bold," Tiro said after a prolonged silence, placing both fists upon the table. "Sir, I must admit I don't like it very much, but if it works...well, there is the very real chance we can make a difference for our brothers in the Third and the rest of the army."

"I can't say I'm..." Varus swallowed and then started again. "I can't really say I'm too fond of being caught on the road by cavalry, sir. Also, I'm none too thrilled about plunging back into the forest either. I say we stick to the road and do what we can for the Third. It is the right thing to do."

Stiger let out a relieved breath.

"Thank you," he said, pausing briefly before continuing. "Mind you, this is all speculation, but I am thinking that the enemy may possibly wait for the rain to stop before leaving the comforts of the plantation. With any luck, the fire will have distracted them. They might even go back to explore the valley. Do you think we can be on the road in an hour? I would like to get marching as soon as possible to put some distance between us and them."

"Aye, sir. We can." Tiro turned to Varus. "Go roust the men. I will be along in a moment to help."

Varus nodded and left the farmhouse without a backward look.

"Do you still want the prisoners executed?" Tiro asked.

Stiger thought on it for a moment, and then nodded. "I think they've earned it, including that one that we brought with us from Cora'Tol."

"What of their lieutenant?"

"All except Crief," Stiger said, unhappily.

"An argument could be made that his men were only following orders," Tiro said. "In their sandals, our boys may have done the same."

"Not while I am in command," Stiger said, and it came out harsher than he intended.

"Sir, if anyone deserves to go, it should be that bastard Crief."

"Agreed. However, I feel duty-bound to turn him over to the general," Stiger said and eyed Tiro for a few heartbeats. "So, you think I should spare the lives of the prisoners?"

"I didn't say that," Tiro said. "It's too dangerous bringing them with us and even more so to let them go. They know our strength and will surely report us. As prisoners, they face a bleak and uncertain future. Slavery is the best they can hope for. Sir, they will look for any opportunity to escape. I've seen it before. This will put anyone assigned to guard them at risk."

Stiger nodded, agreeing with Tiro's logic.

"However, sir," Tiro continued, "dead is dead. Once done, you can't take it back. I want to make sure the lieutenant is certain."

Stiger considered Tiro. As usual, his sergeant was right and onto the heart of the matter.

"Put them to death." Stiger's tone was harsh, but firm. "Do it immediately. Make it fast."

"Yes, sir." Tiro turned and began to leave the farmhouse.

"Tiro," Stiger said, stopping him at the door. "Send Bren and Aronus to me. They will be heading back to the legion. Make sure they have four good horses with plenty of food, feed, and water."

"I will see to it, sir." Tiro turned and left, closing the door behind.

Stiger stared at the closed door for a few heartbeats.

"What am I becoming?" It came out as a whisper. He suspected he already knew the answer to that question.

He pounded the table with his fist. The stones holding the map down jumped a couple of inches into the air.

Stiger turned his gaze back to the map. His eyes found the final fort. He hoped it was a good one, for he was staking his life and those of his men on this bold gamble.

"So be it," Stiger said, snatching up the map and folding it back up. He had rolled the dice.

CHAPTER NINE

"Who the bloody hell are you?" an irritated voice called down from above. The inflection in the speaker's voice spoke of someone raised in the patrician class.

In the dim moonlight, Stiger glanced over at Tiro and shared a knowing look.

"They sure took their time," Tiro said with a shake of the head. "I was growing old just standing here."

"Old man." Stiger grinned.

"Now, sir," Tiro said, "that wasn't kind, not one bit."

Stiger grunted and looked back up at the four men thirty feet above leaning over the lip of the wall just above the fort's main gate. The wall did not seem all that impressive, and it lent the impression that the fort itself was on the small side. The speaker was in the center, while the man on his left held a torch out to better see those below. Stiger assumed the man who had called to him was the garrison's prefect.

It'd taken the watch more than ten minutes to summon their officer. Such a delay in a legionary encampment would have been an unforgivable sin.

"Well?" the voice above asked. The tone was a little shrill and laced heavily with impatience. "I asked you a question, man. Speak up."

"Lieutenant Stiger, Seventh Company, Third Legion," Stiger called back up, before glancing backward at his company. Tiro had given the order for the men to relax. A number had simply sat down on the ground and fallen immediately to sleep. The march to the fort had been exhausting, and it was nearing midnight. During the march, Stiger had only permitted a handful of extended breaks. His men needed a prolonged rest.

There was an exclamation above that brought Stiger's head back around. It was nearly inaudible and was almost immediately followed by hurried muttering. The speaker began gesticulating in his direction. It only served to increase his irritation.

"Stiger?" the voice called back down to him, at first unsure and then a little more firm. "Did you say Stiger?"

"Yes," Stiger said, anger finally overcoming what little was left of his reserve. "I am a bleeding Stiger. Now who are you, sir?"

Next to him, Tiro chuckled. Stiger spared his sergeant a black look, which only served to amuse the old veteran further.

"Sorry, sir," Tiro said in a low tone so those above couldn't overhear. He gave a shrug. "Such is the way with auxiliaries, sir. Best get used to it."

"I am Lieutenant Hollux," the officer called down, "Ninth Light Foot Taborean Cohort. May I ask your purpose?"

"Where is your prefect?" Stiger asked, surprised that the garrison commander had not made an appearance.

"He is not present," Hollux said. "In his absence, I am in command here."

"Well," Stiger said, lowering his voice so that only Tiro could hear, "that makes things a little easier."

"How so, sir?" Tiro asked.

"I should think that obvious," Stiger said. "A legionary lieutenant always outranks the equivalent in the auxiliaries.

Besides," Stiger shot him a smirk, "I am an acting captain. Strictly speaking, I would even trump the prefect."

"Strictly?" Tiro gave a shake of his head. "I would not want to be in the lieutenant's boots should he feel the need to give a cohort commander orders."

"Well," Stiger said, "let's hope it does not come to that."

"Knowing you, sir," Tiro said, "it just might."

"Lieutenant Hollux, open the gate," Stiger called back up, with a sour glance thrown at Tiro.

"How do I know you are who you say you are?" Hollux called back.

Stiger looked to Tiro, eyebrow raised. In the darkness, Stiger understood it would be hard to see his company, most of which was stretched out behind in the darkness.

"Have him throw a torch or two down, sir," Tiro suggested. "We can show him our men, and standard."

"Good idea." Stiger wished he had thought of it first. He turned back to Hollux. "Toss down a couple of torches and we will show you our standard and men."

There was some discussion above and then the man holding the torch dropped it down before the gate. Hissing, the torch landed in the dirt with a soft thud. Another torch was thrown over. Stiger picked one up, while Tiro grabbed the other. He walked back down his column of men, who were mostly off their feet. Stiger held the torch out so that its light fell upon his men.

The standard-bearer had remained standing, using the staff to support himself. He straightened as his officer approached. Stiger held the torch close enough that it illuminated the Seventh's standard and battle honors, which fluttered ever so slightly as a light breeze passed them by.

"Good enough?" Stiger called back.

"Open the gate," Hollux ordered. He disappeared from view.

A few moments later, Stiger could hear the locking mechanism being moved aside. With a great groan and a loud creaking, the heavy wooden gate began to slowly open. Stiger moved back to the front of his column. He dropped the torch, where it sputtered in the moist dirt.

Without orders to do otherwise, those of his men who were awake simply watched. Stiger was in no hurry to order them to their feet. They had marched hard to get here.

When the gate was fully opened, Stiger was pleased to see several files of men standing in a battle line, with short round shields held at the ready. Stiger surmised this was why he had been kept waiting. The ready file had been rousted from slumber, and it had taken them some time to equip themselves and assemble.

"Don't they just seem ready for anything," Tiro commented, irony creeping into his voice. "So far from the fighting, it's heartening to see they are so well prepared."

"That's proper procedure is all," Stiger said, feeling the effects of the march and lack of sleep. Taking out his canteen, he took a hearty swig before returning it to his harness. He rubbed at tired eyes.

"As an old friend of mine was fond of saying," Tiro said, "there are auxiliary cohorts and then there are auxiliary cohorts."

Stiger looked over at his sergeant, wondering if his leg was being pulled.

"Honest, sir," Tiro said. "It was an elf thing, really. Well, I supposed it was a saying amongst their kind, comparing the same thing against itself. Just never had use for it until now."

"You know an elf?" Stiger was highly skeptical.

"Served alongside one of them," Tiro said, becoming slightly indignant. "His name is Eli and we became fast friends. A good one, that elf. I was sad to see him return to his lands."

Stiger eyed his sergeant for several heartbeats. He decided Tiro was not jesting.

"I tell you, sir," Tiro continued wistfully, "it was a sad day the elves withdrew to their own lands."

Hollux and a sergeant stepped out through the gate.

Hollux was a tall man. He stood several inches above Stiger. Wearing auxiliary chainmail armor did nothing to conceal the other officer's painful thinness. Despite that, Hollux had a refined and pampered look about him, which served to confirm Stiger's suspicion that he was from a good family, even though the name was unfamiliar. Likely a second or third son sent off to make his own way in the world. It seemed he had been unable to excel at that and had ended up in the auxiliaries.

He was older, perhaps ten years Stiger's age, which was not a good sign for any junior officer in service to the empire.

The sergeant appeared Tiro's age. He walked with a slight limp and had a hard look about him. The sergeant's neck had been thickened like any other long-service veteran, a mark of the heavy legionary helmets. His eyes were sharp and seemed to miss nothing.

"Lieutenant Stiger, welcome to Fort Footprint." Hollux offered his hand, which Stiger took and found surprisingly firm. Despite that, Hollux seemed uncomfortable. Stiger chalked that up to his family name.

"Lieutenant Hollux," Stiger said, "it is a pleasure to meet you."

"I was not aware that there were any legionary companies operating in the area." Hollux glanced to Tiro and then at Stiger's men. "What brings you out so far from the action?"

Stiger saw the lieutenant's face harden and followed the man's gaze. Cloaks torn and unshaven, his men appeared far from impressive. But Stiger had learned that it wasn't looks that mattered. He saw no judgment mirrored on the auxiliary sergeant's face, only a calm, competent appraisal.

"We were sent to Cora'Tol," Stiger said brusquely. "However, when we got there, we found the town burned and the garrison overrun. I am afraid it is my duty to report Cora'Tol has been destroyed."

"What?" Hollux snapped, shrill tone becoming even more penetrating. "Cora'Tol is gone?"

"Yes, and that's not the worst of it. There is a Rivan army marching this way. They could be here any time."

Hollux and his sergeant exchanged a look.

"Surely that can't be right?" It was apparent Hollux was hoping Stiger was pulling his leg.

"I'm afraid it is." Stiger read the disbelief in Hollux's eyes. He looked over at Tiro. "Sergeant, if you would bring Crief forward."

"Yes, sir."

Hollux watched Tiro step away and then turned his gaze back to Stiger.

"I simply don't believe it." Hollux exchanged another look with his sergeant. "The last we heard, the fighting was well over a hundred miles away. A dispatch rider came through just last week with news Third Legion had won a victory and forced a crossing over the Hana. And you expect me to just trust you that the Rivan are coming? Really?"

"By the gods, you better believe it," Stiger said, anger boiling over as he became hot. This man had just questioned his word. Should he desire it, Stiger would be justified challenging him to a duel. "How dare you question my honor?" Stiger poked Hollux in the chest. The other stepped back, blinking. "I've marched more miles than I can bloody count, and with precious little sleep to boot. We've been pursued and hounded for days by the Rivan. Despite that, we managed not only to elude our pursuers but also to successfully assault an enemy company's encampment at Cora'Tol. Oh, and we learned yesterday there's an enemy cavalry regiment operating just south of the valley. They are probably looking for us for what we've done. How dare you question my word? I've had about all I am going to take from you, sir."

Hollux took another step back and shook his head in dismay at Stiger's outrage. "I...I..." Hollux swallowed and then drew himself up. "Ah, it was not my intention to question your honor, sir. It is apparent you have been through a lot. You caught me by surprise is all. Will you accept my apology?"

Stiger's anger rapidly cooled at the abrupt and seemingly sincere admission. He let out a ragged breath and then nodded.

"I accept your apology, sir."

Tiro and Legionary Asus returned, dragging a battered and bruised Crief between them. The two released the enemy officer just before Hollux. Crief collapsed to the ground, moaning and rocking slightly.

"This bastard," Stiger said, with more than a little disgust, "is Lieutenant Crief, Second Horse Regiment. We caught him and his troop just twenty miles from this here very spot."

"Is he the only prisoner you took, sir?" Hollux's sergeant asked, speaking up for the first time.

"No," Stiger said. "We took others. I had them put to death before we marched."

Hollux seemed surprised by this admission, but his sergeant did not bat an eye. Hollux's eyes traveled from Stiger down to Crief.

"Tell him," Stiger said, nudging Crief with a boot. "Tell Lieutenant Hollux what is coming our way."

Crief stopped moaning and rocking. He looked up at Stiger. His eyes narrowed and Stiger read hate. Crief then turned to Hollux, and his cracked and swollen lips split into a wicked grin.

"My father is coming," Crief cried, then cackled madly. "My father is coming." His voice rose. "He is coming to kill you all." Crief was nearly screaming. "You will all die. Do you hear me? The Rivan are coming for you! I promise—"

Tiro stepped forward and gave Crief a solid kick into his side, which sent him sprawling into the dirt. Crief rolled onto his back and continued to cackle madly. Tiro made to kick him again, but Stiger checked his sergeant with a hand to the chest.

"Take him away," Stiger said.

Crief had done what he had wanted and more. He turned back to Hollux as Tiro and Asus dragged the enemy officer away.

"I take it that settles that?" Stiger said.

Hollux simply nodded and opened his mouth as if to say something, but no words came out.

"What is your name, sergeant?"

"Pazzullo, sir," the sergeant replied and pulled himself to attention. "I served with Eighth Legion for twenty-five years before accepting an assignment with the auxiliaries."

Stiger understood the man's meaning. He had completed his service and been eligible for retirement. Instead, he had taken the position of lead sergeant for an auxiliary cohort, a prestigious post for a ranker. It was possible that after a number of years he might even achieve promotion to lieutenant and be made a gentleman, even if it was only with the auxiliaries. Such a promotion would never have been available to the regulars in the legions. It was an extremely rare thing for a ranker to be elevated.

"Sergeant Pazzullo," Stiger said, "I want you to prepare your men for march. We leave in two hours."

"Yes, sir," Pazzullo said, and Stiger could hear the audible relief in the veteran's tone.

"Full kit," Stiger said to Pazzullo, "and whatever rations the men can carry. Destroy everything else and prepare the fort to be burned."

"What?" Hollux looked to Stiger, eyes wide as if he had suddenly come to his senses. "Hold on a moment. You can't do that. We can't give up the fort."

Pazzullo's eyes snapped to Hollux in alarm.

"Why not?" Stiger said as Tiro returned.

"I don't have orders to do as you say," Hollux said.

Stiger barked out a laugh. "We're well beyond your orders. Do you really want to wait here for the enemy to come marching down that road? By the gods, man, you only have one cohort. Besides, I believe I am the senior ranking officer here. And as such, I am now giving you your orders."

"But you are only a lieutenant," Hollux sputtered, "no better than I."

"A *legionary* lieutenant," Stiger said, "and acting captain of my company."

"But I just can't…"

Stiger had had enough. He turned to the Pazzullo. "Sergeant, do you have any questions concerning your orders?"

"No, sir." Pazzullo did not even glance at his lieutenant this time.

"Then, without further delay, kindly carry out your orders."

"Yes, sir," Pazzullo said and snapped off a salute. He spun on his heel and jogged back into the fort.

"Tiro," Stiger said, "get the men on their feet. They can fall out inside the fort. See what you and Varus can do to help Pazzullo. We march in two hours, whether they are ready or not. Understood?"

"Yes, sir," Tiro said and moved off to deal with the men.

Stiger turned back to Hollux, who looked thoroughly lost by what had just occurred. Stiger felt some sympathy for the man. His life, so far from the fighting, had likely been a quiet one. The worst he had probably had to deal with were bandits and the occasional troubles spawned by greedy tax collectors. Stiger had just turned his world upside down.

"Listen, Hollux," Stiger said and softened his tone. "They are still your men. I don't want to leave you or them behind to face an enemy army alone. Understand me?"

Hollux nodded, swallowed once again, and then met Stiger's eyes. "Where are we going?"

"South," Stiger said. "I have a map, and it shows two more forts down the road. Can you tell me if they have active garrisons?"

"Yes, they each hold a garrison," Hollux said. "Forts Ida and Covenant."

"Good," Stiger said and ran his eyes over the dark walls of Fort Footprint. There could not be more than two hundred men inside. "Is the last fort like this one? On the smallish side?"

"Oh, no," Hollux said. "Fort Covenant is actually quite large and well-fortified. There are two infantry cohorts stationed there. Fort Ida is about the size of this one."

Stiger felt immense relief at hearing that bit of news. It increased their chances of holding until the Third could arrive and relieve them. Stiger's thoughts momentarily strayed and he wondered how Bren and Aronus were faring.

Stiger rubbed at his tired eyes again. They were dry. He blinked several times before focusing back on Hollux.

"What type of cohort is yours?"

"We're a mixed bag, really," Hollux said. "Fifty archers and one hundred light infantry."

Archers would come in handy, Stiger thought.

"You know," Hollux said, taking a dismal turn, "my prefect will be pissed when he learns that I burned his fort."

"We can't leave it for the enemy," Stiger said. "General Treim would have my balls for breakfast if I did. Fort Footprint must be destroyed. I hope you can understand that?"

"I still think he's gonna be unhappy," Hollux said. "Prefect Lears is the kind of man who holds grudges. He won't thank you or I for doing what was necessary."

"I expect not," Stiger said. On the political side, the Lears family was not on friendly terms with the Stigers. "Speaking of which, where is your prefect? Why isn't he here?"

"Lieutenant Aggar from the Cora'Tol Garrison came through with orders for him to report to Fort Covenant for a meeting of cohort commanders."

"Lieutenant Aggar was here?" Stiger felt himself grow cold. "When?"

"Two days ago," Hollux said.

Stiger rubbed his jaw as he considered this news. After a moment, he looked back up at Hollux.

"Do you have any maps?" Stiger asked.

"Yes," Hollux said, "back in headquarters."

"When we set out, we had no plans of coming this way. The only map I have of these parts is one that I took from the enemy. Do you mind if I take a look at them?"

"By all means," Hollux said, having recovered some measure of himself. "We do have several jars of fine wine. Truthfully, it belongs to my prefect, but seeing as how we can't bring it with us and we can't leave it for the enemy..."

"I could use a cup or two," Stiger said with a genuine smile. Hollux was beginning to grow on him. "I haven't enjoyed a good cup of wine since we set out from the Third."

Hollux gestured toward the fort, where Stiger could hear the garrison being rousted. Stiger followed Hollux through the gate, thinking on Lieutenant Aggar and what lay ahead. Behind him, Tiro and Varus had gotten the men to their feet.

CHAPTER TEN

With hands cupped, Stiger brought the water to his parched lips and drank. He took another mouthful and savored the cold chill from the river. Kneeling on the riverbank, he leaned back and closed his eyes a moment. The rain had given way to clear morning skies, and with it, the unseasonal heat had returned with a vengeance. His canteen had run dry several hours ago, and it felt wonderful to drink.

Stiger paused and listened to the sound of the river as it gurgled happily by. The sound was disturbed by the chink of armor and excited voices around him as his men moved to the riverbank.

He let out a slow breath and opened his eyes. He glanced around. The road had entered a small patch of woods, leading them to this ford. Stiger studied the crossing. The depth of the water looked to be around four feet, perhaps a little less. To either side of the ford, the water appeared much deeper, maybe seven or eight feet. That meant the crossing was likely artificial.

Stiger took another handful of water and threw it over his face. He did his best to wipe the grime and dirt of the road away. Having sweated heavily, he felt thoroughly dirty and longed for a good bath. That, he thought, and some well-needed rest.

He had given the order to fall out. His men were crowded around the riverbank, refilling canteens or drinking directly from the river. Stiger could see Hollux's men coming down the road, their standard, which displayed a boar, held proudly to the front. Unaccustomed to such a hard pace, they had been dragging ass a bit.

Stiger unclipped his canteen and filled it. He was tired. No, that was incorrect. He was bone weary. His men were in a similar state. Having left Fort Footprint burning, Stiger had pushed through the night and just beyond sunrise until they had reached this spot. He looked over his men as Hollux's formation came to a halt. A moment later the auxiliaries were given leave to break ranks. They eagerly moved forward toward the water.

Stiger's gaze returned to his own. They were splendid men, he reflected. They had done all he had asked and then some. He felt a moment of pride.

He spied Hollux a few feet away. Hollux dismounted from his horse and handed the reins to one of his men. He then made his way stiffly over to the riverbank, where he squatted down and filled his canteen before drinking deeply. Would Hollux's men have given their all for their officer?

Stiger's legs shook with exhaustion as he pulled himself to his feet. It took an effort not to groan. Tiro was speaking with Pazzullo just a handful of feet away. Both sergeants turned at his approach, abruptly ending their conversation.

"This is a fine spot for a break, sir," Tiro said. "Plenty of water for all, especially considering everyone's canteens have run dry."

"I am pleased you approve," Stiger said, with no little amount of irony. "We will cross the river and take an extended break on the other side."

Tiro turned and looked on the other bank for a brief moment, as did Pazzullo.

"If that enemy cavalry shows up," Tiro said, "I suppose this is as good as any place to stop."

"That is my thinking as well," Stiger said, gesturing with a hand. "They would have to cross the river to get at us. The ford is rather narrow before the depth increases to either side. The trees will also serve to limit mobility. With Hollux's archers, and our shield wall, we would be able to hold them at bay."

"We also have those nice short spears that we picked up back at the fort," Tiro said. "Pazzullo told me they'd been stored there since the legionary company that built the fort handed it over."

"I'm guessing they've been in crates at least twenty years, sir," Pazzullo said. "As good as they were when first delivered. We've just never had a use for them."

Stiger ran his eyes over his men. As they refilled canteens, or splashed water on themselves or each other like children on a hot day, the potent missiles had been laid upon the ground or leaned against trees. The important thing was that now each of his men was armed with a ranged weapon, one they were intimately familiar with. Stiger nodded and rubbed at eyes that were dry and scratchy.

"The men sure need a rest," Tiro said, eyeing Stiger. "I don't think they can go much farther without a few hours' sleep and some food."

"You are correct," Stiger said, realizing that Tiro had been speaking about his officer as well. There were times that Stiger felt as if Tiro mothered him a little too much. "We've gone as far as we can."

Lieutenant Hollux joined them.

"That cold water sure was good," Hollux said pleasantly with a nod to Stiger. "It's gods awful hot out."

"We will cross the river," Stiger said to Hollux and pointed. "Once on the other side, we will take an extended break."

"I could sure use it, and I am confident my men could as well," Hollux said. "Pazzullo will agree with me. Won't you, sergeant?"

"Yes, sir," Pazzullo said in a neutral tone that neither conveyed respectfulness nor disparaged his officer.

"You set a hard pace there, Stiger," Hollux said. "A very challenging one."

"It was no more than necessary," Stiger said and then turned to the two sergeants. "I want to get to Ida today. Tiro, do you think four hours will be sufficient?"

Pazzullo covered his surprise well, but Stiger read it in the sergeant's eyes, which abruptly blinked. Amongst an officer corps, which mostly disdained the rank and file, Stiger understood where it came from.

Pazzullo turned his gaze to Tiro, who shrugged and then replied, "I think so, sir."

"Pazzullo?" Stiger asked, seeking the sergeant's input. If this man was half as wise as Tiro, Stiger would be smart to seek his advice. "I would appreciate your thoughts as well."

Pazzullo hesitated. "My men are not in the shape yours are, sir, but I judge four hours rest to be sufficient. We're only four to five miles from Ida, a short walk at best."

"Very well then," Stiger said, satisfied. "Let's get the men across. I for one would feel a bit safer with that river between me and the enemy. With any luck, it is the only crossing for miles around." Stiger paused and looked at Hollux and then Pazzullo. "You wouldn't know, would you?"

"No, sir," Pazzullo said. "This land is Fort Ida's responsibility. I am afraid I don't know it all that well."

"Hollux?"

"I can't recall seeing another crossing on a map," Hollux said. "That doesn't mean there isn't one. I had no cause to study the terrain in this area."

Stiger rubbed at his stubbled jaw and looked back up the road they had just marched down. He gestured toward the mule train and captured horses. "Well, there is no helping it then. Tiro, Pazzullo, once across, see that the mules and horses are properly secured. When that is done, the men can fall out and grab what rest they can. Everyone is to eat. Is that understood?"

"Yes, sir," Tiro said. "Might I make a recommendation, sir?"

Stiger nodded for the sergeant to continue. Stiger noted that Hollux stiffened slightly, most likely due to Tiro's boldness. Pazzullo, to his credit, did not bat an eye. Stiger's respect for the auxiliary sergeant was increasing by the moment.

"The road cuts through the woods," Tiro said, pointing back the way they had come, "and opens up to that large grass field we passed through about three hundred yards back. I would like to set a watch detail with horses just inside the trees, concealed from view. If they spot anything, they can get back to us quick."

"Good thinking," Stiger said, wishing he had thought of it himself. "See that it's done." Stiger paused a moment, thinking things through. "Since we have mounted scouts ahead, I don't see a need to send anyone forward. However, make sure we put sentries out just the same."

"It will be done, sir." Tiro moved off with Pazzullo, leaving Stiger with Hollux.

There was a prolonged moment of silence that could almost have been described as uncomfortable before Hollux shifted. Stiger looked at him, wondering what the other officer had to say.

"With the pace we set," Hollux said, "you really expect the enemy to come riding down that road?"

Stiger regarded the other lieutenant for a few heartbeats as he considered his response. Despite being rather new to the military, Stiger realized that in the last few weeks he had almost certainly seen more action than Hollux had with all his years of service behind him.

"Do we dare take the chance?"

Hollux shifted his stance again before glancing down at his feet. He looked back up at Stiger. "No, you're quite correct. Better to be safe than sorry."

"Your men marched well today." Stiger clapped the other officer on the shoulder.

"Truth be told," Hollux said with a good-natured chuckle, "had you not called a break, I was unsure that they could manage much more. Prefect Lears is not one inclined to order extended patrols. Gods, you know, most of my time was occupied by administrative duties. I can't recall the last time I left the fort and led a patrol." Hollux shrugged and raised his right hand. "I am cursed with an affinity to write, you see, and my prefect loves his reports. By the gods, my ass hurts something awful."

Stiger chuckled at Hollux's honesty. Despite his age and likely failure at being any semblance of a good soldier, he was a likable sort.

"Regardless, you and your men did very well today," Stiger said. "Almost as if they were regulars and not fortbound. You should tell them that when you have a moment. It is good for the men to hear such praise from their officers."

"I will," Hollux said.

"Well," Stiger said, returning Hollux's honesty in kind, "I am at the end of my rope too."

"Truly?"

"Truth."

Hollux became serious. "May I ask you something?"

Stiger gave a curt nod.

"You have horses," Hollux said, gesturing back up the road. "Your feet must be killing you. Why did you not ride?"

The question took Stiger by surprise. A few weeks ago, he would have thought as Hollux. Heck, he would have ridden while his men slogged along mile after monotonous mile, had it not been for Tiro's prodding.

"I am setting an example for my men," Stiger said. "With the heat, it was a long and difficult march. The least I could do was show them that their officer can handle the discomfort of the road. It is one of the things that helps keep them going under trying circumstances."

Stiger read the astonishment and disbelief in the other's expression.

"I also left my horse back with the Third," he continued. "We were ordered to cut through rugged terrain to get to Cora'Tol instead of going around the long way by road. It was not practical to bring my horse." Stiger let slip a smile. "Besides, riding one of those captured nags somehow doesn't seem worth the effort."

Hollux didn't seem to catch Stiger's tired attempt at humor, as he glanced back at the captured horses and then returned his attention to Stiger. "You've marched all the way out here, then? From the Third, I mean?"

Stiger gave a weary nod, paused, and turned to look at the ford. He had tired of the conversation. "How about we lead the way like good, proper officers and cross the river first, eh?"

Hollux wiped sweat from his brow with the back of his arm as he considered Stiger's suggestion. After a moment, the serious look on his face softened and a slight grin emerged. "I think a dip into the river would be most welcome, especially considering this heat."

Stiger started off for the river crossing. He removed his boots before he plunged in, holding them high. The river bottom was slick with slimy muck. Hollux followed a few moments later, splashing along behind. Around ten feet from the bank, the water rose rapidly from his calves to above his waist. Stiger found the current strong, but easily managed. The cold snap of the water was at first refreshing, but after a few heartbeats turned to discomfort as Stiger's feet began to rapidly ache. Then he was across and out, thoroughly soaked through, wet from his lower chest downward; the heat no longer seemed as oppressive.

Hollux emerged from the river, a full grin upon his face. "I must say, that felt quite good, my man. Quite good, indeed."

Stiger turned and surveyed his men on the other bank. He then looked south and followed the road with his eyes. He could see two pairs of hoof prints in the mud and dirt that led outward from the river and down the road. These were probably left by the two mounted scouts he had sent ahead.

Trees stretched out before him and crowded both sides of the dirt road for several hundred yards. The woods had seemed small from the other side, but Stiger now wondered how big they were. The road took a turn ahead and disappeared from view.

After a moment's more study, Stiger unclipped his cloak. It was heavy with water. He used the part that was not wet to quickly dry his feet, then wrung it out and hung it on a nearby tree limb to dry. Stiger examined the frayed and torn ends, a little mournfully. This expedition had been extremely hard on his kit. Once he returned to the Third, he would need to see to its replacement.

As he slipped the boots on, he noted sourly, he could see his big toe. He wiggled it a little, poking it up through the hole. The boot too would need to be mended or, more likely, replaced. The damage to his meager funds would be significant. The prize money from the captured strongbox and horses would offset it some, but he wondered if it would be enough.

Putting such thoughts from his mind, Stiger slipped his sword and dagger off, leaning them both against the same tree that he had hung his cloak from. He unfastened his helmet, which hung from his chest, and set it on the ground. Next, he pulled off his packs one at a time, including his haversack, and began undoing his armor. Once unlaced, he shrugged out of it, setting the heavy deadweight carefully down against the trunk. The armor needed some serious attention, at least several hours of cleaning. He was not looking forward to that.

Stiger took a tentative step and felt light on his feet, as if he weighed barely a feather. Despite his armor having become a near second skin in recent days, it was a tremendous relief to be free of it. He never seemed to cease marveling at the feeling of near weightlessness that came after shedding it.

The men were beginning to cross, splashing into the river. Stiger watched them, running a hand through his sweaty and matted hair. Next to him, Hollux had also slipped out of his armor—a much easier task, as the auxiliary officer was wearing only a simple chainmail shirt.

"Who's the girl?" Hollux nodded back toward the river at the wife of the farmer.

Stiger followed the lieutenant's gaze and saw Varus leading a horse across the river. The woman was riding upon the horse's back, clinging to its neck. At the sight of her,

Stiger let out a slow breath. She was much too young to be a grieving widow, somewhere in her early twenties. She was also moderately attractive. Stiger had initially worried what trouble this might cause amongst the men. That concern had given way, as Varus had taken it upon himself to keep an eye upon her and divert the men's attentions. However, with the amount of attentiveness the corporal had been paying her, he was beginning to wonder if there was more to it.

"We rescued her," Stiger said unhappily. "The enemy troop we ambushed had holed up at her farm. On Lieutenant Crief's orders, her husband and two small boys were tortured and killed."

Hollux sucked in a breath at that, face flushing with anger. "The blackheart!"

Stiger continued in a weary tone. "I caught Crief in the act of violating her."

Hollux said nothing at this, but shot a heated glance toward the captured enemy officer being led across the river. Crief's hands had been secured behind his back. Two men, each with a firm grip on either arm, made sure he did not try to escape by throwing himself into the river.

"I felt that I could not leave her behind," Stiger said. "Especially considering that an enemy army was approaching."

"Quite right," Hollux said, with conviction. "It was the gentlemanly thing to do."

Stiger said nothing to that, but sat down on the side of the tree trunk that faced the river. He let loose a soft groan as he settled into a comfortable position. Placing his back against the rough bark of the tree, the groan passed over to a contented sigh.

Stiger said nothing more as he watched the column of men continue to move across the river. The horses and mules brought up the rear. Stiger's eyes grew heavy. After a moment, he leaned his head back and closed them, giving in to a deep sleep that pulled him into oblivion.

"Sir? Will you kindly wake up? Sir?"

Stiger's eyes snapped open. He blinked several times before focusing on Tiro. The sergeant had been shaking his shoulder. Pazzullo stood at his side.

"What is it?" Stiger stretched slightly, glancing around. Was there trouble? From the sunlight filtering through the trees, it appeared to be somewhere between noon and early afternoon. Hollux lay against a tree several feet away, snoring softly.

"Time to get moving, sir," Tiro said. "We've been here for four hours. The scouts returned ten minutes ago and said that Ida is maybe five miles away at most. They saw no enemy between here and there."

"Right." Stiger held out his hand to Tiro, who gripped it and hauled him to his feet. Stiger stretched out his back, tortured muscles protesting badly. He yawned deeply. "Roust the men, will you?"

"Yes, sir," Tiro said and then turned, cupping his hands to his mouth. "On your feet, ladies. Up and about!"

"Come on, you maggots," Pazzullo roared, joining in and moving forward. He kicked a man who had not yet stirred. "Time to earn your pay, like proper bastards."

There was a loud chorus of groans. The men began pulling themselves to their feet. As Stiger reached for his armor, he stifled a groan himself.

CHAPTER ELEVEN

"I still can't believe I am hearing this. You burned your own fort?" Lieutenant Teevus exclaimed, an incredulous look passing over his face as he gazed upon Hollux, who abruptly appeared uncomfortable. "Are you mad? Tell me you did not do that!"

Stiger thought furiously on how he could sway Teevus, another older man who had never advanced beyond a lieutenancy. Stiger could not place the family name, but that troubled him little. Teevus was not as refined as Hollux in manner and speech, and his tunic wasn't as well-cut either. This could have been a sign his family had recently been admitted into the nobility or, more likely, Teevus had fallen upon hard times.

"He did it on my orders," Stiger said, thoroughly irritated at how the conversation had turned. They had been arguing for the last thirty minutes with no progress to show for it. "Teevus, allow me explain this again. The enemy is out there. They are coming here, to Fort Ida. I feel very strongly that our only chance is to consolidate our forces at Fort Covenant and hold until the Third arrives. I've sent—"

"I get it, I get it. You don't need to repeat yourself," Teevus said, resting both hands palm-down on the table where Stiger had placed his map. Teevus looked it over as a silence fell around them.

Stiger, Hollux, and Teevus were in Fort Ida's headquarters, if it could be described as such. It was a small square room with a battered desk pushed against the back wall. Two large trunks lay to either side of the desk. A table sat in the center of the room, taking up much of the free space. The flooring was wood plank that creaked and groaned dangerously with every step. There were no chairs, only one rickety stool by the desk. A single lantern hung overhead and a candle burned on the desk, providing adequate but muted light.

A door off to the right undoubtedly led to the prefect's personal quarters. It was closed, as were the shutters that would have allowed in fresh air.

"However," Teevus continued, "I've seen no solid proof other than your roughed-up prisoner and this map. I readily admit both are compelling, but at the same time, it is slim evidence. This could be nothing more than a diversionary raid." He paused and glanced meaningfully at Hollux. "As such, I simply cannot abandon this fort without proper orders. It would violate the trust placed in my hands and, I daresay, put my personal honor at risk."

Hollux swallowed and averted his gaze. Stiger felt his brows draw together at Hollux's behavior.

"How many men do you have here?" Stiger asked, drawing Teevus's attention.

"I don't see how that is relevant," Teevus said, straightening up.

"How many?"

"As of this morning's count," Teevus said, "one hundred eighty-two."

"Do you really believe you can hold this fort with an entire army out there? How long will you last against twenty to thirty thousand Rivan heavy infantry?"

"What I think I can and can't do is immaterial," Teevus said, tapping the table with his right index finger. "My orders are to hold this fort. That is what I shall do."

"I've told you I am changing your orders," Stiger said firmly.

"No, you are not," Teevus said, voice just as firm. His eyes slid over to Hollux. "Is that how you got him to abandon his fort? You pulled rank?"

"I outrank you," Stiger said, jabbing a finger at the other officer, "as I outrank him."

"Only technically." Teevus held up a hand, forestalling any further heated protest. "I concede you are correct. However, it changes nothing. I will not give up my fort without orders from my local command, the tribune at Fort Covenant, or at the very least my prefect."

"Your prefect is not here," Stiger said.

"Yes, as I've said, he is not."

Stiger sucked in a deep breath. "Nothing I say will change your mind, will it?"

"No," Teevus said. "And I would ask while you are within my fort not to try to order my men about either. They are loyal, and such an attempt will only serve to embarrass."

"Why not come with us?" Hollux prompted. "Come on, Teevus. You know me. We've been friends for at least five years. I would not do this unless I thought the threat very grave."

"I have no doubt you believe in what Stiger here has told you." Teevus hesitated again, glancing down at the table before looking back up. "This is my career. It is not much, but it's all I have. I do not hail from a wealthy family. I could barely afford to purchase an auxiliary commission, let alone consider an appointment to the legions." He fell silent a few heartbeats. "I am muddling through as best I can. I cannot give up the fort. If I do, I stand to lose everything if the news you bring is wrong. That includes what little I make, which I subsequently forward on to my wife and child. Though it is not my intention to disparage your honor, Stiger, I hope you understand I cannot do what you ask of me. The truth is, I would like nothing more than to come with you. But I dare not."

Stiger could appreciate Teevus's position, but it did little to quell his irritation. If Teevus remained, he and his cohort would die or, at the very least, end up as Rivan slaves.

"When the Rivan get here," Stiger said quietly, in a tone that was part whisper, "you will lose everything."

Teevus closed his eyes for a long moment, breathed in deeply, and then slowly let it out. When he opened his eyes, his gaze was firm. Stiger knew, in that moment, it was done. There would be no budging the man. For certain, no argument would sway him, for Teevus had inner strength to see through his resolve. It was something Stiger could respect, even if he vehemently disagreed with Teevus's position.

"I will dispatch a messenger," Teevus said. "It is only ten miles to Fort Covenant and, as I've said, my prefect accompanied Lieutenant Aggar there for a meeting with the tribune. I should have a response within a few hours. That is the best I can offer."

Stiger rubbed his jaw and gave a reluctant nod. A little concession was better than none. Though he did not like it, he could see no other way.

"We set a hard pace," Stiger said, heat draining from him as he accepted defeat. "With luck, once your orders arrive, you will have time to evacuate the fort."

"I hope so," Teevus said, glancing down at the map on the table. "I sincerely hope so."

The small room fell silent once again.

"I would like to send along a written report with your messenger," Stiger said. "That way they can start preparations to receive the enemy before we arrive."

"I see no issue with that," Teevus said and then glanced over at Stiger and Hollux. "You both look exhausted. Can I offer you and your men refreshment before you move on?"

"That would be most welcome," Stiger said. "With your permission, I would like to bring my men into the fort and allow them to rest. We will march out in two hours."

"Granted," Teevus said, then hesitated. "I am relying upon your honor that you will not cause trouble with my men."

"You have my word." Stiger folded up his map, slipped it into a pocket in his cloak, then turned and left. Stepping out into the afternoon light, he found Tiro and Pazzullo waiting just outside. Without any shutters thrown open, the air inside the fort's headquarters had been hot and stale. Stiger took a deep breath of fresh afternoon air and looked around.

Much like Footprint, Ida was a small affair. There were only seven buildings in total, surrounded by a simple tree trunk palisade, backed by an earthen rampart. The interior was neat and orderly. The men manning the walls looked professional; their kits appeared well-maintained. It spoke of the quality of the auxiliaries here.

Tiro and Pazzullo stepped over to him.

"Well, sir." Tiro's tone was careful when Stiger said nothing. "How did it go?"

"Bloody awful," Stiger said. "Though he fully understands the threat, Lieutenant Teevus refuses to leave. The best he will do is send a messenger to Fort Covenant seeking orders, but beyond that he is going to sit tight."

"That's not good," Tiro said.

"No, it is not." Stiger slapped a palm against his thigh, letting some of his frustration show, and pointed toward the gatehouse. "Once the Rivan get here, the walls will not long hold against a determined attack."

"No, sir," Pazzullo said. "They most certainly will not. Without an outer trench or pits, the Rivan engineers will be able to overcome these defenses with ease."

"What about us, sir?" Tiro asked.

"Let's get our boys into the fort," Stiger said. "We will rest for two hours and then we depart."

"The men could use a little more rest, sir," Tiro said. "They are almost blown."

Stiger considered Tiro's words, but then shook his head.

"We can't afford to become trapped here." Stiger lowered his voice as a pair of auxiliaries walked by, heading toward the latrines on the back side of the fort. Stiger waited until they had passed beyond hearing. "I want us back into the forest. We move a few miles down the road and take another break before pushing through to Fort Covenant."

"Yes, sir," Tiro said.

"I wouldn't stay a minute longer if I thought I could avoid it, but as you've rightly pointed out, our boys are almost blown."

Teevus and Hollux stepped out of the headquarters behind them.

"Stiger," Teevus said, "I will have my dispatch ready to—"

"Rider approaching," a shout rang out from the platform above the gate. All heads turned.

"From which direction?" Stiger shouted back up and started making his way toward the gate. He suspected he knew the answer to his own question. The others followed.

"North, sir," the man called back, bringing Stiger to a stop in his tracks. "And he is riding hard."

"That would be one of our scouts, sir." Tiro threw a look of concern at Stiger.

Stiger's eyes connected with Teevus's. He held the other officer's gaze a hard moment before turning away. Stiger hurriedly made his way through the gate.

What he had taken for a small wood had proven to be a good-sized forest. Ida had been cut out of the forest and sat astride the road. Unlike other forts that Stiger had come across, there was no civilian village or town here. Stiger figured it was probably due to Ida's remoteness.

The trees around the fort had been pushed back six hundred yards in every direction. Low-lying scrub and brush choked the cleared fields. From the height of the vegetation, Stiger suspected the auxiliaries regularly pruned it down, but the forest was relentless. It sought to reclaim the land it had lost. Should the auxiliaries pack up and one day leave, Stiger had no doubts that within a handful of years Ida would be fully overgrown.

Stiger's column of men, mules, and horses was lounging about, enjoying the respite. Under the afternoon sun, and without shade, they fairly boiled in their armor. Discomfort was something anyone serving in the legions rapidly became accustomed to.

Stiger's gaze shifted to the rider. He saw it was Asus as Hollux, Teevus, Tiro, and Pazzullo stepped up next to him. Stiger searched for his other scout. Tig was nowhere to be seen. Asus's horse was lathered with sweat and kicking up great clods of dirt. Asus yanked hard on the reins, pulling his horse up just short of the officers. The animal's breathing was heavy and labored.

"Sir." Asus slid off his horse and offered a salute.

Stiger returned the salute. "Let's have it."

"Enemy, sir. Heavy infantry, along with a good-sized column of cavalry coming down the road." Asus gestured behind him. "They are four, maybe three miles away by now. Tig is staying just ahead of their advance scouts. I told him not to take any chances and ride back here direct-like should he get spotted."

"You are certain you saw heavy infantry?" Stiger had hoped the enemy's main body was farther away. A cavalry regiment was bad enough, but this was even worse. The rain and fire had apparently not slowed the enemy up much.

"Yes, sir," Asus said. "Tig and I were able to hide in the trees, eyeballed them good, and then were able to work our way around to get ahead of them. Once on the road, I came straight back, sir."

Stiger rubbed at his tired eyes. There would be no rest. It was time to push onward.

"Sergeant Tiro, Sergeant Pazzullo." Stiger rounded on them. "Get the men on their feet."

"Yes, sir," Tiro said, moving toward the men. "Fall in!"

"Let's go, you maggots," Pazzullo roared, striding forward like a human hurricane. "Time for another pleasant walk through the woods, ladies."

"You're leaving?"

Stiger looked at Teevus, who had paled considerably. "I am certainly not staying."

"But you will be leaving us to the enemy," Teevus said, apparently aghast at the concept.

"And you, sir," Stiger said, sucking in a heavy breath, "made clear your intention of remaining to hold the fort. Now, I daresay, you will have that chance."

"I, uh ..." Teevus looked away, eyes searching the forest to the north, almost as if he expected the enemy to emerge from the trees. After a moment, he drew himself up and looked Stiger square in the eyes. "I will hold my fort, but I will also send the messenger to Fort Covenant."

"You do that," Stiger said and then softened his tone. "Maybe there is still time."

"I wish you luck, Stiger," Teevus said, a grim look coming over his face. He extended his hand.

Stiger took Teevus's hand and shook firmly.

"Don't do this," Hollux said as he took Teevus's hand.

"I have to."

"Fight well," Stiger said.

Teevus gave a curt nod, spun on his heel, and reentered the fort.

"They will surely, die," Hollux said with exasperation. "This is utter madness."

"Yes," Stiger said, feeling weary and sick at heart as he looked over the walls of the fort.

"Make them come with us," Hollux said, and it almost came out in a pleading tone. When Stiger failed to respond, Hollux reached out and grabbed Stiger's shoulder, spinning him around so they faced one another. "We can't leave them."

"We can and will," Stiger said. "Teevus has made his choice. We've made ours."

"But their sacrifice is meaningless," Hollux said in a near whisper. "They will die for nothing."

Stiger turned back to the wooden fort, where he could now hear someone shouting orders from within.

"Perhaps not so meaningless," Stiger said.

"What do you mean?"

"Well," Stiger said, "Teevus means to hold, and I have to believe that should delay any pursuit."

Hollux shifted his gaze onto the fort. "You mean he and his men will sacrifice themselves for us?"

"Yes. In a way, they will," Stiger said and looked on Hollux. "Our escape shall only prove temporary, for the enemy will catch up to us. Whether that is somewhere on the road or at Fort Covenant, there are hard times ahead."

The men had fallen in and were ready to march. They were exhausted and covered with dirt from the road, but they were ready to move out.

"Tiro," Stiger called and drew the sergeant's attention. "Give the order."

"Forward march!"

The column began to move, the front at first and then, like a snake, the middle of the column. The sound of many feet on the sun-dried dirt of the road was almost rhythmic.

An auxiliary leading Hollux's horse made his way over. Hollux glanced once at Stiger, chewed his lip, and then looked back to the auxiliary.

"I think I shall walk for a bit," Hollux said to the startled man. "I will call you when I have need of you."

"Yes, sir." The auxiliary led the horse back to the column, which was mostly moving now.

Stiger smiled grimly at Hollux, who returned his gaze.

"I would like to march with you," Hollux said. "If you don't mind, that is."

"Your company on the miles ahead is welcome," Stiger said, and he meant it. "I can promise you one thing though."

"What is that?"

"Tonight your legs will be sore, not your ass."

CHAPTER TWELVE

"I believe I have come to the conclusion that marching is not all that fun," Hollux said by Stiger's side. They were marching in the middle of the column as it snaked its way through the forest.

It was late afternoon. Under the thick canopy of leaves, the heat of the day was kept at bay somewhat. Still, the high temperature, along with the humidity, could almost be described as oppressive. Stiger was looking forward to the cooler temperatures that would come with nightfall.

"You can say that again." The exertion from the march and the heat had Stiger sweating heavily. He unclipped his canteen, which was beginning to run low again, and took a quick swig of warm water. "I don't think truer words were ever said."

"Ah, come on, sir," Tiro said, a few steps behind them. "Marching is good for the constitution."

"Spoken like a true sergeant," Stiger said, noticing Hollux's surprised expression.

"Thank you, sir," Tiro said, somehow managing to sound upbeat. "I've heard it said marching builds character, sir."

"Are you implying I lack character?" Stiger said, without giving the wily old sergeant the courtesy of a glance backward.

"Oh no, sir," Tiro said. "I would never say that, sir. It's just that the holy scriptures teach there is room for improvement."

Stiger actually stopped at that and half turned to face Tiro, who returned his look with one of innocent equanimity. "That is the first I ever heard you directly refer to scripture." Stiger resumed his pace, as did Tiro.

"Being pursued by an entire army gets one thinking on the gods, sir," Tiro said. "Especially with you in command, sir."

Stiger chuckled at that. Tiro was teasing him. It was a game they routinely played. And yet, from Hollux's stiffened posture, Stiger sensed he was scandalized by the exchange. Stiger let out a slow breath. Hollux did not understand that banter like this helped to pass the monotony. It was time to end the game before Hollux said something unfortunate.

"Sergeant, shouldn't you be checking on the rear of the column?" Stiger turned slightly so that Tiro could see his face and jerked his head toward the back.

"Aye, sir," Tiro said, picking up on the cue. He stepped to the side and allowed the men to continue by, thereby giving the two officers space.

Stiger and Hollux marched in silence for some time. Hollux had his jaw set in a manner that suggested he was put out. Stiger considered his options. Perhaps there was an opportunity here, he thought. Would Hollux be open to listening? He was an old dog, in a manner of speaking. Could he learn something new?

"He's right, you know," Stiger said, casting the other a sidelong glance.

"Your sergeant is impudent," Hollux countered. "He's very insolent."

"Maybe," Stiger said. "But I wouldn't change or trade him for any other."

"Why ever not? A sergeant should be subservient. If Pazzullo spoke to me in such a manner, by the gods, I would have him flogged."

"If you did," Stiger said, "you'd be making a mistake."

"How so?" Hollux turned skeptical.

"I've learned that a good sergeant is worth his weight in gold," Stiger said. "You have to begin thinking of them differently. Sergeants like ours are seasoned men who have been promoted for their intelligence, dedication, reliability, and aggressive nature."

"Bah," Hollux said. "You don't know what you are talking about. They are little more than uneducated louts that require their betters to keep them in place."

"Are they?" Stiger asked. "Really? Tiro may be uneducated by our standards, but that makes him no less intelligent or capable." Stiger pointed ahead. "Take your man Pazzullo there. I am confident he has much to teach you. I am sure he could even show me a thing or two."

"What can he teach me that I don't already know?"

Stiger allowed a moment of silence to grow before he replied.

"That man that you so casually dismissed has a lifetime of experience behind him," Stiger said. "He's likely been in more fights than either of us, perhaps even a real battle or two. I'd wager he has been marching under the eagles since before I was even born. Is it possible he has seen and done things you and I have never considered?"

Hollux frowned.

"Listen to me on this. And believe me. I once thought as you. Your sergeant isn't meant to simply act as a middleman for dealing with your men," Stiger continued. "He's there to provide you his insight and advice on how to better handle them, and to ensure that your orders are carried out as best as possible.

Good sergeants should act as a crutch, someone to lean on under difficult circumstances, such as in the heat of combat." Stiger jerked a thumb behind them. "Tiro has proven incredibly valuable. I permit him liberties because he has earned my trust and respect. And more importantly, I have earned his."

Hollux's eyes narrowed, but he said nothing.

"Trust goes both ways." Stiger wondered if he was getting through to the man. "Without Tiro, I would not be the officer I am today."

Hollux threw Stiger a sharp look. They continued on for a bit, neither saying anything. Stiger allowed Hollux to ruminate on what he had just said. Hollux nodded several times. He opened his mouth to speak and then closed it, his eyes traveling to Pazzullo marching several yards ahead.

"I ..." Hollux hesitated. "I've never thought of it that way."

"Neither had I," Stiger said, "until Tiro opened my eyes."

"You are saying that, on occasion, I should seek my sergeant's advice? It seems so unnatural."

"It doesn't hurt to listen. You may find yourself a more effective officer for it," Stiger said. "The final decision always rests with you. If you judge the advice sound, act upon it."

"Make way," Tiro shouted from behind. "Move aside, man! Make way!"

Both Stiger and Hollux turned. Stiger felt his stomach do a backflip. With men stepping out of the way, Trio jogged back up to him. Legionary Tig, one of their mounted scouts, rode forward, just behind Tiro. He would not have returned unless there was trouble.

Tig dismounted and offered a salute.

"Report," Stiger said, dreading what was coming.

"Cavalry, sir," Tig said. "About a mile behind us. When I last saw them, they was walking their horses. They seemed to be giving their horses a break."

"By the gods, so close," Hollux breathed.

"How many?" Stiger asked.

"No more than a light troop, sir. Twenty at most, but I think they number less."

"Were you spotted?"

"No, sir," Tig said. "I was careful-like."

Stiger had to assume these were scouts. He had no idea how far back the enemy regiment was, and he could not dare assume that they were still at Ida.

Stiger studied the terrain around them. Where he was now, the road climbed a small forested hill and snaked its way around the side. Twenty yards to the rear was a sharp bend that the column was still working its way around. Without orders to stop, the column of men continued by, though all eyes were on the officers as they passed.

Stiger scanned both sides of the road and found there was a good deal of brush that might act as cover. A plan of action was forming in his mind.

Stiger stepped across the road and looked down the slope. It was fairly steep, easy for a man, but it would prove incredibly difficult for a horse. After a moment more of studying their surroundings, he decided it suited his needs.

He returned to Hollux and Tiro. Varus and Pazzullo joined them.

"What are you thinking, sir?" Tiro asked.

"How far do you think we are from Fort Covenant?" Stiger asked Hollux.

"Maybe four miles," Hollux said. "It is hard to be sure. I only come through this way once a year to meet with the tribune who commands the auxiliary cohorts and forts. I can't imagine it is much farther."

"Right," Stiger said. "Tiro, call a halt. I've decided we are going to hit this troop."

"Halt!"

Shouts were passed forward and back. The column ground to an uneven stop.

"They can't be allowed to find us and report back," Stiger said, placing his hands on his hips. "I don't believe we will be able to outrun them. This means we must ambush the bastards. Hollux and Pazzullo, I want twenty of your best archers. Tiro, select forty men who still have enough left in them for a fight. No shields, please, but I want spears. The rest of the column will continue on. Hollux, you will lead the column to Fort Covenant. I will catch up just as soon as I can."

"I should join you in this fight." Hollux sounded somewhat indignant, as if Stiger had slighted him.

"Hollux," Stiger said, "this isn't the time for such nonsense. An officer must lead the rest of the column. If there are more cavalry behind this bunch, I will do what I can to hold them for as long as possible. You have to get everyone else to the fort. The more men they have when the time comes, the better. It is the only thing that matters at this point. Fort Covenant must hold until the Third arrives. Got that?"

Hollux thought a moment. "Yes. All right, I will get them there."

"Good man," Stiger said.

"Pazzullo and Varus, you both are with me," Stiger said. "Tiro, you go with Lieutenant Hollux and render him what assistance you can."

Tiro did not appear to like that too much, but gave Stiger a "yes, sir" just the same.

"Daylight's burning." Stiger clapped his hands together. "Let's get moving."

Tiro, Varus, and Pazzullo moved out, shouting orders.

Hollux hung back a moment. "Are you certain about this course of action?"

"Certain? No," Stiger said with a short laugh. "But I feel it is the right thing to do."

"You are taking a serious risk," Hollux said, "especially if there is more than a light troop."

"I know," Stiger said. "Get to the fort. Listen to Tiro. He won't steer you wrong."

"I will do as you ask," Hollux said. "Good luck, Stiger. I will see you in a few hours."

"Good fortune to you as well."

Hollux gave the order for the column to move out, even as Tiro and Pazzullo called for men to step out.

"Sir," Pazzullo said, returning to Stiger's side. His archers formed up a few feet away. They were road-dusty and appeared just as worn as Stiger's men. Varus was busy organizing those selected from the Seventh.

"Tiro..." Pazzullo lowered his voice slightly, "suggested that you might find my advice of value, sir."

"He did, did he?"

"Yes, sir," Pazzullo said. "He did."

"I expect you to give me advice when you see fit," Stiger said. "Even if you know it will displease me, I want to hear from you. Understand?"

"Yes, sir," Pazzullo said. "Perfectly."

"Let's have it, then."

"I assume you plan on ambushing the enemy from this spot." Pazzullo gestured from their current position and back to the bend in the road.

"Yes, that is correct," Stiger said.

"Sir, I would advise against placing men on both sides of the road."

Stiger cocked his head to one side, intrigued. He gave a nod for Pazzullo to continue.

"If you place my bowmen up the slope and above the road—the natural firing position for them, given the elevation..." Pazzullo continued and swung his arm from there toward the downward slope. "Any wayward missiles may strike our boys on the other side of the road. I prefer my men not have to worry about that possibility."

Stiger glanced up the hill and then down the slope across the road, thinking the problem through. Though it would be difficult for a horse to escape that way, it was not impossible. He had been planning on placing a handful of men on the down-slope side of the road. Pazzullo's reasoning was sound, and it certainly gave him pause for thought.

"That makes sense to me," Stiger said.

Relief flashed through Pazzullo's eyes.

"Varus," Stiger called, seeing that the line of legionaries was almost set.

The corporal jogged over, dodging around a team of mules as the last of the column passed them by.

"We're going to keep this simple," Stiger said. Keeping things simple was something that Tiro harped on a lot. "This is how I want the ambush laid out. We will position most of our boys upslope and above the road in two lines, say about five feet apart. The brush should conceal us quite well. Pazzullo's men will be our first line. Right behind them I want twenty legionaries in our second line." Stiger turned and pointed up the road. "Just to the north, we will put ten men off the road and hidden above the bend. The other ten, right down the road, say at thirty yards. Got that so far?"

Both Pazzullo and Varus nodded.

"Good," Stiger said and turned to face north. "With all of our men hidden and out of view, we will let the enemy round the bend. Once they are completely around it, the archers will loose their missiles. The second line will follow up with a volley of short spears before going in to finish off any survivors. When the attack starts, the men positioned at either end of the ambush will close the trap by moving onto the road and neatly blocking any easy exit to the north and south."

"Sounds simple enough, sir," Varus said, to which Pazzullo nodded in agreement.

"To be clear, we cannot allow any of the bastards to escape," Stiger said. "Impress that upon the men. If even one rider gets away, we could have that entire regiment on our backs before we can make it to the safety of the fort. We must get them all."

"What if they ride off and down into the forest?" Pazzullo asked.

"The brush is thick," Stiger said. "If any do, they won't be able to move very fast. I am counting on the archers to hit their marks and my men to finish them off before they can even have a thought on flight. With luck, our ambush will come as a complete surprise."

"My boys will shoot true, sir," Pazzullo said. "Don't worry about that."

"Varus, I want you with the north blocking force," Stiger said before glancing around once again. "That position is critical. You must stand your ground. None can escape."

"You can count on me, sir."

"I know I can. Hoot like an owl when you have the enemy in sight." Stiger glanced around once more, taking a deep breath. He held it a moment before letting it out in a long stream. "I am not sure how long we have. Let's get the men into position and hidden while we have the chance."

A short while later and the men were off the road and into the trees and brush.

"Place your line where you think they will be most effective," Stiger told Pazzullo as he climbed the slope of the hill. "You give the order to fire when you think best."

"Yes, sir."

Stiger moved his legionaries into position right behind the archers, who were sticking arrows point-first into the forest floor. Pazzullo addressed his men, giving them instruction. Once he had them in position, Stiger walked his line, working his way through the undergrowth, speaking encouragements as he went. Satisfied his men were dressed in a good line, he returned to the center and faced them.

"After the archers shoot," Stiger told them, "I will call for a volley of short spears. Aim for the horses, not the men. I don't want any of the enemy to escape. If one does, I'd rather him be afoot than on horseback. I will order us in right after the toss. Keep your heads and stick it to them good."

Stiger paused, considering adding a few rousing words, but in the end decided against it. They were all weary and run down. Despite that, they knew what needed doing. He had said enough.

"Now, get down," Stiger ordered, "as close as you can to the ground, and stay there until ordered. No one gets spotted."

Stiger placed himself in the center of his line and laid down on his belly, a man immediately to his left and another to his right. The scent of dirt and vegetation was strong. A moment later, he saw Pazzullo's men press themselves down. Pazzullo gave Stiger a thumbs up before he too got down and disappeared from view.

Nothing happened for some time. Stiger rolled onto his back and looked up at the tree canopy above him. It was a spectacular view. The dwindling light of a cloudless sky was interspersed by leaves that blew in a gentle breeze. It had a calming feel to it. A bird called and another answered.

But for the coming action, Stiger almost felt at peace. His thoughts turned inward and he offered up a prayer to the High Father. He asked the great god to spare as many of his men as possible and see them to victory. Satisfied, Stiger finished by commending his spirit into the High Father's keeping.

Prayers complete, Stiger lay on his back for some time. He began to ponder on his plan and wondered if he should have done more or if he had missed something. Perhaps he should have kept additional men instead of sending them on to the fort. What if there was more than one enemy troop? Or worse, what if the entire regiment was riding up the road? The what-ifs began to plague him, and the peace of the moment fled.

He heard the hooting of an owl, which sounded a little out of place before dusk. Stiger abruptly realized it was the signal from Varus. Enemy in sight. He rolled over onto his belly.

"Pass it along," Stiger hissed to the men next to him. "The enemy is in sight."

Stiger strained to hear something, but couldn't. He resisted the urge to look. So he remained where he was, listening. Absently, Stiger began silently counting. When he hit two hundred fifteen, the slow, steady clop of multiple hooves reached his ears. With each passing breath it got louder. Voices speaking the language of the Rivan, at first faint and then much clearer, came from below and along the road, which he could not directly see. Someone down on the road laughed. Another coughed.

Pazzullo and his men silently rose to a kneeling position, almost as if they had grown from the ground. They raised their bows. As they reached for their arrows, Stiger pulled himself up to a knee. The men beside him did the same, and Stiger's line came up also.

Below him, less than fifteen feet away, were the blue-cloaked Rivan. It was shocking to see the enemy so close, so oblivious to their presence. They were riding their horses, which plodded along in boredom, heads hung with the heat. Each man carried a lance, the points of which occasionally caught a ray of the fading sunlight and glittered wickedly. The enemy had bundles of hay, forage bags, and nets affixed to the rumps of their horses, along with their small round shields. Stiger counted sixteen of the enemy. He glanced to the right toward the bend and could see no additional horsemen. Was it a light troop, as Tig had said? He certainly hoped so.

There was a loud *twang* from twenty bows firing in unison. Stiger almost jumped. He had missed Pazzullo's silent order to loose. The air was abruptly filled with the sounds of impact, cracks of arrows penetrating armor and flesh. This was immediately followed by screams, cries of agony, and shouts of alarm.

"Loose at will," Pazzullo roared.

"Spears!" Stiger called, standing and pulling out his sword. He glanced along his line as his men came to their feet. "Aim for the horses! Aim for the horses, boys! Make your toss count!"

Stiger's men grunted as they threw their deadly missiles, which sailed over the heads of Pazzullo's bowmen.

"Draw swords!" Stiger didn't wait to see the results. He held his sword high, even as there was a scattered series of additional *twangs* from Pazzullo's bowmen as they fired down into the enemy. Stiger pointed toward the road with his sword. "At them!"

Moving through and by Pazzullo's line, he led the way forward, his men just steps behind. Once past the bowmen, he picked up his pace and crashed through the undergrowth. Stiger burst from the tree line and emerged into a setting of devastation and chaos.

Injured horses screamed, with a number down and kicking wildly about. Spears protruded from several. Riders hung limply from saddles, arrows sticking out of chests, sides, and backs. In some cases, the arrow had penetrated clean through and poked out both sides. A number of the enemy lay on the ground.

It was a slaughter. Despite that, there were several of the enemy still mounted.

One rider, unscathed and just ten feet away, spotted Stiger. He wheeled around and lowered his lance. With no time to formulate a better plan, Stiger ran at the horse, screaming wildly as the rider kicked his heels in and the animal lunged forward, hurtling at him.

At the last moment, Stiger dove aside and stabbed his sword into the horse's neck, plunging the blade as deeply he could. Hot wetness sprayed him in the eyes as the razor-sharp edge of the lance passed within a hairsbreadth of his face. Then the horse was past and Stiger's sword was violently ripped from his hands. As Stiger crashed hard to the ground, the horse let loose a scream of agony. This was almost immediately followed by a solid thud as the wounded animal lost its footing and went down.

Stiger lay on the ground, stunned slightly from the impact. Feet thundered around him as his men arrived and tore into the remains of the troop. Shaking his head, Stiger slowly picked himself up, glanced around, and found that, for the most part, barring the enemy wounded, the ambush was already over.

A sense of satisfaction settled over him. He had given the enemy another bloody nose, albeit a small one.

The pounding hooves brought his head around. A lone trooper was riding for all he was worth back the way the troop had come. Varus and his legionaries blocked the road. Varus shouted an order, and short spears arced out. One spear hit the horse. Two struck the rider in the upper chest and neatly plucked him from his saddle. He seemed to hang in midair for a heartbeat, as if he were a puppet attached to a string, before he slammed to the ground, kicking up a cloud of dust and dirt. A heartbeat later, the horse, maddened by its injury, crashed into Stiger's men. Bodies flew as the animal plowed through them before it collapsed several yards beyond.

"Great gods," Stiger breathed, heart in his throat. "Great bloody gods."

He glanced around to make certain it was all over and then jogged over. Two of his men were on the ground. They were still. Two others pulled themselves to their feet. As Stiger approached, he saw one of those not moving was his corporal. Legionary Erbus, having dragged himself to his knees, moved to Varus and leaned over him. The other man down, Barrath, was clearly dead. His head hung at an unnatural angle.

Varus's helmet was badly damaged. Blood covered the corporal's face, though Stiger could not see a wound. It seemed to be leaking out of the helmet and onto the dirt of the road, where it pooled.

"He's alive, sir," Erbus said, looking up at Stiger. "He breathes."

Stiger did not know what to say to that. Varus looked to be in a very bad way. The men gathered around, looking concerned.

"This is my fault," Stiger whispered to himself as he knelt by Varus's side. His corporal looked close to death. The pain of the moment almost overcame him. A man was dead because of his orders, and another who had become dear to him was gravely injured.

"We have to get this off him, sir," Erbus said, "and examine the wound."

Erbus untied Varus's helmet and then carefully removed it, while Stiger supported the corporal's neck. Stiger's hands quickly became slick from blood. Erbus gingerly felt the back of Varus's head, which elicited a groan from the corporal. Varus's eyes popped open and he attempted to sit up, but Erbus and Stiger held him back. A moment later, Varus lost consciousness and went limp.

"Help me turn him on his side, sir," Erbus said.

Stiger rolled the corporal over. Erbus studied the back of the Varus's head. After a prolonged moment, he sat back and breathed a sigh of relief.

"He's got a nasty bump," Erbus said. They rolled the corporal onto his back. "I think he should live, sir."

"What of all the blood?"

"A scalp wound. I am not a surgeon, but it doesn't seem too bad. The skull under the cut seems sound enough," Erbus explained. "Cuts on the head tend to bleed a lot, sir."

"Right," Stiger said, standing. He studied Barrath and felt a wave of exhaustion and sadness overtake him. Barrath had been a good legionary, always doing as asked with no disciplinary issues. He had not deserved to die like this, run down by a maddened animal.

"How is Varus?"

Stiger looked over, blinking. It took him a moment to realize that Pazzullo stood before him.

Stiger sucked in a shaky breath and cleared his throat. "Erbus says he should live."

"That is good news," Pazzullo said. "It was a fine ambush, sir."

Stiger looked down the road. A couple of horses walked aimlessly about as his men and Pazzullo's looted the dead.

"Any other injuries?"

"No, sir," Pazzullo said, glancing down. "Just these two."

"That's good," Stiger said, a little dazed by what had occurred. He rubbed at his eyes a moment and told himself it was only the exhaustion. "That's good."

"I think we should get moving, sir." There was a hard edge to the sergeant's tone. "Before more of the enemy come down that road."

"Yes, of course," Stiger said, snapping back to his duty. He felt somewhat guilty that Pazzullo had needed to remind him. "Erbus, get Varus on one of those horses. Barrath comes too. We have to go."

"Yes, sir," Erbus said. "I will see to it, sir."

"Pazzullo, get the men formed up."

"Yes, sir."

Stiger looked around. He had lost his sword. He spotted it down the road, still sticking out of the horse he had stuck. With a glance at the injured Varus, Stiger made his way over to the deceased animal. The rider lay a few feet away, lying on his stomach. A sword thrust to the back of the neck had ended him.

Varus's injury and Barrath's death weighing heavily upon him, Stiger blew out a heavy breath. As the men formed up, he pulled his sword free. It was time to move on.

CHAPTER THIRTEEN

"That is a very welcome sight," Stiger said, and he meant it. Under the light of a full moon and cloudless sky, he and Pazzullo were gazing down into a large valley. To their backs were the forest and the men. In the center of the valley, around a half mile distant, stood a large square fort. Stiger could see sentry fires and torches flickering in the darkness. Each of the four walls was easily six hundred yards in length, with covered towers on each corner. Off farther to the south, Stiger could see the lights of what he assumed was a small town. "A sight for sore eyes."

"It sure is, sir," Pazzullo said and then cleared his throat. "I think it might be better to admire the fort from the inside. Don't you think, sir?"

"I completely agree," Stiger said. He turned to look behind at the weary column of men, which snaked back into the forest along the road. "Forward march."

The column started forward once again, with Stiger and Pazzullo moving alongside.

Stiger was exhausted. His legs trembled slightly with each step, and he now had a persistent headache. He longed to lie down and catch up on some sleep. What kept him going was the example he felt compelled to set for his men. In a way, as long as he kept going, so too would the company. There were times he felt as if he were their willpower.

They covered the distance rapidly, following the road, moving down the hill and into the valley. With nightfall, the hot temperatures had finally eased. With the setting sun had come light gusts of wind. The cooler temperatures were more than welcome and made the long march just a tad bit easier.

Fields of wheat ready for harvest spread out to either side of the road. The wind rippled through the fields like ocean waves. Under the bright moonlight, it was a ghostly scene. Stiger was reminded of the man he had set afire during the assault back at Cora'Tol—an image he would not soon forget. One he knew he would carry to the end of his days.

He felt immense relief as they neared the front gate. Placing one foot in front of the other was becoming a real effort. His men were in a similar state. Stiger was so tired now, he felt as if his mind had become shrouded by a thick fog. Even so, he noticed that despite the late hour, the fort's gate stood fully open. At night, procedure called for the gate to be sealed.

"There seems to be a lot of activity inside," Pazzullo said as they crossed a wooden-planked bridge that ran over a deep defensive trench with steep sides. Stiger glanced over the side and saw spikes and obstacles below. "An awful lot of activity, sir."

Now that Pazzullo mentioned it, Stiger could hear quite the commotion coming from inside the fort. It sounded as if the garrison were being called out.

"I am sure that Hollux's arrival got their attention, if not the dispatch rider from Ida first," Stiger said.

Pazzullo did not reply to that. His eyes were on the four files of auxiliaries waiting before the gate, formed up into two lines. An officer stood to the right side of the formation. He spoke to a man and sent him running into the fort.

"What do you suppose that was all about?" Stiger asked Pazzullo as he and his men began crossing the second and final defensive trench. Stiger's boots rang with a hollow sound on the planking.

"Dunno, sir," Pazzullo said. "They couldn't have just spotted us. Under this moon, we would've been visible clear up to the top of the hill."

Stiger rubbed his jaw. He considered the situation as the distance closed. Pazzullo was correct. Stiger and his men could not have been missed, especially with the news that had preceded them. The garrison would have lookouts scanning the darkness for any hint of the enemy.

The auxiliary officer stepped out into the road and before his formation. He held his hand up, signaling for Stiger to halt his men. For some reason Stiger could not identify, he was irritated by the man's manner, which was almost arrogant. So, Stiger decided to close the distance further. Ominously, a sergeant behind the officer snapped an order. The auxiliaries raised their shields, the bottoms of which had been resting upon the ground.

Irritated by their reception, Stiger waited until he and his men were almost on top of the auxiliary officer, a youthful lieutenant, before he called out a terse halt.

"Identify yourself," the officer demanded in a haughty manner that dripped with hostility.

"Lieutenant Stiger, Seventh Company, Third Legion." Stiger was surprised at the other's tone. "And who, sir, are you?"

"Lieutenant Tride," came the curt reply. "You are to remain here. I have sent for Tribune Declin."

"Now listen here," Stiger snarled, stepping nearer the man. "I don't know what your game is, but—"

"I have my orders," Tride said. He pointed at the ground. Though his tone was firm enough, Stiger thought he detected a little unease. "You are to wait here."

Stiger ground his teeth in frustration as he swung toward Pazzullo with a questioning look. Pazzullo gave a rough shrug.

"Sir," Pazzullo said, drawing Stiger's attention toward the fort.

A man in a richly cut tunic had emerged, clearly the tribune. The line of auxiliaries parted to let him through. He was flanked by another officer, this one wearing the armor of a prefect, and three large auxiliaries. Stiger felt Pazzullo stiffen at his side and guessed this was Hollux's commanding officer, Prefect Lears. The Lears family were no friends of the Stigers, nearly outright enemies.

"Stiger, I presume?" the tribune asked.

Stiger offered a salute to the tribune, who waved it away.

"Yes, sir," Stiger said. "You are Tribune Declin?"

"I am." The tribune walked right up to Stiger and gave him a hard look. Stiger read a deep, burning anger in the man's eyes and sensed danger.

"You, son," the tribune said, biting off each word, "have a lot to answer for."

"Excuse me, sir? I am afraid don't understand."

"Your orders?" The tribune held out an expectant hand.

"What?" Stiger's tired mind attempted to grapple with the situation that was threatening to spiral out of control.

"You have orders?" the tribune asked. "Come on, man, I don't have all night."

"Yes, sir, I'm sorry, sir," Stiger said. "My orders come from General Treim."

"Well, then," Declin said, "let's see them."

"I'm sorry, sir," Stiger said, face flushing. "I'm afraid I destroyed them back at Cora'Tol."

"To what end?"

"I did not want them to fall into the hands of the enemy, sir," Stiger said. "General Treim made it plain I was to destroy them if necessary."

Tribune Declin eyed Stiger for a few heartbeats, then made a point of slowly looking him over. Stiger knew his appearance was dreadful and very unlegionary. With a look of contempt, the tribune's gaze returned to Stiger's face.

"You are a disgrace, sir," the tribune said. "An utter disgrace and a poor excuse for an officer."

Stiger said nothing, though he very much desired to rebut that statement.

"Just as I had surmised, sir," the prefect said, drawing the tribune's attention. "He is operating without orders."

Stiger felt his mouth fall open. Surely the tribune did not think that. Did they truly believe he was without honor?

"Sergeant," the tribune said to Pazzullo, "step aside."

The sergeant did as he was bid, casting a sidelong glance at Stiger that was filled with worry.

"What is going on here?" Stiger, having recovered from his surprise, rapidly became angry. With the onset of his anger, the exhaustion fled. "I am operating under the direct orders of General Treim."

"If you were," the Tribune said, "then you would have your orders."

"I don't need written orders," Stiger said. "The general gave me my orders himself, personally."

"And what were they?" The tribune's eyebrows rose, as if he were dealing with a small child telling a fib. "I want to hear what great task the general set for you that you needed to be dispatched so far from the action."

"I was to travel to Cora'Tol and take Lieutenant Aggar into custody, sir."

The tribune shared a meaningful glance with the prefect. They both turned their gazes, far from friendly, upon Stiger.

"The general could have sent a messenger," Declin said. "I would have easily been able to apprehend Aggar if required. Why send you instead?"

"Those were my orders, sir."

"Is that so?" the prefect asked.

"It is," Stiger said. "Upon my honor, it is."

"Why was Aggar to be detained?"

"I was not privy to that," Stiger said. "I was to locate the lieutenant, secure the prisoner, and return him to headquarters for questioning."

"Then your orders don't mention commandeering the Fort Footprint garrison, do they?" the tribune asked.

"The enemy is coming," Stiger countered. "When I could not find Aggar, and learned of the threat, I took the initiative. It was the only sensible thing to do."

"Really?" The tribune cocked his head to the side.

"We must concentrate all available forces here, sir, where there is the chance of holding off the enemy," Stiger said. "I could not leave them behind to be slaughtered."

"And what of Fort Ida?" Declin's eyes narrowed. "Why are they not with you?"

"Lieutenant Teevus refused to give up his fort," Stiger said. "I gave him the chance, but he refused."

"I see." Declin sucked in a deep breath. "Well, at least one of my officers has some sense."

"Remaining to fight and die for nothing does not strike me as very sensible, sir. By rights, he should have come with us, especially when I ordered him to do so."

"You freely admit to exceeding your orders, then?" There was a sense of triumph in Declin's tone. "Very well, I have heard enough. Prefect Lears, you may arrest Lieutenant Stiger."

Stiger took a step back and glanced between the two officers. He couldn't believe what he was hearing. Were they mad? Were they so out of touch? It did not seem possible.

Lears motioned his men forward. Stiger took another step backwards. Behind him there was a commotion. Swords were drawn. Stiger's men began moving forward toward the auxiliaries, who suddenly checked their advance.

"Now, Lieutenant Stiger," Declin said, "don't make this worse than it is. I will not hesitate to order the slaughter of your men."

With swords drawn and shields out, Stiger's men meant business. Even Pazzullo's men had raised their bows, arrows at the ready. Stiger's gaze swung back on Declin and the auxiliaries, who appeared somewhat uncertain but had also drawn their swords. He wasn't so sure it would be as one-sided as the tribune had suggested.

Stiger was moved by the loyalty of his men. Despite that, and even for his own sake, he could not allow them to shed imperial blood. He was simply not his father. Stiger was certain this was a terrible misunderstanding on the tribune's part. He was confident that when tempers cooled, he would be shown innocent and the tribune would take his news seriously.

"Stand down," Stiger said. His men did not move. He hardened his voice. "I said stand down, now."

Reluctantly, swords were sheathed and the men moved back and away from him.

"I would not have enjoyed ordering the deaths of your men," Declin said. "Prefect Lears, if you would?"

"Take him," Lears snapped, seeming to relish giving the order.

The three auxiliaries who had accompanied the tribune and prefect moved forward. Each of Stiger's arms was seized in a vice-like grip. His sword and dagger were removed. He was roughly searched for other weapons.

"There is an army on the march," Stiger said, directing himself to the tribune. "It's coming here. I sent word to the general. With luck, the Third is already on her way."

"Lieutenant Hollux informed me of your actions," Declin said in a sad tone. "You should know I have already dispatched a note to your general advising him that we are dealing with raiding parties you mistook for more, something my men are fully capable of handling."

"You can't be serious, sir?" Stiger exclaimed.

"I am," the tribune said with a sneer. "Take him from my sight."

The men began to drag Stiger into the fort.

"But, sir," Stiger said as he was pulled past, "I took an important prisoner. He will confirm what I've told you. Ask him."

"Stop," the tribune called and then walked up to Stiger. "I interviewed your Lieutenant Crief and I can assure you he is quite mad. Whatever he has told you is purely nonsense. Nothing of value can be gained from the man."

"How do you explain the Rivan heavy infantry that we attacked at Cora'Tol or the enemy cavalry, sir? They are not figments of my imagination."

"Listen here, Stiger." Acid dripped from the tribune's tongue as he spoke. "You are a traitor's son. In my mind, you are no better than a dog. I don't care what your initial orders contained, but I can tell you that I will get to the bottom of it, and when I do, you shall hang as your father should have. I would rather trust Lieutenant Aggar, whom I view as a second son, than the likes of you. Now take him from my sight."

"You are making a mistake," Stiger yelled back as he was dragged into the fort. "There is a Rivan army coming! Don't be a fool! You are making a mistake!"

A cohort was assembling on the parade ground. Stiger saw that activity ceased as all eyes turned their way.

"You made the mistake," Prefect Lears said, walking alongside as Stiger was dragged roughly along. "You are nothing more than a filthy bastard, no better than a mad dog."

Stiger struggled to break free, but the hold on him was simply too strong. The third man came up from behind, grabbed Stiger's hair painfully, and forced his head forward so he was looking at the ground.

Stiger managed to catch a glimpse of Tiro and a few of his men watching from a barracks doorway, and then he was past. A few moments later, they entered a building that smelled bad and was poorly lit by a single lantern. The man from behind still had a firm grip on his hair, keeping Stiger's gaze fixed onto the battered wooden floor. It was badly in need of a sweeping. He heard a rattle of keys and the mechanism of a lock turning.

The grip on his hair was released. Stiger looked up and found he was in a small single-room building with three metal-barred cells. The cell door he was standing before was opened and he was thrown inside. He landed in a tumble on the wood-planked floor. Before he could pull himself to his feet, Prefect Lears entered the cell and knelt down beside him. A fist from the prefect slammed into Stiger's jaw. For a moment, Stiger saw white, and then his vision cleared. He reached up to his jaw, which hurt something awful.

"How dare you?" Lears hissed, voice shaking with ill-concealed rage. "How dare you order the burning of my fort? When it comes time to stretch your neck, I promise you I will be in the first row to watch. Perhaps I shall even volunteer to assist the hangman. Won't that be a kindness?"

"There is an army coming," Stiger said, tasting blood from a split lip. It ran down his chin and dripped onto the floor.

"There is no army," Lears spat. "They are only raiders, you dumb fool. We've seen their likes before in these parts. You allowed your imagination to get the better of you. Now, I have to go and rectify the damage you've done." Lears sucked in a breath and released it. "Since my cohort is exhausted from the march here because my fool lieutenant was taken in by your madness, I have to take one of the Covenant cohorts to put this raid down."

"Don't go," Stiger said. "Please listen to me. You—"

Lears punched him again. The force of the blow caused the side of Stiger's head to slam into the floor. Stiger found he was dazed for a moment, and struggled to regain his wits. Lears stood.

"I shall return to watch you hang." Lears stepped out of the cell. "The tribune has promised me that singular honor. All I have to do is beat back the enemy's raiding parties and you are mine. It's nothing I've ever had a problem doing before and shouldn't prove to be much of a challenge."

Stiger sat up as the door to his cell was closed and locked.

Lears chuckled darkly. "You know, even if you had served honorably, and had been falsely accused, I would still have been in the front row to watch you hang. You understand, family business, but a pleasure just the same."

"You are a fool." Stiger spat out blood.

"Maybe so, maybe not. But you both shall hang nonetheless." With that, the prefect left. Lears looked back once, smiling as the outer door was closed.

Stiger got to his feet. He heard a scuffing off to his side. He glanced around and spotted Hollux in the next cell over, looking rather miserable. There was no one else with them in the jailhouse.

"Fancy meeting you here," Stiger said.

"I'm going to hang," Hollux said numbly.

"No, I don't think you will." Stiger began untying his armor.

"How can you say that?" Hollux stood.

"Oh," Stiger shrugged out of his armor, "I think the Rivan will get here before they have the chance to put the hangman's noose around our necks. In the end, I shall be proven right."

"Really?" Hollux looked suddenly hopeful. "Do you think so?"

"I am certain." Stiger placed his armor carefully against the bars of the cell and then laid down on his bench. He gingerly touched his split lip, which still freely bled. "To be honest, I don't think it will help us very much."

"What?" Hollux stepped up to the bars, gripping them.

"The Rivan will be the ones that get us," Stiger said and let out a heavy breath. "Tribune Declin has sent a message to General Treim that will see the Third turned back." Stiger paused and felt his jaw where Lears had struck him. It ached terribly, but what hurt even more was the knowledge that all of his efforts had come to naught. He glanced at Hollux. "We shall die all right, but at the hands of the enemy."

Using his arms for a pillow, Stiger closed his eyes.

"What are we going to do?"

"At the moment," Stiger said, "nothing much. If I am to die, then I intend to do it well-rested."

"Sleep?" Hollux fairly screeched. "You're going to sleep?"

"Yes, and I would appreciate it if you kept it down," Stiger said. "It's been a good long while since I've had a full night's sleep and I intend on getting it."

With that, he surrendered and allowed blissful oblivion to overtake him.

Chapter Fourteen

"All you do is sleep," Hollux said, sounding thoroughly put out.

Stiger cracked open an eye and turned his head to look over at Hollux, who was sitting on the bench in his own cell. Without a fire, the small jailhouse was cold with the early morning chill. They had passed an uncomfortable night, with only their tunics for warmth.

"So?" Stiger asked. "What's your point?"

"It's been two days," Hollux said, the frustration leaking into his voice. "We've been stuck here for two entire days."

"So?" Giving up on the idea of further sleep, he sat up. "What else is there to do? Besides, I've not gotten this much sleep in weeks." Stiger yawned, stretching. "I feel fully rested. You know, it might not be a bad thing to get locked up now and again."

Hollux shook his head in disgust. "How can you joke at a time like this?"

"It's about one of the few things we are free to do at the moment," Stiger said. "Get it? Free?"

"This sitting around is driving me mad." Hollux stood and began pacing his small cell. "I want out."

"I didn't realize that you were so eager to greet the hangman," Stiger said, letting slip a slight grin. "That or the Rivan, whoever comes first."

Hollux chuckled, finally giving in to the black humor. He stopped pacing. "Anything seems better than just sitting here. They only come in once a day to give us food. We've had no visitors. It is boring."

"Are you saying my company is tedious?"

"Don't start that again," Hollux said. "Seriously, all we've been able to do is talk."

"It has afforded us time to become better acquainted," Stiger said.

Though Hollux was at least ten years his senior, Stiger felt like the older lieutenant was his junior in age. The man talked incessantly, a byproduct of his nervousness at their current condition. Despite that, Stiger found Hollux an affable fellow who was honest almost to a fault.

"I've learned more about you and your family," Stiger said. "Your father is an honorable man, your mother a lovely woman. They had two sons and a daughter. Your brother…ah…" Stiger snapped his fingers. "Terguna, stayed home to help run your family's interests. And you've told me all about your sister Amelis, whom you adore. Her marriage to that Meklen fellow, a good prospect that turned out not to be so respectable. 'He's a real bastard,' I think is how you put it."

Hollux spared him a rueful look, but refused to be drawn out.

Stiger pursed his lips as he contemplated his fellow prisoner. He had learned that, as he had expected, Hollux had not thrived in the legions. Hollux had been transferred to the auxiliaries, where he'd finally found a place but, in Stiger's estimation, not a home. Unable to advance, Hollux had settled in, seeking nothing more than to complete his service and obtain his pension. He was an embarrassment to his father, who had effectively disowned him.

"You have told me so little about yourself," Hollux said suddenly, turning it back on Stiger. "Your father, next to the emperor, is the most famous man in the empire."

"Infamous is more like it," Stiger said, suddenly feeling uncomfortable.

"During the civil war he defeated army after army," Hollux said in a tone that was somewhat awed. "I've studied his exploits."

"Only to lose in the end," Stiger said quietly.

"His battles have become legend," Hollux said. "It must have been glorious to see."

"Glorious?" Stiger said, glancing down at the floor and shaking his head slowly. "I don't think so. Glory is a word that those who have not known combat freely bandy about."

Hollux did not look convinced by that.

"What was it like growing up under such a man?" Hollux asked. "It must have been incredible."

"It was far from that," Stiger said, thinking back upon his childhood, the latter end of which he viewed as an unhappy time. "My father is a hard, unforgiving man."

Hollux was silent for several heartbeats. "I think there is some of him in you."

"Perhaps," Stiger said, and though he wished to deny it, he understood the truth in those words. He was very much like his father.

"Come on, it could not have been all that bad," Hollux said. "I've heard you were the childhood playmate of our emperor. Is that true?"

Stiger nodded, feeling even more uncomfortable with the turn of the conversation. "After the war, it was likely the only reason my family was spared. That and my mother was the emperor's sister," Stiger paused, the hurt at her loss pulling at his heart. "She did not make it through the war."

"Oh," Hollux said, a little lamely. "I am sorry. I did not know…"

Stiger looked up at Hollux and saw that he was sincere. This man dealt with him for who he was, not his family name. It was a rare thing.

"So, let me get this straight," Stiger said, seeking to divert the conversation. "After your term of service is completed, you're going to find a woman?"

"It hardly matters now," Hollux said with a heavy sigh and sat down on his bench.

"Raise a family?" Stiger said, a grin finding its way back onto his face.

Hollux scowled at Stiger. In the dim light, Stiger thought he saw the other color. After a moment, the expression softened. "Yes, a family would be nice, but I also intended to petition the court for a civil service position. I am sure my father will do nothing to help me. Perhaps a lower level provincial judge, or something like that. Enough to live comfortably."

"A peaceful life then?"

"Until you arrived, I led a very peaceful life," Hollux chuckled and then made a show of glancing around his cell. "Now, it seems I am destined to face either the hangman or end my days on the point of a Rivan sword."

"Now you're getting into the spirit of things," Stiger said with a chuckle. "I've found that humor can be a soldier's best friend."

"Is that so?"

The outer door rattled. They only brought food around midday, but bright morning sunlight flooded into the interior of the dim jail from the small slit windows. Stiger and Hollux shielded their eyes against the penetrating light as the door swung open.

"Been getting some rest, sir?"

"Tiro," Stiger exclaimed, lowering his hand and standing. He was pleased to see his sergeant healthy and well. "How are the men?"

Stiger's sergeant walked up to the cage.

"Doing well, sir," Tiro said, studying Stiger and then Hollux. He gave an unhappy scowl at what he saw. "They've been enjoying life some, resting, eating, and generally getting soft. Since we got here, they've not had an officer to push them."

"Guilty as charged, I am afraid," Stiger said. "I've been shirking, you see."

"I would never dream of accusing an officer of dodging his duty, sir," Tiro said. "Besides, we both know you are not the type."

"Varus?" Stiger asked. "How is he?"

"He's mending," Tiro said. "Still recovering his wits with that nasty knock on the head. He's got one heck of a bump, but Nera's been taking good care of him."

"Nera?" Stiger was immensely relieved to hear that Varus was doing well. "Who?"

"That woman we rescued back at the farm," Tiro said. "She's become quite attached to our corporal."

Stiger had never learned the woman's name and now felt slightly embarrassed that he had not made the attempt. It had been nothing overt on his part. He had just had a lot on his plate at the time.

"Any news?" Hollux asked, stepping nearer.

"That's why I'm here," Tiro said. "A messenger, along with a troop of cavalry, has arrived from the Third. Can you believe it? The general sent a ranger. I've not seen one since the Wilds. Along with the troop commander, he's with the tribune now."

Stiger stepped up to the metal bars of his cage and gripped them. "What word does he bring?"

"I don't know," Tiro admitted. "I was in the barracks and heard word that he had arrived. They were in with the tribune before I could learn something."

Stiger wondered what it meant. Was the messenger here with a reply accepting the tribune's report? Or did he bring word of something else? Was Stiger to be delivered to the general to face trial?

"Why didn't you come sooner?" Stiger asked, eyes narrowing. "Why wait so long?"

"I was ordered to stay away from you, sir," Tiro said. "Well, really the jail. The tribune gave orders for all of us from the Seventh. He even put extra guards on this building and on our barracks."

"So, the tribune lifted the orders then?" Stiger asked.

"No, sir," Tiro said and shifted about uncomfortably.

"Sergeant, you're willfully violating orders?" Hollux said with a deep frown.

"No, sir," Tiro said, suddenly looking very offended. "I would never violate orders, sir. Without the lieutenant here, my boys have been idle too long. I am looking for busy work that needs doing, is all. It occurred to me that the jailhouse may need to be swept, the waste buckets emptied. That sort of thing, sir."

Hollux's frown deepened, if that was possible.

Stiger swallowed, as Tiro's gaze returned. The old sergeant had violated his orders to check on his officer. Stiger found that he was touched by Tiro's concern.

"Sergeant," Stiger said, "though I welcome your visit, I would not want you to fall under a charge. You need to go."

"Aye, sir," Tiro said, with a glance behind him. "In good time, I will."

"I meant it," Stiger said. "You need to go, now."

"I was let in by the sergeant of the guard, sir," Tiro said. "He will warn me when it is time."

"Why'd he violate orders?" Stiger raised an eyebrow.

"It's a sergeant thing," Tiro said, shifting his stance.

"Tiro," Stiger said. "What's the real reason?"

"The auxiliary sergeants are getting a tad concerned, sir," Tiro said. "We talked and they believe without a doubt the Rivan are headed this way."

"I see," Stiger said, eyes narrowing. There was more to the story than Tiro was telling.

The sergeant gave in with a heavy sigh. "Prefect Merritt, he leads the Twenty-Fifth Toldean Cohort that's stationed here," Tiro explained. "He's a good sort, sir. A bit old like me, but he fought in the Wilds and knows which end of a sword is the correct one to jab an enemy with." Tiro took a deep breath. "It seems he believes the enemy is coming, especially after he and I spoke, sir. He asked me a lot about you, and I answered honestly, sir. Among other things, I told him you was one of the best officers I've ever served with and that what you'd told the tribune was the gods honest truth. I told him about Cora'Tol, the farm, and what Crief said about the army that's comin'. Well, that got his attention. He's put his men and ours to work on the defenses, sir." Tiro paused for another breath. "When the tribune asked what they were doing, Prefect Merritt explained the need to get his idle boys to work...like we do with the legions, sir. Busy boys means less trouble, sir." Tiro paused. "To be honest, it might've been my suggestion, but you'd never get me to admit that. Well, he sort of sent me to see the sergeant of the guard, sir."

Stiger was amused with the long, rambling explanation on what had been going on while he had been confined. It was good to know that there were defensive preparations underway.

"What of the cohort that marched?" Stiger asked. "Has there been any word from Lears?"

"Nothing, sir," Tiro said. "It's one of the reasons I came. They marched to Ida and were supposed to send a messenger back. When none came, the tribune dispatched a rider. He didn't come back either, sir. So the tribune sent another rider." Tiro shook his head at that. "We know what's coming, sir."

Stiger closed his eyes, feeling helpless behind the bars. He was stuck here doing nothing, when he should be out there helping to strengthen the defenses of the fort.

"Once the enemy arrives," Tiro said, "the tribune should let you out. Then there will be plenty to do."

"Thank you for your visit, Sergeant," Stiger said. "It is much appreciated. Now, I would ask that you leave. I don't want to see you placed on a charge."

"Aye, sir," Tiro said and turned toward the door when a commotion outside caused him to freeze.

A man wearing a richly cut brown cloak stepped through the doorway. The hood was pulled up. The dim light of the jailhouse served to conceal his features. Though he had never met one before, and despite the man not wearing the uniform, Stiger realized this was the imperial ranger. Stiger could not help shake the feeling that he had seen this man before.

The ranger glanced around before his gaze settled upon Tiro. Using both hands, he pulled the hood back. Stiger sucked in an astonished breath.

"Eli!" Tiro exclaimed with excitement. "By the all the gods and the High Father's beard, is it really you?"

"You've become old," came the reply in a pleasantly soft, singsong kind of voice. It sounded almost human, but was tinged with something alien at the same time.

Stiger blinked, not quite believing his eyes. Before him stood an elf. And not just any elf, but a friend of Tiro.

Eli was tall, standing several inches above Stiger. He was whipcord thin. His face was that of a young man, barely out of his teens, with blue, almond-shaped eyes and sharp, pointed ears that poked out from his sand-colored hair. Eli's face, framed by his long hair, was almost too perfect. Carved by a master of unparalleled skill and flawless to a fault, it was like one of the numerous marble busts that adorned the palace back in the capital.

Tiro and Eli embraced, the sergeant patting the elf heavily on the back. After a moment, Tiro stepped back, holding Eli by the arms.

"I've become old," Tiro said, "but you've not aged a day."

"It is but a curse of my race," Eli said.

The sergeant turned and Stiger was surprised to see tears in the old veteran's eyes.

"Eli," Tiro said, wiping them away. He gestured toward the cage. "I would like to introduce you to my commanding officer, Lieutenant Stiger."

Eli stepped past Tiro and up to within a foot of the cage. Stiger felt as if he were being studied. He did not like the feeling.

"I've come a long way to find you, lieutenant," Eli said softly. "General Treim sends you his greetings."

Eli reached into his cloak and withdrew a dispatch, which he passed through the bars. Stiger opened the dispatch, tilted it toward the light from the door, and scanned the contents. He looked up at Tiro and over to Hollux, then back to the dispatch.

"Our boys got through," Stiger said excitedly to Tiro. "The Third is on her way."

"The legion should be here in two days," Eli said. "General Treim thinks you cause ..." Eli paused, clearly contemplating his words. "No, that is not the right word. He thinks trouble finds you."

"It seems the general might be on to something, sir," Tiro said with a chuckle.

"But the tribune sent a messenger to turn the Third back," Stiger said.

"I was with the general. He became ..." Eli paused and looked at Tiro. "Mad or angry? Which is the better word?"

"I bet he became angry," Tiro said, with a satisfied look thrown to Stiger.

"Yes," Eli said, "the general became angry. The legion is still coming. I offered my services to ride ahead with the advance party and act as a representative."

A cavalry officer strode into the jail, the heels of his riding boots conking off the wooden floorboards. The sergeant of the guard who delivered the meals followed closely on his heels.

"Carbo," Stiger exclaimed in surprise at the sight of the cavalry officer who had become his friend over the past few weeks.

Carbo's expression turned thunderous and he rounded on the sergeant. "Get them out of there. Now!"

"But, sir," the sergeant sputtered, "I have orders from the tribune holding these two prisoners for trial."

"Sergeant," Carbo lowered his voice, "your tribune has been relieved of his command. If you don't get them out of there this instant, I promise you that I shall see you broken back to the ranks. Furthermore, I shall personally see to it that you spend the rest of your days in service to our emperor mucking out the latrines with your tongue."

The sergeant didn't even bother to reply. He fumbled with the keys on his belt, untied the loop, and then hastily unlocked the door to Hollux's cage before turning to Stiger's.

Once the door was swung open, Stiger stepped out. Carbo offered his hand, which Stiger took in a firm, friendly grip.

"Carbo," Stiger said, "I would like to introduce you to Lieutenant Hollux. I consider him a friend."

"Any friend of Stiger is a friend of mine." Carbo shook Hollux's hand. "It is a real pleasure to meet you, sir, and an honor."

Hollux seemed taken aback slightly, but handled it well. "It is my pleasure, sir, especially since you got us out of these damned cages."

Carbo suddenly stepped back, holding his nose, looking between Stiger and Hollux.

"You both need a bath," Carbo said, "and badly."

"That I do," Stiger admitted. "It's been far too long since I properly bathed."

"Well, let's get you cleaned up and into a fresh tunic," Carbo said. "I am afraid there is a lot to be done, and not much time."

CHAPTER FIFTEEN

S tiger strode out of the officers' quarters and into the bright morning sunlight. The temperature was much cooler than the day before—it could almost be described as crisp. It was possibly a sign that the unseasonably hot weather was finally giving itself over to fall. Stiger certainly hoped so, for he was more than tired of the oppressive heat.

He was wearing a freshly laundered tunic, drawn from the fort's quartermaster. The coarse wool itched only a little. The tunic was the kind reserved for a ranker, but it was clean and for that he was grateful. Slightly larger than he would have liked, it also wasn't quite his size. If he kept the tunic, it would have to be tailored for a better fit. The military typically held a jaded view of the enlisted man's tunic and took the one-size-for-all approach. Officers, men generally of some means, had their tunics custom-made from better-quality wool.

Stiger had also taken the opportunity to bathe. Being clean for the first time in weeks felt wonderful. To be free of the dust, dirt, and grime was a small mercy in itself. He had even managed a shave, using hot water, not the usual frigid river or pond water he had made do with over the past few weeks. Combined with the sleep he had caught up on while being confined, he felt like a new man.

"Better watch it, old boy," Stiger said to himself with a slight chuckle. "If you keep this up, you may just spoil yourself."

Stiger surveyed his surroundings. The officers' quarters opened onto the parade ground, which was situated behind the main gate. Fort Covenant was a large one, as rear echelon garrisons went. Built to hold two cohorts by necessity, there were more than a dozen single-story structures. The buildings of the fort spread out to his left and right. They included several barracks, a warehouse, cold cellar, stable, barn, smithy, mess hall, and centralized keep that housed the headquarters and the tribune's personal quarters. Three stories tall, the fortified keep towered over the other buildings. It backed up to the parade ground and was built upon a raised mound. The keep reached higher than the outer walls, and from the top he presumed one would have a clear view in all directions.

The buildings were made of timber, using whole logs from the nearby forest. Stacked one atop another and interlocked at right angles, the logs formed solid walls that had been plastered over for insulation. The outer defensive walls of the fort were also constructed of these logs, each of which was at least three feet in circumference. These had clearly been selected not only for their thickness, but also their height.

Starting from the edge of the parade ground and traveling around the entire fort, an earthen rampart backed up to the outer wall. The rampart was thick with trimmed grass. The top of the rampart served as a platform for the defenders to walk upon, with the defensive wall rising another three feet above it, forming a protective barricade.

Stiger found the fort itself neat and orderly. Nothing seemed out of place. It spoke of either a fanatical devotion to order or a disciplined garrison. He wondered which one applied to Tribune Declin.

"Excuse me, sir." An auxiliary had come up, interrupting Stiger's musings, and gave a smart salute.

"Yes?" Stiger returned the man's salute.

"Prefect Merritt requests your presence on the wall above the gatehouse." The auxiliary pointed. "He's right there, sir, with the other officers."

"Thank you," Stiger said and started off.

There were few men about as he made his way across the parade ground. The grass in the center had a distressed look to it, a sign that it potentially saw frequent use for drill. Stiger wondered where everyone had gone, for the interior of the fort was mostly deserted. There was only a handful of men on the walls.

The near absence of the garrison made Carbo's troopers stand out. Horses saddled, and with reins in their hands, the troopers waited near the gate. Stiger wondered where they were off to as he strode over to the gatehouse and up the back side of the rampart.

"Ah, Stiger," Merritt said, turning at his arrival.

Carbo, Hollux, Tride, and Eli were there, but the tribune was absent. Since Declin had been relieved, Stiger found his absence hardly surprising.

Hollux gave Stiger a welcoming nod. He also wore a fresh tunic and had washed.

"Good of you to join us," Merritt said. "I assume you feel much improved at having been given the opportunity to clean up."

There was only stiff formality in the prefect's tone. It was suffused with neither malice nor friendliness, but instead a controlled professionalism. In his late forties, Merritt had short-cropped hair that had thinned and long since grayed. He had a large reddish scar that ran down the left side of his neck and disappeared into his tunic.

The prefect was in excellent shape and seemed a no-nonsense kind of man. There was a hardness in his manner and a distant look to his eyes that Stiger had come to associate with veterans who had seen hard times. He instantly liked the older officer.

"Yes, sir," Stiger said. "After so long in the field, it was a welcome change."

"I can well imagine, having been there myself upon occasion." Merritt sucked in a deep breath. "Let's begin, shall we?" The prefect paused a moment, as if he were gathering his thoughts. "There is undoubtedly an enemy army coming our way. In addition to Lieutenant Stiger's report, General Treim has only recently confirmed that through intelligence from other sources. He has charged me with the defense of this fort. Furthermore, he has asked that *we*," Merritt said with emphasis, "hold until the Third arrives. It is the general's intention to bring the enemy to battle, preferably here in this valley. He does not want them to break out into open country. With any luck, the Third is expected to be here sometime tomorrow evening, perhaps a little later." Merritt paused briefly. "Now for the bad news. Upon my request, Lieutenant Carbo sent scouts up the road in search of the enemy. They encountered advanced elements less than two miles from the edge of the forest."

"Infantry or cavalry, sir?" Stiger asked.

Carbo stepped in. "Cavalry. A strong column too, followed closely by infantry."

"Yes," Merritt said. "We have to assume that the infantry represents the beginnings of the enemy's main body." Merritt turned to Carbo. "That means you must depart shortly, before the fort is surrounded."

"You are leaving?" Stiger was surprised by this.

"Yes," Carbo said in an unhappy tone. "I was instructed to deliver the general's orders, see that the change of command was carried out, assess the situation, and report back."

"What of the tribune?" Stiger asked, curious as to Declin's fate. "Is he going with Carbo?"

"No," Merritt answered with a slight frown. "Though he has been relieved, the tribune has elected to remain a few days before returning to the capital. He has not said so, but I believe he intends to hold the line with us. I believe him to be an honorable man."

Stiger understood Merritt's meaning. The tribune was in disgrace and would likely face a trial when he returned to the capital. Fighting alongside the defenders might be a way for him to partially redeem himself.

"If you would not mind, Prefect," Eli spoke up, drawing their attention, "I would prefer to remain also."

"Eli," Carbo said with a look of concern, "the general expects you to return with me."

"I shall, in good time," Eli said, then added a slight shrug. "But not now. Prefect, I request the honor... 'honor' is the correct word, right?" Merritt gave a nod. "Yes, I request the honor of fighting alongside you and your fine men."

"It's been a long time since I've had the pleasure of serving alongside elves." Merritt's stern expression cracked a little and he let slip a smile. "I welcome the services of a ranger. However, with what's coming, I urge you to consider going with Carbo. I cannot guarantee I can hold this fort."

"I feel I can be of better use here," Eli said. "I will stay if you will have me."

"Very well, then," Merritt said. "I am honored to have one of the High Born with us. Thank you."

"It pleases me much to fight alongside such gallant men." Eli gave a slight bow of his head.

"Well," Merritt said and bounced on his heels, "that's settled. Let's review our defenses and the challenge ahead of us."

The prefect stepped up to the barricade. The other officers followed. Stiger placed his hands upon the top of the wall and looked over. Beneath him, at least a hundred men worked in the two trenches that stretched clear around the fort. They were busily cleaning out debris and replacing old stakes with fresh ones.

Beyond the outer trench, several men moved with large canvas bags, tossing bits of metal into the long grass. It looked as if these men were sowing caltrops. Simple yet vicious, caltrops were incredibly hard to spot. When tossed, one side of the four-headed, spiked weapon always managed to point upward. Should an unwary person step on one, it was certain to cripple.

A man working below in the first trench spotted them and pointed up at the officers. He shouted something and a hearty cheer went up from those nearest. Stiger realized after a moment that they were his men. He waved back. They cheered even louder. Tiro was below among the men, grinning like a bear.

Stiger felt a lump form in his throat as he looked down upon his cheering men. His gaze then shifted to the road north. He loved his company, and yet he had led them here to a place that would soon see them locked in a desperate struggle. The likelihood of many of them ending up fodder for the worms was high. And yet, Stiger felt as if he had made the correct decision. This fort had been until recently an isolated backwater. Now, because of his direct actions, Fort Covenant had become a critical position that had the potential to affect the course of the war.

"Back to work," Tiro snapped. "Bend your backs, you bastards."

The cheering ceased, and the men returned to their tasks.

"I've heard a great deal about you," Merritt said to Stiger. "The general even mentioned you in his orders to me. It seems you show real promise as an officer. It is good you are with us."

"Yes, sir," Stiger said, feeling slightly embarrassed by the unexpected praise. Merritt did not seem to begrudge his family name, something until recently he had not come to expect in anyone serving. Stiger noticed, however, that Tride looked like he had swallowed a frog. The lieutenant carried a small wax tablet, which he tapped on the palm of his hand.

"I fought under your father," Merritt continued, "before the civil war, that is."

"I did not know, sir." This was the first time Stiger had spoken with the prefect.

"It was a long time ago, and I was a junior officer much like yourself." Merritt became unfocused, as if reliving a different time. His gaze sharpened. "Well, that's in the past. It is time we speak on what must be done going forward." He pointed out into the field as he addressed those gathered around. "To assault these walls, the enemy must get past the two outer trenches. Make no mistake, they will do so. We have neither the artillery nor sufficient numbers of bowmen to make such an effort a costly venture to our enemy. Nor do we have the ability to hinder them in any meaningful way. Once they have overcome the trenches, they will either assault the walls or the gate. It is possible they may attempt both simultaneously. Any attempt to break through the gate shall prove futile. We will deny them that opportunity by shoveling dirt up behind the gate, thereby rendering a battering ram ineffective. With luck, this will buy us some time before they switch all of their efforts to the walls."

"Sir?" Lieutenant Tride spoke up. "What if they just bypass us? Wouldn't it be easier for them if they went around us? We're so few, hardly enough for an army to worry much about. I should think they have nothing to fear from us."

"There is little chance they will bypass us," Merritt said with a heavy breath as he regarded his lieutenant with disappointed eyes. "Our enemy cannot afford to leave us to their rear. This north-south road is their lifeline. Moving around us would pose an unacceptable risk to their communications and supply. More importantly, this fortification is all that stands between them and open country. Have no doubt, they will attack. They must reduce and overcome this fort before they move on." Merritt paused for a breath. "In a few weeks, winter will arrive and all campaigning for the season will end. The winters so far north are terrible. Our enemy knows this only too well. Their goal by coming here is an attempt to outflank our army that is mostly to the northwest. They mean to cut off supply by thrusting around and to the rear of the legions. Should their effort prove successful, it will mean a military disaster on a near unimaginable scale."

Merritt fell silent a moment. "I want to be plain. This is a grave threat, not only to the war effort, but to the empire as well. The Third is on the march, as you already know. General Treim has informed me our legions farther north have also begun pulling back, giving up the hard-fought ground they have taken this summer. Should the Third be defeated in battle, it will fall to the rest of the army to hold off the enemy until winter ... that is, if the enemy does not get behind them first and cut supply. Should that happen, there is the very real possibility that the enemy's two armies may combine."

"But if the Third is defeated," Tride said, "then that means we will be also."

"Yes," Merritt said. "Now you understand the true nature of our position."

"Yes, sir," Tride said.

"Good. We have two auxiliary cohorts," Merritt said. "Mine the Twenty-Fifth Toldean and Hollux's Ninth Light Foot Taborean. We also have Stiger's Seventh, with just enough men to be considered a light company. That gives us nearly seven hundred with which to hold this fort. Are there any questions so far?"

There were none.

"Lieutenant Tride," Merritt said, "you may give us your report on our supplies and available equipment."

"Yes, sir." Tride began to read from his wax tablet. "We have plenty of water, since it is well-drawn. Food will not be a problem. Our stores are sufficient for months. Concerning missiles, we have two thousand two hundred short spears and twelve large barrels of arrows." He paused and glanced over at Hollux. "I would think that plenty for your bowmen. Do you not agree?"

"Maybe," Hollux said, tapping a finger against his chin. "My men can shoot awful quick. Twelve barrels means perhaps four thousand arrows combined with what we brought. Well ... it may not last us all that long." Hollux stood straight as he looked over at Merritt. "I will impress upon my men to make their shots count, sir."

"That will be much appreciated, lieutenant." Merritt nodded for Tride to continue with his report.

"We have the equivalent of five barrels of oil," the lieutenant continued, "which must be used sparingly. And, of course, we have pans for cooking sand and boiling water. Our four bolt throwers are being assembled as we speak. We have nearly nine hundred bolts." He pointed to the covered towers on each corner of the fort. Hammering could be heard from inside the nearest tower. "They should be completed within a couple of hours. Our single catapult is also being assembled." He pointed down toward the parade ground. "We have plenty of round shot."

Stiger could see several men working to assemble the machine. He let slip a slight frown. The catapult was on the smaller side, perhaps capable of tossing a two-pound ball. It would do little to frighten the enemy or cause damage.

"That completes my report, sir."

"Gentlemen," Merritt said, "we don't have much with which to hold back the tide, other than sheer grit and determination. Since that is all we have, that is what we shall use. I am counting on each of you to do your duty. You must reach deep and pull forth courage. For courage is what you will need to set an example for your men to follow. Do that and we might just hold until the Third arrives. Fail in that…" Merritt fell silent for a moment, looking each in the eye. "Well, that will not happen, will it?"

"No, sir," Hollux said. "It will most certainly not."

Tride voiced his agreement.

"Stiger." Merritt turned to him. "I understand your men have seen considerable action?"

"Yes, sir, they have."

"Then you shall act as our reserve," Merritt said. "We shall use your legionaries to reinforce where needed, to plug the holes and force the enemy back over the wall. Think you can manage that?"

"Yes, sir," Stiger said. He had expected as much. "My boys and I will stand ready."

"Enemy in sight!" The shout ripped across the fort.

The officers' heads turned to the north. A column of riders had emerged from the tree line and was working its way down the hill, following the road. Several riders had pulled off to the side and remained on the hilltop as the column continued to ride from the forest and stretch down the hill.

Stiger supposed these were officers. They were clearly studying the fort as the bulk of the column continued past them. Stiger could hear the enemy cavalry singing a melodious tune, but at this distance could not make out words.

"Carbo," Merritt said, turning to face the cavalry lieutenant, "it is time for you to depart."

"Yes, sir," Carbo said.

"I would appreciate it if you rode through the town on your way out of the valley," Merritt said, gesturing vaguely toward the south, "and let the good people know it is time to evacuate."

"Yes, sir." Carbo gave a salute, which Merritt returned. "Take care, sir."

"Tell the general to hurry."

"I will, sir," Carbo said.

Carbo gave Stiger a nod before working his way down the rampart to where his troopers were waiting. Stiger watched as Carbo pulled himself up into the saddle. The cavalry lieutenant raised his hand and let it fall, pointing forward, giving the soundless order to ride. Amidst the sounds of heavy hooves, they trotted through the gate. Stiger continued to watch as the troop crossed the trenches, turned to the west, and rode hard around the fort, before angling south and being lost to view.

"Lieutenant Tride," Merritt said, "kindly issue the recall for our men outside. Also, see that the bridges are pulled up from the trenches. I see no point in making it easier for the enemy."

"Yes, sir." Tride hurried away. A few moments later, a man atop the gatehouse blew his horn, sounding the recall.

The notes were nearly pure and rang out on the cool morning air. The men outside immediately dropped what they were doing and started for the protection of the fort.

"Well," the elf spoke up, drawing their attention. Eli was looking out toward the hill where the road emerged from the forest. The cavalry column had given way to enemy infantry, marching four abreast. They too were singing. Like a snake coming out of a hole, they began to work their way down and into the valley. "Things are about to get interesting."

CHAPTER SIXTEEN

"It's clear, sir," a lookout yelled down from above, having leaned over the outer wall, eyeballing the other side of the gate. "No enemy closer than the nearest trench, and they are just standing around bored-like. Only a handful, sir."

"Open the gate," Merritt ordered.

Several men standing by to do just that raised the locking bar, which landed with a heavy thud. They began pulling the gate open.

"Stand ready," Hollux, who was atop the gate, called to his men. The bowmen stepped up to the barricade and nocked their arrows.

"Are you sure about this, sir?" Stiger stood to Merritt's side.

Hinges creaking, the gate began to open. Stiger had his company formed up into a two-ranked battle line just behind the gate.

"Raise shields," Tiro ordered. "Draw swords."

The shields came up off the ground and swords seemed to jump out of scabbards.

"Unfortunately, I am," Merritt answered with a sidelong glance at Stiger. Absently, the prefect drummed the side of his chest armor as he shifted his gaze to the gate.

The prefect's armor was of an older style. It was lovingly cared for and yet had also clearly seen some action, for there were little dents, scrapes, and nicks from battle damage.

"Yes," Merritt said, drawing a long breath, "we must attend this parley. Anything to delay our enemy serves our needs."

"You don't have to go personally, sir," Stiger said. "I could represent you well enough."

"Our enemy is generally known to be honorable in these situations," Merritt said. "We should have little to fear."

"Except when they are not," Stiger said with some heat, "like in Cora'Tol. Crief is a good example of that."

Merritt was silent a moment.

"You must understand, victory is everything," Merritt said. "Nothing comes second. War must be waged in a terrible, total, and complete manner. There are times in pursuit of victory when we are called to do terrible things. Almost anything—and I mean anything—goes. Rules don't apply. The sacking of villages and towns, though repugnant, is an acceptable means to an end." Merritt paused and his look became quite hard. "Even small farms are fair game, like the one your prisoner took. We don't have to like it, nor condone it, but this is the world we live in. To the victor goes everything."

Merritt paused, his eyes flicking to Stiger's men. "I for one would rather the empire be the conqueror than the vanquished. There are times when that means ordering the death and destruction of that which we love." Merritt stepped closer and put a hand on Stiger's shoulder. "To be successful at our chosen craft, you must take this lesson to heart, no matter how distasteful it is going down."

Stiger sucked in a breath and let it out as he thought carefully on the prefect's words.

"In all this chaos and madness that war brings with it," Merritt continued, "there are times when gentlemen from both sides are able to come together and treat each other

honorably in parley. For a brief moment, we can set aside
the horrors of what we do and pretend that we are not the
monsters we have become."

The gate ceased its movement with a loud thud.

Merritt gave him a meaningful look. "Do you follow?"

"I understand, sir."

"Good," Merritt said, taking a step back. "It was a hard
lesson for me as well, but having learned it made me a better
soldier."

"Tiro," Stiger called. "You and Tig are coming with us.
In the absence of Varus, Asus, you have the formation."

Asus looked startled for a moment, then recovered. He
drew himself up and saluted as Tiro hurried over with Tig.
Both carried their shields.

"Yes, sir," Asus replied.

"Might I join you also?"

Stiger and Merritt turned to see Eli had joined them.
The elf's ability to move about unnoticed was uncanny.

"Why would you wish to expose yourself to the enemy?"
Merritt asked. "The elves as a people have parted ways with
the empire. You may inadvertently give the impression that
is not so."

"I have no compelling desire to do so," Eli said, "other
than curiosity."

"You are bored already?" Tiro said, incredulous.

"Sergeant," Merritt snapped, "mind your tongue with
our guest."

"Sorry, sir."

"It's quite all right," Eli said to the prefect. "Sergeant
Tiro and I are old acquaintances. You see, we previously
served together. I consider him a good friend."

Merritt glanced between the two of them. "The Wilds,
then?"

"Yes, sir," Tiro said. "Eli and I have been through some rough times."

"Addressing your concern on impressions," Eli said, "today I only represent myself."

"I see." Merritt released a breath that was almost a huff. "Very well. If you wish to join us, then so be it."

Merritt started forward through the gate, with Stiger and Eli trailing. Tiro and Tig followed a couple steps behind. To their front, at around five hundred yards, Stiger saw a few hundred enemy heavy infantry.

The enemy was busily erecting a camp, including the beginnings of a defensive berm. Stiger could hear the muffled cracks that signified ax parties at work in the forest. As they walked out of the fort, a second column of infantry was starting to snake its way down the hill.

Merritt strode up to the edge of the first trench. A delegation waited on the other side. Stiger saw two officers and what he took to be a sergeant waiting patiently. Their manner was relaxed, as if they had not a concern in the world.

"You requested a parley," Merritt said curtly. It was not framed as a question, but a simple statement of fact.

"Yes, I did," the officer Stiger took to be in charge replied in fluent Common. His armor was more ornate and expensive than the other's. There was not even the hint of an accent in his tone, and he sounded quite cultured. "I am Senior Captain Golves."

Golves was perhaps five years older than Stiger. He had the look of a hardened soldier, but also the refinement of a noble. A thick scar on his lower lip marred his features. Golves paused and gestured to the officer standing next to him. "This is my lieutenant, Ocal. And you, sir? May I have your name?"

"I am Prefect Merritt, in command of Fort Covenant."

"It was my understanding that Tribune Declin held that esteemed honor," Golves said. A slight hint of curiosity hung in his tone.

"Your intelligence appears to be flawed and out of date," Merritt said.

"So it seems," Golves said, his eyes sliding to Stiger and then Eli, who had pulled the hood of his cloak up. "And these gentleman, I know not their names. Would you be considerate enough to introduce me?"

"Of course," Merritt said. "May I present Lieutenant Stiger and—"

"Stiger?" Golves said. An amused look came over him. "Aren't you are supposed to be in disgrace and under confinement?"

"More faulty intelligence," Stiger growled. Golves's manner was beginning to irritate him.

Golves brought a hand up to cover his mouth as he gave a slight chuckle.

"You, sir, I have been chasing a good long way," Golves continued, lowering the hand. He pointed a finger. "Lieutenant Stiger, you have left a trail of destruction with your passage that honestly has been quite surprising. May I say, it is truly an honor to finally meet you face to face after so many weeks on the chase. You are such a formidable opponent that it seems a shame to have finally run you down..." Golves paused and gestured at the fort with both hands. "Here in the middle of nowhere."

Stiger wasn't at first sure how to take that. Initially he thought the enemy officer was playing with him, but then decided otherwise, as Golves appeared quite serious.

"Stiger," Merritt hissed after several heartbeats of silence, "do the gracious thing and accept the bloody compliment, would you?"

"It is an honor to meet you as well," Stiger said, drawing himself up. "And if you must know, I am precisely where I intended to be."

Golves offered a slight bow, but looked far from convinced.

"If I am correct in my thinking," Stiger said, having thought on the enemy officer's words, "it was your company that has dogged our heels something fierce. Is that so?"

"Yes. After you attacked a section of my men out on forage, I happily gave chase," Golves said, seeming rather pleased with himself. "But now I have finally caught up. All hunts must come to an end. You've nowhere to run."

Stiger gave a shrug rather than reply.

"What do you want?" Merritt asked.

"In the interest of saving lives, I ask humbly that you give up the fort," Golves said.

"I was a guest of the Rivan once before," Merritt said in a hard tone. "I will not subject myself to that indignity again."

"I see," Golves said and made a show of thinking, stroking his jaw. "In that case, I am prepared to offer you and your men free passage, provided you surrender your standards and weapons first."

Stiger glanced to Merritt, hoping the prefect would not consider such an offer. To surrender one's standards was an unforgivable offense. It would effectively end their careers or, possibly worse, sign their death warrants.

"Captain Golves," Merritt said, "I am afraid I will have to decline your generous offer. If you want them, you will just have to take them."

Golves let slip an unhappy scowl. Then his face lit up as if he had stumbled upon a fantastic idea. Stiger understood the enemy captain was playing a game, which he seemed to be enjoying.

"What if I permitted you to keep your standards and weapons?" Golves asked. "Would that satisfy your honor?"

"I would be compelled to decline your generous offer," Merritt said. "I intend to keep my fort. The only way you can have it is by seizing it forcefully."

Golves let slip another unhappy scowl, sharing a look with his lieutenant. "I am but the tip of the spear. In my humble estimation, you have no hope whatsoever of holding. If you compel us into an assault, I will tell you honestly, none shall be spared. Death will be your only escape."

"That may be so," Merritt said stiffly, "but I will not give up my fort. Unless you have other business, I believe we are done here."

Merritt turned to go.

"I understand you are holding a prisoner," Golves said. "A Lieutenant Crief."

"Your information is correct," Merritt said.

"We want him back," Golves said. "I have two of your officers. I propose a trade."

"Who?" Merritt's eyebrows rose. "Who do you have?"

"Prefect Lears and Lieutenant Teevus," Golves said. "I am afraid Lieutenant Teevus made the mistake of thinking he too could hold his fort."

"And you let him live?" Merritt asked. "What other prisoners do you have?"

Golves's expression hardened. "Alas, we did not take any. The only reason the poor lieutenant escaped his fate was for intelligence purposes. Now that we have all that we need from him, a destitute noble is of no use to us, other than in trade, of course. Should you refuse, I will have him immediately executed in the most brutal fashion I can think of."

Merritt became very still.

"Which is why I suggest you seriously consider my previous offer," Golves said. "You all have an opportunity to walk away with your standards and your lives."

"I will think on it," Merritt said, appearing to give a little.

"You have an hour," Golves said.

"Two hours," Merritt said.

"An hour," Golves said. "If I don't have it then, I shall put my prisoners to death."

"An hour," Merritt agreed. "You shall have my answer at that time. I will take you up on the offer of the prisoner exchange."

"Sir?" Stiger said. "You can't give them Crief."

"Be quiet, Stiger," Merritt snapped. "This is my decision, not yours."

"When do you desire to conduct the exchange?" Golves asked.

"In an hour's time, when I give you my answer. Will that be sufficient?" Merritt said.

Golves nodded.

"Lieutenant Stiger shall deliver the prisoner and my answer."

"Very good." Golves's eyes moved to Eli. "I was not introduced to this other gentleman."

"I am no gentleman," Eli said, and drew back the hood of his cloak. "Eli'Far at your service."

Golves made no show of surprise, other than the blinking of his eyes. Stiger noticed the enemy officer became quite still. He then shifted his stance and seemed to relax.

"I thought you elves had quit the empire," Golves said, giving Eli a slight bow, which the elf returned.

"Again," Stiger said, "it would seem you are receiving faulty intelligence."

Golves's eyes turned to Stiger and narrowed.

"I will see you in an hour," Golves said frostily. With that, he began walking back to his budding encampment, his lieutenant and sergeant following him.

"Sir," Stiger said to Merritt, "we cannot give up the fort."

"Lieutenant," Merritt said, "I have no intention of doing that. I was simply buying us time and playing his game."

"What of Crief?" Stiger said. "He is an important prisoner and the son of—"

"I know who he is," Merritt snapped. "I will not leave two of our own in the enemy's hands. I've been their guest. Trust me, it is not a pleasant experience."

With that, Merritt began making his way back into the fort.

Stiger watched the prefect go before stepping over to Tiro. "What do you think?"

"I think," Tiro said with a glance at the enemy column coming down the hill, "we are in the shit, sir."

"That was my thinking as well," Stiger said. "As soon that army comes up in its entirety, they will attack."

"I agree, sir," Tiro said. "However, they will not need their whole army. What with the moon being almost full, they may even try our walls this evening."

"I say," Eli said cheerfully, having sidled up to the two of them, "isn't this exciting?"

Tiro shot a frown at the elf. Stiger just shook his head.

Eli pointed towards the hill, where the road exited the forest. Another formation of heavy infantry had emerged and was moving down the hill toward the encampment. Stiger almost felt sick at the sight. There would be hard hours ahead.

"Exciting is not how I would characterize it," Stiger said.

✤ ✤ ✤

An hour later, Stiger stepped through the gate. Tiro and two legionaries dragged Crief along. As they neared, Crief took one look at the waiting Golves and the rapidly growing Rivan encampment and began laughing, nearly hysterically.

"I told you, Stiger," Crief said. "My father is coming to kill you all."

Tiro reached over and slapped Crief hard on the face. "Keep your tongue."

Golves did not seem at all fazed by Tiro's treatment of Lieutenant Crief. He just stood there and waited patiently. With him were his lieutenant, Lears and Teevus. He also had two men who each carried a long wooden plank.

Both Lears and Teevus appeared to have been worked over fairly well. Teevus looked up. His right eye was swollen shut, but his left widened at the sight of Stiger standing across the other side of the trench. After a moment, he averted his gaze and looked at the ground, clearly shamefaced.

"Stiger," Golves said, all business, "do I have your permission to run these planks across the trench to affect our exchange?"

Stiger gave a curt nod, at which Golves motioned his men forward. Once it was done, Golves looked expectantly at Stiger.

"My men first," Stiger said. "Then I will send your man."

"Do I have your word of honor on that?"

"You do, sir," Stiger said. "Though I'd prefer nothing better than to gut this murdering and raping bastard, I will send him to you. What you do with him after is your concern."

Golves's eyes slid from Stiger to Crief. A look of contempt and disgust washed over the enemy officer's face.

"Go," Golves snapped, pulling his gaze away from Crief to Lears and Teevus. "Return to your own."

Teevus started across first. Lears, appearing worse for wear, needed a prodding before he too shuffled along. Halfway across, he stumbled and almost toppled into the trench below. Tiro moved forward and assisted him.

"Right," Stiger said once the two imperial officers had safely crossed, kicking Crief lightly with a boot. "On your way."

Crief didn't even hesitate. He walked boldly over the planks, stopped on the other side, and offered Stiger a mocking salute.

"See you soon," Crief said.

"If you do," Stiger said, still angered that the man had been freed, "I will be sure to give you a few inches of steel."

Crief laughed at him. "I think it's you who will be the one stuck with Rivan steel." He started walking toward the enemy encampment. Golves motioned for his lieutenant to accompany Crief.

"I take it your prefect's answer is no?"

"Did you really expect us to capitulate?" Stiger asked.

"No, I most certainly did not," Golves answered and looked over the fort's walls. "We were always going to have to do this the hard way."

"Lieutenant Aggar." Stiger said. "He's one of yours, isn't he?"

"Oh no," Golves said with an amused chuckle. "I am afraid he's one of yours. It's just that we pay him better."

"So, Aggar's your source of information then?"

"Perhaps." Golves offered a smile of sorts and then sobered. "I am sorry that you will have to soon die. You have proven to be a worthy and honorable adversary."

"I shall be sorry to have to kill you," Stiger replied. "You seem honorable as well."

With that, Golves offered Stiger a nod and left with his two soldiers, trekking their way back toward their camp. They had left the planks in place. Stiger used his boot to tip them over and into the trench.

He swung his gaze across the two freed prisoners. Lears had collapsed to the ground. The prefect had a broken arm, and his face was hardly recognizable from the pounding he looked to have taken during questioning. The man's nose was broken too, as were several teeth. Dried blood had darkened his filthy tunic.

"Thank you," Teevus said, tears in his eyes. The lieutenant's face was nearly purple from bruising. "Thank you for trading us."

"Had it been up to me, I would not have traded. You owe your thanks to Prefect Merritt."

"What?" Teevus said, incredulous. "You would have left us in their hands?"

"I don't think either of you was worth trading," Stiger said.

"That's because you are a bastard," Lears glared at him, "just like your father."

"I am," Stiger said. "Tiro, see that the prefect is helped along. In his current state, I doubt he can make it on his own."

"Aye, sir," Tiro said.

With that, Stiger strode through the gate to the fort.

CHAPTER SEVENTEEN

66 I would've expected them to attack last night, sir," Tiro said, his gaze straying out towards the enemy camp. The early morning air was crisp, just like the day before. A fog that had partially shrouded the land had mostly lifted, revealing the full extent of the enemy's camp and its activities throughout the night.

Stiger, Tiro, and Eli were standing on the north-facing wall. The enemy army had encamped just beyond the second trench, their camp filling up the entire north side of the valley. There were thousands of tents and even more smoke trails that drifted slowly up into the sky. Stiger had to admit it was an impressive sight. What was more incredible was that the enemy army was still arriving with long columns of fresh formations marching out from the forest road nearly every hour.

Though the fort's catapult could easily reach the enemy's camp, the prefect had held back from opening hostilities. He did not wish to speed up the unpleasantness that was sure to come.

The sun had been up for maybe an hour. Stiger had finished walking the wall and found Tiro and Eli studying the enemy. Overnight, with thousands of men working by moonlight, the Rivan had thrown up an impressive defensive berm that was threatening to completely encircle the fort.

"It seems they don't want us getting out, either," Stiger said, surveying the defensive works.

"Would you?" Tiro asked. "If things were reversed."

Stiger shook his head.

The enemy had brought up some artillery and set it up in a small field. Stiger counted four large machines that appeared capable of firing four-to possibly six-pound shot. Wagons had been moved up and teams were busy unloading shot, trampling the wheat as they went about their work. Worse, there was significant activity in the camp beyond, as a number of formations were assembling. A few had marched out and were working their way around the east side of the fort.

Stiger let out a slow breath. The enemy did not seem to be in any pressing hurry to launch their assault, though from what he was seeing, it would likely come sometime this morning.

"Let's be grateful for the time they've wasted," Stiger said. "Every moment squandered brings the Third that much closer to relieving us."

"I am sorry, sir," Tiro said, "but that army across the way is much larger than the Third and her auxiliary cohorts. Will the general even be able to relieve us?"

"It is," Stiger said, "and he has to."

"I'm just sayin', sir."

"I know," Stiger said. "I know."

"This is much more exciting than remaining at headquarters with your general as an observer," Eli said, speaking up. "I am so very pleased that I came and even more so that I made the decision to remain."

"Eli gets bored easily, sir." Tiro shook his head. "You have to watch him or he gets himself into trouble, and sometimes others too."

"Get myself in the trouble?" Eli said, aghast, turning on the sergeant. "Why, Tiro, I ne—"

"It's the help he needs getting out of trouble that is the problem, sir," Tiro said, flashing Eli a grin. "I could tell you a few stories, sir. Believe me, he bears watching." Tiro looked as if he were about to say more, but paused and slowly turned his gaze on Stiger. The sergeant's eyes narrowed as if something had just occurred to him. "You know... he is very much like you, sir. Sort of attracts trouble."

"Do you?" Eli asked with interest. "General Treim mentioned something about that, but I wondered if he was jesting. He is a hard man to read. Do you really attract trouble?"

Stiger rolled his eyes.

"He does," Tiro said. "And don't bother denying it, sir. Like when you ordered the company to attack that isolated section of men back at that farm? Only they weren't so isolated, were they? Golves got on our trail and chased us something good."

"Oh my," Eli said. "We're going to have so much fun together. I can just tell."

"Wait a moment, you can't blame—"

Stiger was interrupted by a loud creaking, followed by a thud that came from out beyond in the field. This was immediately followed by a high-pitched whistling.

"Down!" Tiro pulled Stiger to the ground behind the barricade. Eli dove and covered his head with his arms. A heartbeat later, there was a deep, shuddering impact behind them. Stiger looked and saw a great gout of dirt fall in a shower. When it settled, a crater three feet around had appeared where moments before there had only been grass. Stiger could see the white ball, partially exposed, sitting in the middle of the crater.

Thankfully, no one had been injured. A horn sounded the call to arms. After a hesitation, the horn blew again. Barracks doors burst open. Like angry ants, auxiliaries began to boil out, making their way to their posts, tying helmet straps or slipping on their swords.

Stiger looked up and over the edge of the barricade at the enemy, just as there was another loud creaking out in the field, followed almost immediately by a *thud*. Stiger tracked the ball with his eyes as it arced up into the sky, whistling. The round contacted the tower to his left on the corner of the fort. It was a dead-on hit, and before he could blink, the wooden tower came apart. With a great splintering crash, it tumbled backward into the fort.

Before Stiger could pull his eyes away, another ball slammed into the wooden wall just below them with a loud crack. Stiger felt the impact. The ball bounced back and out into one of the trenches.

The fourth machine let fly with a ball that sailed clean over the wall and into the parade ground. It landed several yards from Stiger's men, who were forming up. They scattered.

"Tiro," Stiger pointed, "get down there. Move our men back to the other side of the fort, preferably behind the keep. Have them shelter there until called."

"Yes, sir," Tiro said and started off. "I'm on it."

"Tiro informs me when you learned of the enemy army, it was your idea to come. I now see why you wanted to remain here."

Stiger turned an astounded look upon the elf, wondering if he had gone barking mad. He supposed that Eli was teasing him. "Well," Stiger said with a chuckle, "we're both crazy for having decided to stay, aren't we?"

"Undoubtedly," Eli said and bared his teeth in a full grin at Stiger. Small and needle-sharp, the teeth looked like they belonged in the mouth of a predator. Stiger resisted the urge to shudder and turned his gaze back toward the enemy, who were reloading the four machines to fire anew.

Beyond the field, a large number of the enemy had lined the edge of their camp. They gave a great cheer to the artillery crews. Several waved back but quickly returned to their work.

There was a crack off to the right. From the last remaining tower on the north wall sprung a bolt. The overly large dart shot out toward one of the enemy machines. The aim was low and it struck the defensive berm, harmlessly kicking up a spray of dirt.

Auxiliaries on the wall gave a defiant shout. A number of catcalls were sent the enemy's way. The crew down on the parade ground began loading the fort's only catapult.

When it finally released, the ball sailed upward and out of the fort, whistling toward the enemy's camp. Stiger tracked its path. In a rather anticlimactic fashion, the ball landed somewhere in the middle of the camp. He could not tell if it had done any damage, but hoped it had.

The artillery duel continued for more than an hour. Lieutenant Tride stood atop the north wall with a pair of white flags. He used them to signal the crew below in an attempt to direct the fire towards one of the enemy machines. The more he worked at it, the more it seemed the fire became evermore erratic. To Stiger's disgust, the friendly shot landed farther and farther away from the intended target.

"They don't seem to shoot fine," Eli said as he and Stiger gazed upon the catapult.

"Did you mean good?"

"Yes," Eli said, "that is the word. They are no good, yes? The Common Tongue is a little confusing. It's not like Elven."

"They are rear echelon auxiliaries," Stiger said, hoping the elf caught his meaning so that he did not have to explain further.

"There are auxiliaries and then there are auxiliaries," Eli said.

A crack from the tower signaled another bolt loosed. Stiger followed the deadly missile's flight as it shot toward the same target. It impacted the ground around ten feet away. The crew reloading their machine paused only briefly before returning to their work.

The bolt thrower was a relatively accurate machine. However, like the catapult, the crew operating it did not appear terribly skilled. Stiger considered sending his men up to take charge, but disregarded the idea. He would step on Tride's toes if he did so. Besides, with so few machines in operation, the artillery duel would have little impact on the overall assault other than a psychological one. Sending his men up to the tower would put them at risk, and right now they were safe. Not only that, it would violate his orders from the prefect. Stiger's men were the reserve. They would be needed when the enemy tested the walls.

Another ball sailed overhead, whistling. It passed through the roof of one of the barracks with a tremendous crash, partially bringing the roof down and nearly demolishing the entire building. A heartbeat later, a ball smacked loudly into the fort's wall off to the right. Crouching behind the barricade and peeking over the top, Stiger had to admit that he did not much enjoy being on the receiving end with not much to do other than spectate.

Prefect Merritt visited the wall, making a point to speak to his men as he worked his way along its length. Like Stiger, the auxiliaries huddled for cover. They had placed their shields against the lip of the barricade in the hopes that, should it be pierced, they would have some limited protection.

At one point, Stiger even saw the tribune come out and climb up the rampart to look from the wall before returning to his quarters. Since he had been relieved of command, Declin had remained out of sight. Whether by design or from shame was debatable.

"Looks like they are finally getting ready to make an assault," Merritt said, coming over. He had brought Tride, Teevus, and Hollux with him. Merritt stood in plain view of the enemy, even turned his back as a ball whistled close by. Stiger ducked with the other officers, seeking the shelter of the barricade. Merritt was the only one who refused cover, even seemed to disdain it.

"Gentlemen," Merritt said, "do try to set an example. Stooping behind the barricade every time a ball sails in doesn't exactly inspire courage or confidence, now, does it? If it has your name on it, there's nothing you can do. So, I ask you, why hide? It is not like those infernal machines are terribly accurate, especially from this distance. The men should see you standing tall and unafraid."

A little shamefaced, Stiger and the other officers stood, fully exposing themselves to the enemy's fire. Stiger looked across the field. Formations of men had been marching from the camp for some time, moving around the fort. Stiger had counted nine enemy companies moving into jump-off positions. A large number of covered wagons had followed behind each company.

"I fear they mean to assault our walls, even as they go after the gate," Merritt said, eyes sweeping the enemy formations that were preparing to attack. "Hollux, I want your bowmen over the gate. They are bound to make a go for it. No matter how successful they are, that mound of dirt piled up behind the gate will keep them from getting through. We might as well bleed them as best we can. See that you do so."

"Yes, sir," Hollux said.

"Tride," Merritt said. "I will take the north side and the west. I want you on the other two sides. Take Teevus here with you. Keep an eye out for trouble. Send for reserves should you need them."

"Yes, sir," Tride said.

"Stiger." Merritt turned to him.

"Sir?"

"You are our reserve. Tride and I will send for reinforcement should we need it. However, I expect you to look for trouble and dispatch men as you see fit. Take the initiative, son."

Stiger nodded his understanding.

"With the exception of the gate," Merritt said, "should the other sides of the fort come under direct assault, we shall conserve our short spears. Use as few as possible in ranged attacks. It is the enemy's second and possibly third attempt at forcing the walls that will prove most serious. Understand me?"

There were nods all around.

"Gentlemen," Merritt said, "we have to hold the wall. There is nothing more important. The Third should be here at the earliest this evening. I expect you to set an example for your men to follow. Show them why we are their betters and why we lead. Are there any questions?"

There were none.

"See to your duty, then," Merritt said stiffly.

The officers broke up. Instead of returning to his men, Stiger elected to remain at the wall to watch. Standing in full view of the enemy, he did his best to keep from cringing every time a ball came whistling in. Just to be safe, he made a point of watching for them as they were launched and sailed through the air. Even so, he moved about frequently to keep from being targeted. He noticed the eyes of fearful auxiliaries who were crouching down behind the barricade track him as he moved by.

After a time, Eli left their original spot and joined him. The elf was carrying a short bow, with a quiver full of arrows slung over his left shoulder. Stiger offered a nod as another ball whistled in. It impacted the wall a few feet to his left, and he felt the vibration through his boots.

"Have you been through this before?" Stiger asked Eli.

"Trapped in a fort, hopelessly outnumbered, and surrounded by an enemy army with no relief in sight?"

Stiger gave another nod.

"I have seen much over the years," Eli said, "but this is a first for me. It will be something to tell tales about, eh?"

"I wish we could silence that artillery," Stiger said with some frustration.

"What do you have in mind?" Eli glanced out into the field.

Stiger had not expected the question. He felt his brows draw together as he gazed out over the machines. It was an interesting question, but one he thought academic. With the enemy massing around the fort and preparing for a direct assault, there would be no way to get at the enemy's artillery. Any attempt would be spotted the moment they left the fort. Besides, any assault force would have to cross the two bridgeless trenches. By the time a team could clear both, the enemy would easily be able to counter such a move, and with superior numbers to boot.

Stiger pursed his lips. He could not see anything that could be done. He glanced over at Eli once more and chewed his lip as a thought occurred to him. He turned back to the artillery and almost chuckled. Eli gave him a curious look.

"A few days ago," Stiger explained, "my company assaulted an enemy encampment in the Cora'Tol Valley. During the attack, the fields of wheat around the encampment caught fire." Stiger gestured out into the field. "Those machines out there are sitting smack in the middle of a wheat field. If we could somehow set the wheat afire, the enemy would be compelled to either abandon or withdraw their machines."

"What an excellent idea!" Eli reached up and pulled an arrow from his quiver. The long shaft was bright green. The feathers on the end were brown and from a bird Stiger was unfamiliar with. Where there should have been a sharpened point, he saw only a rounded tip that was surprisingly thicker than the rest of the arrow.

Before Stiger could question the elf's intentions, Eli's hand brushed the end. The tip of the arrow exploded into flame, which hissed and smoked menacingly. Astonished, Stiger simply stood and watched as the elf calmly nocked his bow. Eli drew the string taut, as if he had not a concern in the world, and then released.

Trailing a line of bluish-gray smoke, the arrow arced up high into the air and landed several feet from the nearest machine. Having followed the missile's path, Stiger almost missed Eli firing a second arrow and then a third in rapid succession. Each time, the elf simply touched the end of each arrow. Obligingly, they burst into flames. Eli shot a fourth missile before lowering his bow and making a show of admiring his work.

Out in the field, where Eli's arrows had landed amidst the wheat, thick smoke rapidly billowed upward. A few heart-beats later, flames could be seen licking their way amongst the wheat as the fire hungrily spread.

"How did you manage that?" Stiger asked, nearly agog.

"Magic," Eli said with a closed-mouth grin. "High Born magic."

"Really?" Stiger had seen small trinkets and lanterns that were true magic. Curiosities more than anything else, these were generally owned by the wealthy as mere status symbols with little use. Stiger had never seen actual magic in use for a practical purpose. Wizards, being the only ones capable of making magical items, were few and cared little for mortal affairs.

"I'll never tell." Eli winked.

"Can you shoot more like that?" Stiger asked.

"Sadly, those were the only special arrows like them that I had," Eli admitted with a slight shrug. "Truthfully, I've been saving them. It seemed like a good time to see how well they worked."

"Fire!" someone along the wall shouted.

Auxiliaries who had been sheltering behind the barricade popped their heads up over the wall for a look.

Great clouds of smoke were rising upward from around the enemy's artillery. The flames were rapidly spreading. The crews of three of the machines ran for cover, almost as if the flames were chasing them. The crew of the fourth machine worked desperately as they prepared to tow it out of danger. A team of horses was run up. Men set about hitching it up, even as flames started hungrily on the other end of the machine. Stiger wondered if they would be successful at saving it as they pulled away, part of the catapult on fire.

He swept his gaze beyond the artillery. Unfortunately, the fields that bordered the fort had been devoted to other crops and appeared to have already been harvested. There was little chance they would burn. They'd been lucky the enemy had set up their artillery amongst the wheat.

"Did you do that?" Merritt had come up. He was looking to Eli for confirmation.

"It was his idea," Eli said, pointing at Stiger. "You can blame him. I only executed his plan."

"Good show," Merritt said, patting the elf on the shoulder as he looked out at the burning machines. "I should've thought of that myself."

A horn from the enemy sounded, one long, steady note that seemed to go on and on before finally falling silent.

"Here they come," came a shout from off to the right.

A large mass of men was moving forward toward the first trench. From the wagons they pulled large bundles of sticks, which they hauled forward and then threw into the trench to act as a makeshift bridge. Others laid planks across. Similar bridges were being built by the enemy at several points along the trench. In a shockingly short time, the first trench was bridged in several places. The shouts of alarm coming from the other side of the fort told Stiger that a similar thing was happening there too.

Those creating makeshift bridges crossed and moved on to the second trench.

"Had we more bowmen," Merritt said, "I would make that a very costly endeavor."

Three heavy infantry companies were arranged neatly in long blocks, their standards fluttering in the breeze. They waited for the work to be completed, having lined themselves up behind the budding makeshift bridges. A shout came from the other side of the fort, calling for the prefect.

"I best go see to that," Merritt said. "Stiger, I believe it's time for you to get with your men. I am sure you will be called upon soon enough to reinforce the walls."

"Yes, sir," Stiger said. "Um, a question, sir."

Merritt nodded.

"I am curious, sir," Stiger said, a thought occurring to him. He realized that he was more than a little curious now that he got around to asking it. "I'd like to know, why is this place called Fort Covenant?"

"Stiger, I've been here ten years," Merritt said. "In all that time, no one has been able to tell me beyond the fact this fort was built over the remains of an older one of the same name. If you ever find out, I'd like to know too."

"Yes, sir," Stiger said.

Merritt left them, running down the slope of the rampart and making his way across the parade ground to the other side of the fort.

Stiger turned his gaze out into the burning field. The flames had thoroughly overtaken one machine and it burned fiercely. Two others were on fire. The fourth had been pulled to safety. It was still on fire, but men were busily shoveling dirt onto the flames. Stiger glanced over at Eli. "What are those magic arrows of yours called?"

"I don't think there is an exact translation in the Common Tongue. However, it comes close to roughly *burning glory*."

"That's fitting," Stiger said. He took one last look out at the field before he started working his way down into the fort. Stiger sensed Eli following. With the threat of the enemy artillery removed, the auxiliaries stood boldly in view, grimly prepared to receive the coming assault. It was a little thing, but at the same time, Stiger understood that Eli's work with his bow for the defenders was a big thing morale-wise.

CHAPTER EIGHTEEN

"How goes it up there, sir?" Tiro asked as Stiger made his way around the keep to where his men were sheltering from the artillery. "We've not heard any shot come in for a good bit."

"Eli's work, I'm afraid," Stiger said. "Three of the four machines are out of action and the fourth is burning, thanks to his magic fire arrows."

"Magic?" Tiro asked of Eli. "I've never seen you do magic before."

"I thought you said how I moved through the forest was 'a magic unto itself'?"

Tiro grinned at Eli. "You never tire of patting yourself on the back, do you?"

"I don't see anyone else rushing to do it," Eli said.

"Well," Stiger said, "there is no reason to keep the men sheltering here. Let's move back to the parade ground."

"Aye, sir." Tiro saw to it that the company was moved out into the center of the parade ground. Once there, Stiger allowed the men to sit, relax, and rest.

"Tiro," Stiger said with a glance around at his men. They were tense, grim even, though there was some talking and light banter. It was clear they knew the stakes of what was to come. He could well imagine that several of his men had upturned stomachs, a result of nerves rather than the normal culprit—undercooked food. Many had likely skipped the morning meal for fear of embarrassing themselves with the runs or upchucking. "The men are to eat and drink. There is no telling when they may get the opportunity once the action starts."

"Yes, sir," Tiro said. "Best to have something in the belly to keep 'em going."

Stiger saw Varus emerge from a barracks building, Nera from the farm at his side helping him walk. His head was wrapped in a gray dressing and he appeared more than a little unsteady. It was clear that he had not yet fully recovered. The corporal wore his armor and carried his shield. It heartened Stiger to see him on his feet. He held an auxiliary helmet that he had obviously requisitioned under his free arm.

"Reporting for duty, sir," Varus said, shooing Nera away and attempting to stand on his own. He wavered precariously.

"You are not fit for duty," Stiger informed him, with a glance over at Tiro. The old sergeant nodded his agreement.

"Sir," Varus said, "I can fight."

"Varus." Tiro lowered his voice. "You'd be more a danger to yourself than to the enemy."

"Please, sir," Varus said quietly so that the men could not hear. "Shortly, you will need every man. We all know this. I can't sit this out. Don't ask me to do that."

"I'm not asking," Stiger said, hardening his voice, though he wanted nothing more than to give in to the man who had almost been killed as a result of his orders. "You will stand down, Corporal."

"Sir—"

"Varus, I have no doubts on your capabilities as a fighter. When you're fit, you may return to duty, not before," Stiger said. "I have made my decision and that is the end of it."

Varus's shoulders slumped, and the movement almost made him topple over. Nera stepped in close, supporting him.

"Make your way over to the keep and remain there," Stiger said. "The prefect has designated it as a hospital. Since you can't fight, perhaps you can at least help by caring for those who need it." Stiger softened his tone. "Can you do that for me? Some of our boys will end up there soon enough. Knowing that you're looking out for them will be a comfort."

"Aye, sir." Varus sounded a little better, but still disappointed. "I don't like it much, but I will do what I can."

"Very good," Stiger said. "I will check in on you later."

With Nera's assistance, he hobbled off toward keep.

Stiger's men were busy pretending they hadn't witnessed the scene when their officer glanced around. Tiro stepped nearer.

"It was the right proper thing to do, sir," Tiro said, voice a little gruffer than normal. "And I appreciate you sending him off. He is the best friend I have. Varus would end up dead if he took his place in the line, sir."

Stiger nodded, feeling terrible about denying Varus the opportunity to stand with the rest of the men and do his duty. But as Tiro had just affirmed, it had been the correct thing to do.

A muffled massed shout from the other side of gate went up. Stiger turned. He could see Hollux's bowmen gathered on the platform above and to either side of the gate. Hollux was pacing slowly behind his men, calling out encouragements as they leaned forward and repeatedly shot down over the wall at the enemy on the other side.

Inside the fort, there was a wall of freshly shoveled dirt behind the gate, which covered the only entrance into the fort completely. It was several feet thick.

"Won't do them bastards no good," Tiro said in amusement. "That's one large mound."

There was a deep thump. The earth behind the gate vibrated from the force of the blow of a battering ram. Muffled screams and shouts could be heard from the other side of the wall as the enemy struggled to overcome the gate while Hollux's bowmen rained death down from above.

An auxiliary atop the wall tilted a large smoking caldron over the side. From the bluish smoke, Stiger knew that the man was pouring heated oil onto the enemy. Another threw boiling water, while a third shoveled dirt that had been cooked over a fire. These were all horrific weapons that were designed to inflict terrible burns. Out of all of them, oil was possibly the wickedest of the bunch. Like water, it would run down and under a man's armor. Unlike water, it would eat away any skin it touched and was nearly impossible to get off.

Stiger fairly itched to go up and lend his support. But he had his orders, and Hollux appeared to have everything in hand. So he stayed with his men and waited, albeit a little impatiently.

"Sir," Tiro said, "might I make a suggestion?"

Stiger looked up at Tiro and raised his eyebrows expectantly. The sergeant cocked his head to one angle and stared at him meaningfully. Stiger realized he had been pacing, which was not good. The last thing he desired was to unsettle the men.

"Well, sir," Tiro said after a long moment, "standing here on the parade ground, we can see the northern wall well enough, a bit of the eastern, and very little of the western. Those buildings block almost all of the southern wall."

"Your point?"

"The roof of the keep will allow you to see in all directions, sir," Tiro said and gestured at the building. "I think you might wish to consider going up there."

The keep, only a few yards away, towered over all the other buildings. Crenulated battlements topped its roof. He itched to go up there and see what was going on, but at the same time, he felt the need to be on the ground with his men. He was torn.

"Sir." Tiro lowered his voice so that only the two of them could hear. "There are times when officers must lead and other times when they must fight. Right now, it's time to provide direction, and you won't be able to do that without knowing what's going on."

"All right," Stiger said. Tiro had made his point. "Let's move the men over to the keep again. I'll go up to the roof and holler down where reinforcements need to go. That sound good?"

"It does, sir," Tiro said, sounding extremely pleased. "It does indeed."

Stiger made his way over to the keep. The main door, heavily reinforced with metal supports, was open. Inside he found the surgeon with an assistant setting up shop in a large centralized room, the space that had been set aside for the fort's administrative work. There were a few closed doors off to the sides that led to what Stiger assumed were offices.

The surgeon had cleared off a table, upon which a number of wicked-looking surgical instruments lay. Several crates filled with bandages and dressings were by the table's side, as were a number of stopped jars, likely vinegar for cleaning out wounds. The surgeon and his assistant were in the process of moving a second stout table next to the first. Both men barely spared Stiger any notice as he made his way past them.

Stiger almost stumbled over Varus, who was sitting on the stairs that led upward to the second floor and looking quite miserable. Nera sat on the step above and was leaning her head against his. He made to get up, but Stiger waved him down and moved around the corporal and up the stairs.

Passing the second and third floors, Stiger followed the stairs all the way up to the top, where he came upon a trapdoor that lay open. Eli was already up there, having slipped away unnoticed some time before. He spared Stiger a glance before turning back to watch the action to the north.

The view from the top of the keep was impressive. Not unsurprisingly, Stiger found he could see in all directions. It was, however, more than a little shocking to see the enemy arrayed around the fort in orderly blocks, two blocks for each side, with the exception of the north side, where the enemy had lined up three. Stiger figured each block represented a single company of heavy infantry. The trenches directly to the front of each company had been filled in with bundles of sticks or bridged by a series of planks. These makeshift crossings should have been critical choke points or avenues of death for the assaulting companies. Instead, the enemy would cross all unopposed. The imperial fort was short on defenders and the tools with which to make such crossings hazardous.

The only action was around the gatehouse. Stiger moved to the north side, next to Eli. He gripped the top of the battlement, feeling the coarse wood on the palm of his hands. Hollux's bowmen fired missile after missile down into the enemy out of sight. Hot oil was repeatedly poured over, as was the boiling water and cooked sand. Stiger could only imagine the horror being wreaked upon those attempting to force the gate.

An enemy horn sounded to the east, cutting over the noise of the fighting. Stiger moved over to that side to see what was going on. He arrived as a mass shout went up from out in the field. The two enemy companies there broke formation and surged forward and over the bridged trench.

Apparently, traversing the bundles of sticks was trickier than it appeared. Several men lost their footing or were inadvertently knocked by their mates and tumbled over into the trench, where sharpened stakes lay waiting. Most, however, made it across. They brought with them numerous makeshift ladders.

Auxiliaries along the eastern wall raised their shields and prepared to receive the enemy. They wielded a mixture of short spears, swords, and large poles with metal hooks on the end that were designed to push ladders off and away from the wall. Pazzullo moved amongst them, which meant some of Hollux's light infantry were present. The sergeant's voice could be heard as he shouted to his men. Over the noise of the fight around the gate, Stiger could not make out the words.

Lieutenant Tride was there too, watching the enemy surge forward. Where the defenders should have been tossing their short spears, there was no ranged fire. The prefect had made his point and the spears were being conserved for later action.

Stiger's eyes followed the enemy as they began to cross the second trench. Then the lead elements disappeared from view, shielded by the wall. Another horn sounded to the west, then to the south. Stiger felt his gut clench. He resisted at first the urge to look in any other direction, as he wanted to see how it played out initially on the eastern wall.

It wasn't long before Stiger saw the tops of the first ladders land against the barricade. Auxiliaries struggled desperately to push ladders back, while others dropped large stones over the side on those below. Men armed with short spears sparingly threw them down at the enemy attempting to climb the ladders.

Stiger could hear shouts and screams. It was a loud and confused jumble of noise.

Having successfully scaled his ladder, the first enemy came into view at the top of the wall. The Rivan soldier made to climb over the barricade. He was immediately set upon and stabbed by an auxiliary and fell backwards and out of sight. Another immediately took his place.

Stiger tore his gaze from the east to look to the western wall and then the southern. He saw a similar scene there, with men struggling to keep the enemy from coming over the top. For a time, Stiger felt like his head was on a swivel as he scanned in each direction, waiting for the moment when the enemy would get over the wall and he would need to commit some of his reserve. He was surprised that it hadn't happened yet. The auxiliaries were holding.

Sucking in a breath, Stiger looked far to the south, squinting in the hope of seeing the first elements of the Third entering the valley. He let the breath out. All he saw was a thick column of enemy cavalry riding south and an infantry company following. Stiger wondered if it was Golves's company.

"It's nerve-racking, isn't it?"

Eli had come up next to him. Stiger looked over at the elf. Was he so transparent? Had the elf seen it so plainly?

"I should be down there," Stiger said, gesturing at the wall to the east. "Not up here."

"Our time to fight, and possibly die, shall come soon enough," Eli said. "However, our place for the moment is here."

Stiger held the elf's timeless gaze as he weighed the words. It irritated him that Eli was right.

"Your duty lies here. When it comes time for you to be on the wall fighting alongside your brothers, you will know."

Stiger gave a curt nod. Though he did not have to enjoy it, his duty was to watch and wait, for surely, as the elf said, his time would come. Stiger turned back to watching the walls and saw the first auxiliary fall. An enemy at the top of the ladder had stabbed out with a sword, striking him in the leg. The injured man lost his footing and rolled back down the rampart to the bottom, where he writhed in pain as his lifeblood poured out, staining the grass and dirt.

Another auxiliary took his place, jabbing a short spear at the enemy and taking him in the neck. The Rivan soldier clung to the ladder in a death grip. The auxiliary stabbed him again, this time in the face, and pushed hard. The force of the strike was so strong that it shoved both the man and the ladder backwards and off the wall, where they crashed out of sight.

The defenders were being pressed hard. Stiger estimated that at least twenty ladders had been thrown up along the eastern wall alone, the tops of which poked over the top of the barricade.

An enemy finally managed to climb over the barricade. He drew his sword and was immediately rushed by three auxiliaries, one of which had a short spear. The Rivan soldier slashed his sword in wide arcs in an attempt to ward them off. Desperate, he even managed to bat aside the spear, but a sword jabbed into his side. Stiger could hear his agonized scream as another sword stabbed him in the thigh. He finally went down when the spear pierced clean through his neck. While he was being cut down, another Rivan soldier had scaled the top, pulled his sword, and jabbed the auxiliary with the spear hard in the side.

Stiger had seen enough. He leaned over the building and looked down at Tiro.

"Tiro," Stiger hollered. The sergeant looked up. "Fifteen men to the eastern wall. The enemy has made it over the top. They are to plug the breach and then render what assistance they can."

"Fifteen men to the eastern wall, is that correct, sir?"

"Yes."

Stiger returned his attention to the east. Several of the Rivan had made it over at that point, but nowhere else. The auxiliaries desperately fought to contain the breach, Lieutenant Tride amongst them. Stiger's men, with shields held to the front, red cloaks brilliant under the morning sunlight, formed a line and began working their way up the rampart towards the enemy.

Satisfied that his men would be enough to seal the breach, Stiger turned his gaze to the south and saw that the auxiliaries there were holding. To the west was a similar scene, with Merritt personally directing the defenses. The northern wall was holding as well. Could he dare hope that they would withstand this assault?

Motion out of the corner of his vision drew his gaze. Eli, who was facing the eastern side, had removed his bow from his back and nocked an arrow. In the blink of an eye, he let fly. Stiger saw the arrow neatly strike an enemy on top of the ladder. The man had been about to clamber over at a spot to the left of where Stiger's men had pushed forward. The arrow took the man right through the throat. He fell backward into space. Another appeared almost instantly. Eli loosed again, striking this man as well. Clinging to the ladder with an arrow sticking out of his chest, he was pulled back and off the ladder by the next man coming up beneath him. This man made to clamber over, but another bolt from Eli hammered him as well. With a bloodcurdling scream, he dropped from sight. Eli struck the next man, and the next after that.

Stiger had heard of elven skill, but had never truly believed it until now.

"Send more men to the eastern wall," Eli said tersely as he loosed another arrow. This one was aimed at a different spot, where several of the enemy had made it over.

Stiger called down to Tiro. The sergeant sent another twenty men on their way.

Stiger returned to studying the situation. The fifteen men he had first dispatched had made their way up the rampart and sealed the original breach. They had thrown the ladder back off the wall. These men then began moving along the wall, assisting the auxiliaries who were hard-pressed.

Eli lowered his bow, dispassionately scanning the action. He had perhaps three arrows left in his quiver. Stiger saw his additional reinforcements moving at the double, making their way up to the rampart, further reinforcing the beleaguered auxiliaries. It seemed to make the difference as his men spread along the wall. Satisfied that the eastern side was under control, Stiger turned his attention elsewhere, sweeping each side of the fort for trouble.

Lieutenant Tride had moved on to the south and was battling bravely alongside his men, helping to force ladders back off the wall. Teevus was there too. Stiger saw the lieutenant from Fort Ida block a blow with his shield before using it to hammer the enemy in the face and knock him off his ladder.

It was an awful struggle, and ugly to watch. The fight seemed to go on and on without letup.

Abruptly, an enemy horn blew a series of blasts. It was repeated and taken up by other horns, each one sounding the same call. The din of the fighting along the walls slackened and then ceased altogether.

The enemy began drawing away from the walls of the fort, streaming back toward their jumping-off points. Many of the defenders cheered at their apparent success, while others slumped to the ground in exhaustion. The wounded who were capable dragged themselves down the rampart or walked toward the keep. It was a pitiful sight.

"Tiro," Stiger called down, "help with the wounded and get them to the surgeon."

"Aye, sir," Tiro called back up and set about dispersing the remainder of the company.

Stiger turned back to studying the enemy that surrounded the fort. By his estimation, nine companies had partaken in the assault. He did the math in his head and thought it amounted to no more than eighteen hundred men. As he looked upon the enemy's camp, he knew without a doubt they had greater than twenty thousand out there. By counting standards, Stiger was able to determine that twelve fresh companies had moved out of the encampment, marching in neat formations as they worked their way around the fort.

With a sinking feeling, he understood the first assault had only been probing in nature. The second assault was meant to swamp the walls, as a wave washing over a child's sandcastle at the beach.

"They mean to overwhelm us with this next assault," Stiger said to Eli.

"It looks that way," Eli said. "Let us hope they don't bring more ladders."

"I'm going to find the prefect," Stiger said and made his way down the stairs. The main level of the keep was already filled with wounded and awash with blood and the cries of the injured. He saw Nera and Varus caring for those they could and the surgeon hard at work with his assistant.

Stiger paid them no mind, moving out onto the parade ground. He went in search of the prefect and found him above the gate with Hollux, looking down on the remains of the enemy's assault. Both men were silent as Stiger came up.

The small area before the gate was filled with bodies. Some had fallen one atop another until they were several deep. Bodies lay heaped atop or sprawled next to the ram, which was crude and had been made from a single tree trunk. Evidence of the accuracy of Hollux's bowmen was readily apparent. The smell of burned flesh and oil hung heavily on the air. Stiger guessed there were at least one hundred of the enemy, maybe even as many as one hundred fifty, dead, dying, or injured before the gate.

"We murdered them here," Hollux said woodenly. "I never imagined such slaughter."

"Sir," Stiger said to the prefect, who was spattered with blood, mute evidence as to how involved he had been. The prefect turned a hard gaze upon Stiger. "The enemy is moving up at least another twelve companies."

"You mean they are finally getting serious?" Prefect Merritt asked with a grim chuckle. "That did not take them long."

Stiger was impressed with the prefect's demeanor. He had not even flinched when given the bad news. Here was a leader of men, Stiger thought, his respect growing for the older officer.

"This wasn't serious?" Hollux gestured at the carnage below.

"They only came in with nine companies," Stiger told him. "Once these fresh companies are in position, I expect we will really be tested."

"How did the other sides fare?" Merritt asked. "Do you know if Tride made it?"

"The eastern wall was breached," Stiger said. "I was forced to dispatch men to contain it. The other sides held well enough and the lieutenant seemed to acquit himself quite well, sir."

Merritt gave a nod to that, then lifted his gaze from the bodies below. He looked out beyond the two defensive trenches. The formations that had just taken part in the assault were busily reorganizing themselves. They were also tending to their injured, at least those fortunate enough to be capable of walking out under their own power. Beyond the companies that were slowly reorganizing, the fresh formations were still in the process of moving into position. He studied them for a protracted time. Stiger said nothing and waited.

"I'd say we have at least an hour, perhaps a little more, until they are in position." Merritt glanced down at the ram. "I don't believe they will try the gate again. It is time to redeploy our bowmen to the other walls. Hollux, I would like you to leave five men here and disperse the rest of your shooters around the fort."

"Yes, sir."

"For this next fight, hold nothing back," Merritt said. "Send plenty of arrows with them."

"I will," Hollux said.

"I am also going to order the remainder of the short spears be dispersed," Merritt said to Stiger. "It is time we use everything we have."

"I agree, sir," Stiger said, though he personally doubted that it would be enough to hold the enemy off. From Hollux's look, he understood the gravity of their position as well.

"Sir," Hollux said, "if you will excuse me, I will see to the disposition of my men."

Merritt nodded and Hollux left them.

"I saw you on top of the keep," the prefect said. "It is a good position. I want you up there again. Dispatch men where you feel the need, and then, when all of the reserves are committed, join the fight yourself."

"Yes, sir." He began to step away.

"Stiger." Prefect Merritt stopped him. "Though I served on the other side during the civil war, it is an honor to fight with you, as I once fought with your father."

"Thank you, sir," Stiger said, with mixed feelings at the prefect's sentiments. "I'm honored to fight alongside you as well."

"Take care, son," Merritt said.

With that, Stiger stepped away to find Tiro and his men, determined to do his duty to the end.

CHAPTER NINETEEN

The assault was thunderous. It was as if more than a thousand voices were shouting, screaming, and crying out in unison, which, Stiger supposed, they were. Add to that the clash of swords and the clatter of shields being battered, and it was riotously loud.

Stiger moved from side to side, watching the struggle along each wall. It was desperate, hard, and brutal. The fighting had been going on for more than an hour as the enemy attempted to force the walls for a second time. They had sent more men, but fortunately no additional scaling ladders. Nevertheless, the assault was intense. Stiger got the sense these men attempting the walls were of better quality than those of the first attack. He had been forced to dispatch almost all of his men, including Tiro, to help plug breaches.

Even so, the defenders were managing to hold the walls of the fort by a bare thread.

Stiger's reserve now consisted of only five men. They waited for his call. When it came time to deploy them, there would be no more help available. Stiger knew he would be going with them.

The twang of a bow drew Stiger's attention. Eli had brought several bundles of arrows with him to the keep's roof. The elf had been firing nearly nonstop since the assault had begun. For each shot, he hit his mark with deadly accuracy. Stiger had seen Eli miss only one shot, and that was because the target had unexpectedly tripped and fallen. Eli reached down to the last bundle of arrows and, one-handed, untied the coarse string that bound them.

Stiger turned his gaze to the south. An ugly plume of smoke climbed high into the sky where the town had been. With mounting frustration, he scanned for the Third but saw nothing of their relief. All that was in view was a column of enemy cavalry leisurely returning from the town they had undoubtedly sacked.

Stiger's frustration with their position gave over to a sinking feeling. It was now abundantly clear. General Treim would not arrive in time.

Stiger kicked the wall. From what he was seeing, the tide could not be held back for much longer. The defenders were not only being worn down, but also steadily whittled away. Stiger's hand strayed to the hilt of his sword. He closed his eyes and offered up a silent prayer to the High Father. He made sure to commend his spirit into the great god's keeping.

"So be it," he growled to himself, accepting what fate had dished out. He trusted in his god.

Stiger opened his eyes. It was time.

He studied the four walls and decided the western side of the fort needed the most help. The enemy had gotten up over the wall, and a large breach was forming around one ladder. Tiro and a handful of his legionaries struggled on one side of the breach, Lieutenant Tride and a number of auxiliaries on the other. They pushed back against the growing bulge, attempting to contain the breach.

The enemy struggled just as fiercely to widen their gain. A sergeant clambered over the barricade. He began guiding men fresh over the wall and into the fight, while at the same time exhorting those climbing up to hurry.

Stiger saw one of his own fall and roll down the inside of the rampart like a discarded child's doll. Stiger could not see who it was, but the sight tore at his heart. When the man came to a stop, the legionary's red cape was wrapped around him like a burial shroud.

"I'm going to the western wall," he said to Eli, anger roiling through him.

"I will be along shortly," Eli said, even as he loosed another arrow at the enemy along the southern wall. The enemy soldier dropped as if the life had simply been plucked out of him.

"Don't wait too long," Stiger said, "or you may just miss the fun."

"I wouldn't dream of missing it." Eli flashed him an open-mouthed grin before reaching down to grab another arrow from the open bundle at his feet.

Stiger took a last look to the south, hoping to see something, anything.

With a shake of his head, he made his way through the trapdoor and then down the stairs. The makeshift hospital was packed. The rooms on the second floor, offices, and personal quarters for the tribune had been opened and were overflowing with wounded men. Blood streaked the floor. It had landed in drops and splashes before being tracked across the wooden boards. The injured sat on the stairs, the floor, or wherever they could find the space, waiting for their turns to be seen by the overworked surgeon and his assistant.

Stiger passed several who were slowly bleeding out, their pale features a testament to the blood they'd lost. Stiger paused at the foot of the stairs, surveying the grisly scene on the first floor. Men had been slashed and stabbed. Some had lost hands, fingers, and even arms.

One man was missing a chunk from his forearm. Bone and mangled muscle were in plain view. He cradled his ruined arm, rocking back and forth and moaning softly to himself for his mother.

Stiger rubbed his jaw as he took it all in. This was the face of war. Those who dreamed of battlefields and glorious charges never cared to imagine it.

On a table, the surgeon's mate held a patient down while the surgeon stitched up a leg wound. The injured auxiliary screamed in torment as the work was completed. The surgeon paid the protests of his patient no mind but continued his work with single-minded efficiency.

Varus and Nera moved around, doing what they could for the wounded—wrapping and bandaging wounds, attempting to staunch blood flows. Two of the walking wounded were doing the same.

Stiger made his way over to Varus. He found he had to be careful of his footing, as blood slicked the wood-planked floor.

"Varus," Stiger said, laying a hand on the man's shoulder armor.

Varus turned dulled eyes upon him. Realizing who it was, his gaze sharpened and he straightened. "How's it going out there, sir?"

"Not good," Stiger said and glanced quickly around. It seemed all eyes were on him, with those nearest listening intently. It was time for plain talk, and these men deserved the truth. "I want you to organize the walking wounded and prepare to defend the keep."

"It's that bad, sir?" Varus asked.

"The enemy will shortly overcome the walls."

The corporal's eyes blinked at that, but he nodded his understanding just the same. Concern washed over Varus's face. "Where are you going, sir?"

"I am taking the last of the reserves to the western wall to do what I can," Stiger said and then cleared his throat. He pointed at the heavily reinforced door. "You must hold the door for as long as possible before sealing it. When the end comes, the survivors will need sanctuary. Keep it open for as long as you can."

"You can count on us to hold the keep for you, sir," Varus said loudly, glancing around. "Isn't that so, boys?"

There was a chorus of agreement. Several of the injured stood.

"When the time comes," Stiger said, "seal the door, even if I'm not here. Hold out for as long as you can. The Third may yet come."

"I will hold the door until you return, sir."

"I know you will," Stiger said, "but close it just the same when the time comes. Understand?"

Varus, looking miserable, gave a curt nod.

"Good luck, Varus," Stiger said. He had the nagging feeling he would never see the corporal again. Worse, Stiger thought he read the same in Varus's eyes.

"Take care, sir." Varus drew himself unsteadily into a position of attention. He saluted. Stiger returned the salute and held the corporal's gaze a prolonged moment, then made for the door.

Stepping outside, the noise of the fight crashed home once again. It was nearly overwhelming in its intensity, but the struggle on the walls did not capture his attention.

Stiger's eyes fell upon the dead just beyond the keep's doorway. Bodies had been carried from the interior of the keep and piled up like firewood. The sight made Stiger ill.

The feeling became worse as he recognized one of his men, Erbus, laid out on one of the piles. The legionary's eyes were open in a death stare, gazing up at the sky. Stiger moved over and gently closed them. He rested his hand upon the man's forehead.

"High Father, kindly take this brave soldier into your care," Stiger said. "He is in your hands now."

"Ah, Stiger, I see you have finally come down from your perch. That's very brave of you."

Stiger turned to his left. Tribune Declin was calmly pulling on a pair of leather gloves as he eyed Stiger. He wore his kit, which included his helmet and expensively engraved chest plate. He wore both arm and leg leather greaves that had been embossed and etched with silver. The polished chest plate shone brilliantly under the late afternoon sun. A breeze stirred the tribune's fine red cloak. His shield leaned against another small pile of dead men.

Stiger felt nothing but disgust for the tribune. Had the man not sent his other cohort to its death, they might have had a chance to hold the fort. Instead, Declin had effectively signed all of their death warrants.

"You are a disgrace," Stiger said bitterly.

"That's right," Declin said in a conversational tone. It was almost as if the fight around them were not happening. "Even after you told me of your orders for his arrest, I made the mistake of listening to that traitor Aggar. I sent him unknowingly back to his masters as Lears's second in command. Worse, I allowed both Lears's and my hatred for your family to color my thinking."

The tribune reached down and picked up his shield. He drew his sword and glanced to the nearest wall, the north side. "I have dishonored myself and my family. So yes, I am a disgrace. Truth be told, I think I have always been one.

For my many sins, I go now to atone in the only way I can."
He looked back on Stiger and managed a smile. "My only
consolation is that you shall shortly follow me over to the
other side. I will see you there, traitor's son."

The tribune turned his back and started across the
parade ground. Anger burning white hot, Stiger watched
the man go.

"Sir," Asus said, drawing Stiger's attention. His five men
were standing just a few feet away, including Dergo, one of
the auxiliaries Stiger had rescued in the Cora'Tol Valley.
They looked unsettled.

"We need to help relieve the pressure on the western
wall and plug the breach," Stiger told them. He pointed to a
discarded legionary shield. "Hand me that, will you?"

Stiger pulled out his sword as Asus handed him the
shield. He took a moment to get a comfortable grip on the
shield before turning to his men.

"Let's go." Stiger led the way across the parade ground. The
closer they got to the rampart, the noisier it got. The enemy had
gotten over in good numbers. The breach had widened considerably, and the imperials were being steadily forced back.

Stiger led his men to just below the center of the breach.
The enemy had completely broken the defense here and
were attempting to clear the rampart so they could get more
men over at additional points.

To the left side of the breach, Lieutenant Tride fought
desperately alongside his men. To the right side, Tiro led
a mixed bag of auxiliaries and legionaries. As more of the
enemy clambered over the barricade, the pressure upon
both groups increased. There was almost a clear path right
up to where the enemy were coming over the wall. The sergeant who was directing the fight and sending men fresh
over the barricade had not spotted Stiger and his men yet.

"Listen up. We're gonna thrust right up there…" Stiger turned to address the men before pointing with his sword up toward the center. "…directly between the two fights, and we don't stop for anything until we reach the barricade. Once there, we push that ladder back over the side and keep any more of them bastards from getting over. We do that and our boys on either side should be able to fight their way to us. Fail at this and I am afraid the fort is lost." Stiger raked his eyes over his men. They were grim-faced, but appeared ready. "All right, fan out and form a line." Stiger stepped into the center spot. "Shields up. Advance!"

They started up the slope of the rampart. Stiger bashed his shield forward into the first man he came across, slamming him hard in the body and knocking him down. He stabbed downward, taking him in the belly, and then twisted the blade as he felt the tip strike bone. The man screamed, blood frothing his lips. Stiger stabbed down again and silenced him.

To either side, his men moved forward and engaged the next enemy soldier several feet up the slope of the rampart, efficiently cutting him down. Stiger stepped over the body of the man he had just killed and advanced up the slope. He caught up to the line as Asus on the right stabbed an enemy, who had been locked in individual combat with an auxiliary, in the ass. Badly wounded, the auxiliary slumped to the ground in relief as Asus finished the Rivan soldier off.

The fight to either side raged unabated. As they advanced up the rampart, Stiger found it surreal. As impossible as it seemed, the enemy seemed completely unaware of their presence. They were allowed to continue uncontested and almost completely unimpeded for a few more feet, until they made contact with those just coming over the wall. The enemy sergeant noticed them for the first time and called out a warning.

"Push 'em," Stiger shouted, charging up the last few feet. The sergeant and five others made ready, though from having climbed up with only swords at hand and no shields, the enemy were at a severe disadvantage.

The fight to either side, just feet away, was so loud it beat down heavily on Stiger's senses. He put it from his mind as he slammed his shield at a man wildly swinging a sword at him in panic. The sword clattered harmlessly off his shield. Stiger hammered forward again, slamming the man back into the sergeant. The sergeant fell, helmet connecting with the wooden barricade. Asus, to Stiger's immediate right, stuck an enemy and then knocked him aside as he went for the next one.

Stiger stabbed the man he had hit with his shield and then pushed him bodily aside. He fell and rolled down the rampart.

Stiger turned on the sergeant.

The sergeant had lost his sword. He leapt up and grabbed desperately for Stiger's shield. The move was so unexpected that the shield was almost wrenched away. Instinctively, Stiger jabbed out and struck the man's chainmail chest armor. The sergeant's breath whooshed out with a grunt. He released the shield before stumbling backwards over the man Asus had just taken down. Stiger pressed forward and stabbed the sergeant in the thigh, neatly taking him down.

Stiger stepped forward to finish the man, clearly an older veteran of some experience and not unlike Tiro. The enemy sergeant was on his back and helpless. He raised a hand and said something that Stiger took to be a "no." It did not matter; he was the enemy and could not be allowed to live.

As he drew back to strike, Stiger was struck a hard blow over his back that knocked him to the ground. Twisting as he fell, he saw an enemy raise his sword for a finishing strike, only to be struck in turn by a killing blow from a short sword that slid deeply into the armpit. Dergo threw the mortally wounded man to the ground before turning to face the next man.

Having lost his shield, Stiger scrambled to his feet and cast his eyes upon the sergeant. He too had gotten to his feet. Their eyes met. Before Stiger could make a move, the sergeant placed a hand upon the barricade and threw himself over the side.

Stunned, Stiger hesitated a couple of heartbeats. He shook off the shock and rushed up to barricade.

A few of those facing the stubborn defenders led by Tride or Tiro finally became aware of the threat to their rear. Stiger's men turned and dropped into combat stances and prepared to receive them.

Trusting the men to have his back, Stiger reached over the barricade and stabbed a man in the process of clambering over in the side of the neck. Silently, the enemy soldier tumbled back down the ladder, taking the next two men with him to the ground. Stiger glanced over the side and saw a mass of enemy below, waiting their turn to go up the ladders. He also saw the sergeant, stirring feebly as his own men stepped over him.

Several of the enemy behind rushed Stiger's men. He heard the clatter and clash of swords, shields, screams, and oaths. Someone bumped into his back. Stiger's men fought off the enemy attempting to fight their way back to the ladder and open the way again.

"Help me!" Stiger called to Asus, who had just dispatched an enemy. Stiger was struggling one-handed to push the ladder off the wall. Realizing he had only heartbeats before the next man clambered up, Stiger dropped his sword and took hold of the top of the ladder with both hands. He shoved with all his might, straining. Those below on the base resisted and worked to hold the ladder in place. Then Asus was there at his side.

Using his shield longways, Asus hooked it between the top rungs and pushed with Stiger. The ladder resisted a moment more, then toppled backwards to the ground and over those below.

"Nice work," Stiger said, picking up his sword.

"Thank—" A sword point exploded through Asus's throat, blood spattering Stiger in a terrible spray. Asus toppled to the ground, a Rivan officer standing over the dead legionary.

Impossibly, it was Crief. The lieutenant's eyes widened in recognition, then narrowed.

Stiger saw red.

Roaring his rage, he charged.

Crief wielded a long cavalry sword. The enemy officer swung downward, a vicious yet clumsy blow that Stiger blocked with ease. The two swords met in a ringing clang. Hand stinging from the impact, Stiger pushed Crief's sword away. As the other attempted to recover, Stiger drove a fist into Crief's jaw, snapping it back. Crief dropped his sword and stumbled back a couple of steps. Stiger was on him in a flash, driving his sword into Crief's exposed arm. Crief screamed as Stiger opened up the arm to the bone.

"I told you if I ever saw you again," Stiger said, "I would give you some steel. Where's your daddy now?"

Cradling his injured arm, Crief took another step back and glanced around for aid. There was none.

Stiger punched out again, this time aiming for the neck. Seeing the blade coming, Crief tried to duck back, but Stiger's attack was lightning fast. The sword went in just enough to nick the artery. Blood immediately fountained from the wound.

Crief staggered, hand gripping his ruined neck in a futile attempt to stop the flow. Blood began to run out of the enemy officer's mouth. He stood there in stunned shock, choking. A moment later, the life left his eyes and he crumpled to the grass.

Stiger stood staring at the body of his enemy. Crief had gotten no more than he deserved.

The sound of the fighting crashed home, jarring Stiger awake to his surroundings. Dergo was the only man Stiger had led in who was still standing, and he was locked in a one-on-one fight. Stiger jumped to his aid, distracting Dergo's opponent by landing a powerful blow along the man's chest armor. It was enough for Dergo to slip in a strike, which dropped his opponent.

"Behind you!" Dergo shouted.

Stiger turned as two Rivan soldiers attacked him, one swinging a slashing attack. Stiger blocked it, the two blades coming together with a powerful ringing. His fingers went numb and his hand started to tingle. Stiger held on tight to his sword and forced the blow aside.

A sword from the second attacker jabbed painfully into his side armor. Stiger took a step backward in an attempt to gain some space. Even as he did so, he blocked a strike from the first man. Their swords met again in a ringing clang that sent sparks flying into the air. Stiger flicked his gaze at the second man. He had started working his way around Stiger's side, only to have Dergo engage him.

Free now to face one opponent, Stiger stepped forward and punched out with his sword, even as he drew his dagger. The enemy soldier dodged Stiger's strike and then lunged. Stiger again forced the strike aside, stepped in close, and stabbed with his dagger into the side of the neck. Stiger's hand was immediately coated in warm wetness as the dagger went in deeply.

The Rivan soldier dropped his sword, sighed once, and fell to the ground, where he twitched his last.

Breathing heavily, Stiger looked around for Dergo and saw him tightly engaged. Stiger was about to step to his aid when motion from his left caught his attention. He looked and saw three Rivan soldiers several feet away and closing in. One pointed his sword at Stiger and said something to the others. Stiger could well imagine them relishing the idea of taking down an officer.

Stiger dropped his dagger. He reached down and picked up a discarded shield, never taking his eyes off the three as they carefully closed the distance and fanned out. Stiger brought the shield up.

The one who had initially spoken shouted and they leapt forward. Stiger took a step back and used his shield to block the first blow. He immediately pushed back, throwing his shoulder into it, and caught the man by surprise, sending him bodily backward to the ground. Before Stiger could fully face the other two, there was a flash of reflected light. Something glinted as it flew in front of Stiger's face. There was a meaty *thwack*. A dagger had taken one of his opponents squarely in the throat. Eyes impossibly wide, the man staggered like he was drunk before falling to his knees and then toppling over. Stiger caught a glimpse of Eli to his left and assumed it had been the elf's dagger, but there was no time to think on it. He focused his attention on the man before him.

Stiger's opponent attacked, forcing him to block with his shield where the sword hammered home. The strike was communicated painfully to his arm behind the shield.

Stiger jabbed out where he thought the other's leg was and felt the tip slide home, sinking in several inches. The Rivan soldier collapsed to a knee, crying out. Stiger's next thrust silenced his voice evermore.

Dergo had dispatched his man. In the process he lost his sword, which had been ripped from his grasp as his opponent tumbled down the rampart. Screaming madly, Dergo jumped on the man Stiger had first knocked down as he was attempting to stand. He pummeled the man in the face, hitting him again and again until he slumped back to the ground.

Stiger turned around, looking for the next threat, and saw Eli engaged with a Rivan soldier. The elf wielded two wicked-looking daggers that could almost have been described as short swords. Eli's opponent did not stand a chance. The elf sidestepped and danced aside, avoiding a strike before landing one of his own, nearly decapitating the man.

There was a shout from behind. Stiger turned and saw Tiro's bunch push forward, cutting down the last of the Rivan facing them. They surged around him and descended upon those still pressing Tride's group.

"That was a bold move, sir," Tiro said, coming up. The sergeant was breathing heavily as he looked over Stiger, who was also just as winded. "You saved the wall, sir."

Stiger glanced down at the body of the enemy officer he had killed. "I got Crief, but not before he killed Asus."

"I saw the bastard come over the wall," Tiro said and spat on the body. "I could not get at him. Shame about Asus. He was a good man."

"Crief should never have come back," Stiger said as the fighting around them died down somewhat. He felt a sense of satisfaction. The breach had been contained. The imperials still held the wall.

"Great gods," Tiro gasped, abruptly looking past Stiger. Stiger followed the sergeant's gaze to the east wall. The defenders had broken, with men throwing down their shields and running for their lives. The enemy was coming over the barricade at several points, and in large numbers.

He glanced around, gaze sweeping the western wall. With the breach contained, the enemy were still trying to overcome the defenders, but they were managing to hold. Stiger was surprised at how few defenders there were holding the wall. Bodies, both friend and foe, were seemingly everywhere.

"Sir." Knuckles bloody, Dergo pointed at the southern wall. The defenders were abandoning their positions as well, as were those to the north.

"It's over, sir," Tiro breathed, and in his tone Stiger heard defeat.

CHAPTER TWENTY

Stiger could not believe his eyes. With men running every which way, the scene before him was one of utter chaos. He was unsure what could be done.

"Whatever you plan on doing," Eli said, coming up beside him, "I suggest you do it quickly."

Stiger glanced at Eli.

"Unless it is giving up, of course," Eli said, with a sour expression. "I don't much care for that. You aren't the kind of man to surrender, are you?"

The elf's words were offensive and stung. His anger flared. Then it hit him. Eli's words had been intentionally barbed.

No, he would not give in. Stiger knew what he had to do.

"It's not over," Stiger growled at Eli and started moving down the rampart. "On me! Form on me!" Stiger waved his sword in the air and shouted for all he was worth. "Form on me! Hurry now."

Tiro shoved men toward Stiger while also taking up the call.

"Form on the lieutenant!"

Stiger picked up a shield as men from across the wall began to rally to him, at first coming in ones and twos and then a steady stream. Stiger glanced back at the wall where Asus's body lay, along with so many others. For just a moment, they had succeeded in holding the wall. But that small victory, purchased at such a high price, had been fleeting. Unhindered, the enemy were now freely climbing over the barricade.

"Form up!" Stiger roared as a few auxiliaries ran for the safety of the keep. One of the fugitives was Lieutenant Tride. He shot Stiger a guilt-filled look but continued on.

"Tiro, I want two ranks," Stiger ordered.

"You heard the lieutenant," Tiro shouted. "Two ranks, quickly."

Stiger estimated he had at least thirty men in his scratch formation. The enemy, having gained the wall, was thoroughly disorganized. He figured they would not likely challenge an organized formation, which was what he had just created. At least, they wouldn't until an officer or sergeant imposed some semblance of control. With the defense of the fort having collapsed, Stiger suspected the enemy's first impulse would be to loot.

His thinking was rapidly confirmed. Stiger was sickened, but also at the same time relieved, to see the Rivan soldiers who had made it over the barricade behind him begin looting the dead. It bought him the time he needed to act.

Stiger swept his gaze around the fort. Everywhere he looked, there was the enemy. They were looting, wildly running down the last few isolated auxiliaries, or locked in individual combat. One of the barracks to the left had caught fire and begun to burn fiercely. Yet amidst the chaos, Stiger's formation was a sea of ordered calm as the last men stepped into place.

Stiger glanced over at the keep. He saw Merritt, along with a handful standing before the entrance, struggling against a mob of the enemy. Stiger spotted Varus in the mix. Lieutenant Tride was almost to them when he was attacked from behind and brutally cut down. He had never seen his attacker, who set about looting the lieutenant's body. Stiger felt a mix of disgust and sadness. Had Tride's courage not fled, he would yet live.

"Your orders, sir?" Tiro sounded nervous. That unsettled Stiger more than a little. He had never known Tiro to be anything but steady.

"We're going to advance in good order to the keep," Stiger shouted at the mixed bag of auxiliaries and the handful of legionaries he had formed up. Stiger pointed with his sword. "The keep is safety, and that is where we're going! We're gonna murder the bastards. We're gonna kill each and every one we come across until we get to the keep. What are we going to do?"

"Kill," the handful of Stiger's legionaries in the scratch formation shouted. Without the auxiliaries adding their voices, it sounded pitiful.

"I can't hear you!"

"Kill!" they shouted in unison, the auxiliaries joining in. "Kill, kill, kill!"

"That's bloody better," Stiger roared at them. "Advaaance!"

The formation started forward.

"Tiro," Stiger said, "pull a couple of men to watch the formation's back. I don't want any of the enemy coming up on us from behind."

"Aye, sir," Tiro said as Stiger turned his attention back to the advance across the parade ground. Holding his shield forward, Stiger joined the end of the line, Eli at his side.

Merritt and the handful of fighters before the keep were hard-pressed. An enemy sergeant had appeared, leading an organized section of men against the defenders. The prefect was doing his best to hold the way open for as long as possible, but that window was fast closing.

Wounded were streaming in ones and twos through the keep's door. Stiger caught a glimpse of a limping Hollux being helped into the keep. Pazzullo was assisting his lieutenant.

Stiger saw Merritt glance his way and wave with his sword before turning back to his defense. Stiger considered ordering the formation to advance at the double, but decided against it. Had he been leading only his men from the Seventh, he could have trusted them to remain organized, but the majority of his formation was made up of auxiliaries Stiger did not know. So, he kept the pace what it was—slow and steady.

The distance closed—thirty yards, twenty, ten. With each step there seemed fewer and fewer defenders before the keep. Merritt and his men were in trouble. Then the prefect went down, stabbed clean through the leg. Varus stepped forward and stopped the killing blow with his sword before deftly flicking the blade around and jabbing the tip of his weapon into his opponent's arm. Unseen, a Rivan soldier punched his sword into Varus's side. The corporal shuddered from the force of the blow and then turned to face his attacker and stabbed back, taking the man in the throat.

"What are we going to do?" Stiger roared to his men.

"Kill, kill, kill!" The shout drowned out the fighting. Those pressing the handful of defenders just steps away turned in surprise at the formation's approach. Then Stiger's front rank made contact, hammering away with shields and jabbing with swords.

"Two inches of steel is all you need," Tiro called. "Just like you do with the whores, give 'em love with your two inches, boys!"

Stiger's line smashed into the enemy, cutting down six or seven, including the sergeant, before the rest turned and broke, running for their lives.

"Hold!" Stiger called. "Stay in line there." Exhausted and nearly spent, the men didn't need much encouragement and responded.

"Dress yourself on your neighbor," Tiro roared. "Straighten out that line or so help me I will put you on a charge."

The formation quickly became ordered.

"Wheel right!" Stiger brought his formation around and stopped it with the shield wall facing outward and their backs to the door of the keep.

"Tiro." Stiger turned to him. "Use the second rank. Get what wounded you can into the keep. Hurry."

"Yes, sir," Tiro said.

Stiger scanned around the parade ground. The enemy had completely overrun the fort, but they were still terribly disorganized. Looting was clearly more important than overcoming the last of the defenders. The Rivan soldiers wanted nothing to do with the organized formation standing before the keep. They gave Stiger and his men a wide berth while they searched for plunder.

Satisfied they were out of immediate danger, Stiger went in search of the prefect. He found him lying on the ground, an auxiliary at his side. The prefect's cloak had been used as a tourniquet on his leg.

"Nice move, Stiger." Sweat beaded Merritt's brow. "Get the men into the keep, will you?"

"I will, sir."

"Don't give up the keep," Merritt said. "I may shortly pass out. Hold unto the last. We hold out for as long as possible. I will not end up a prisoner again. Understand me?"

"Yes, sir," Stiger said and then, with the auxiliary's assistance, helped the prefect up and onto his feet. Supported by his man, Merritt made his way through the door and into the keep.

Stiger was about to order the men inside when he spied Varus lying on the ground a few feet from where the prefect had been. Tiro was at the corporal's side. He looked up, grief etched upon his face as Stiger approached. The sergeant puffed out his cheeks and slowly shook his head.

Stiger stood there in shock, looking down on the corporal's body. There was a deep gash high on Varus's left thigh. Blood stained the ground around him.

"Sir." Tiro stood. He gripped Stiger's shoulder and shook him. "Sir… it is time we bring the boys into the keep."

"But Varus," Stiger said. He did not want to leave the corporal behind. He could not.

"He's dead, sir." Tiro's voice was gruff and filled with raw emotion. "It is time to look after the living."

Stiger pulled his gaze from Varus to his formation. "Get the men inside."

Tiro snapped out an order as Stiger turned back to Varus. The men quickly made their way into the keep, leaving Stiger and Tiro alone.

"Come on, sir, Varus would want us to live." Tiro took hold of Stiger's arm and guided him into the keep.

Several men slammed the door closed and dropped its heavy locking bar in place once they were inside. Stiger saw Nera tending to a wounded man. She looked up and scanned the room, clearly looking for Varus. When she could not find him, her eyes fell on Tiro. The old veteran held her gaze and then looked uncomfortably away.

Shoulders shaking, she covered her face with a bloody rag and sank down onto the floor.

"We need to brace the door," Pazzullo said. The sergeant's armor was covered with blood, and judging from the cuts on his face and arm, some of it was even his own. "They are bound to try to force it."

Stiger gave a nod and glanced around the crowded make-shift hospital ward. Everyone, including the wounded, was looking in his direction. Hollux, with a pasty pallor, sat in a corner holding his leg with his hand. Blood bubbled up from between his fingers. Lieutenant Teevus was also there. He too had been wounded and looked to be unconscious. Stiger's eyes fell upon Lears for a moment, who glared back while cradling his broken arm. Prefect Merritt was nowhere to be seen. Stiger figured he had been carried upstairs. Not counting any of the walking wounded, Stiger had perhaps thirty men, twelve of whom were from his company. It shocked him that was all he had left. At the same time, it reignited his anger.

"Right," Stiger said, thinking fast and pushing his grief for Varus aside. The men needed his strength. "This is what we are going to do. I want the wounded moved upstairs. Break up the tables and chairs to help brace the door. Any man who can carry a sword and shield is to remain here. Pazzullo and Tiro, find anything that is heavy. Select six men and have them start hauling whatever they find up to the roof. When the enemy tries to force the door, we can give them a nice surprise. Also, see if there is any lamp oil… We can throw it over and ignite it." Stiger sucked in a breath. "The Third is on her way, boys. We need to hold for as long as possible." He swept his gaze around the room. It wasn't much, but he had given them a little hope. "Now, it won't take the bastards long to get organized, so we need to hurry. Are there any questions?"

There were none.

"Get to it."

The men set to work. Stiger made his way up the stairs for the roof and found Eli already up there. Stiger looked to the south. There was still no sign of the Third, only the column of smoke rising from the town.

The elf was looking to the north.

"They are getting ready to march." Eli pointed.

Stiger joined Eli and studied the enemy's encampment. Tents were being broken down. Several companies had already formed up. Stiger even saw the enemy's supply train being readied, with horses and mules being hitched to wagons.

"The enemy's general must not like wasting time," Stiger said. "They are marching even before they've taken the entire fort. I guess with all that we have left, they don't need much."

A horn sounded in the distance. The call repeated itself. Stiger felt himself frown. It sounded like a recall. There were a number of shouts from below out in the fort. Though Stiger could not understand the Rivan tongue, they sounded like orders being called by officers and sergeants.

The horn call sounded again. It was taken up by others nearer. The enemy began moving toward the walls. Stiger could not believe his eyes as they started climbing back over the barricade and descending the ladders, first in ones and twos and then lining up in large groups, waiting their turn.

"What's going on?" Stiger asked, confused.

"They are leaving," Eli said plainly.

"Stiger! Is that you up there?"

Stiger glanced off to the north wall and saw an enemy officer standing next to a ladder with men lined up and climbing back over. It was Golves.

"Do you have any arrows left?" Stiger said.

"No," Eli said with regret. "I've used them all."

"That's a shame," Stiger said, before shouting back. "What do you want?"

"I thought that was you," Golves replied. "You are a hard man to kill. I am so pleased to learn you survived."

"Crief didn't," Stiger said.

"His father gave him the chance to redeem his honor by storming the walls," Golves called back and then gave a shrug. "I never much liked him anyway."

Stiger actually chuckled.

"Where are you going?" Stiger called back at him when the last man in line climbed over.

Golves shook his finger at Stiger. "If I told you that, it might spoil the surprise." He clambered onto the ladder. He stopped at the top before climbing down over the other side. "I hope we shall meet again. I have found you a worthy and honorable opponent."

Golves started down the ladder and was lost from sight.

"What's going on?" Tiro asked, coming up behind them.

"They are leaving," Stiger said, elated and at a loss as to why.

"But where is the Third?" Tiro looked to the south.

"I don't know," Stiger admitted.

"I bet they do," Eli said, gesturing out at the enemy encampment.

Stiger had to agree with the elf. They continued to watch as the first enemy companies to march stepped onto the road and turned north, climbing the hill toward the forest. Company after company followed, until a few hours later none remained behind, leaving only the remnants of the enemy camp. Below them, the enemy had also left behind their dead and injured.

"I guess this means we held the fort," Tiro finally said, breaking the long silence. Dusk had begun to fall.

"We did," Stiger said, somewhat numbly, thinking on Varus, Asus, Erbus, and so many others.

"Sir," Tiro said, "permission to go out and find our wounded."

Feeling thoroughly worn out, Stiger gave a weary nod.

EPILOGUE

"This is awful," Stiger said, coughing. "It's really bad."

Tiro took the pipe back from Stiger and sucked in deeply. He let out a long stream of smoke and gave a contented sigh.

"That's right good stuff, sir," Tiro said. "Good old Eastern tobacco that is."

"How can you enjoy that?" Stiger continued to cough, thoroughly mystified. "It burns. Why would anyone want to smoke that?"

"It takes a little getting used to is all," Tiro said, "but trust me, sir, there's nothing better to help you relax after a good day."

Tiro and Stiger were sitting on a couple of stools outside of one of the barracks. A third stool lay off to the side. Pazzullo had left them a few minutes before.

It was the day after the enemy's attempt on the fort and dusk was fast approaching. There still had been no word or sign of the Third.

Stiger had put his men who could walk to gathering up the dead. He had worked alongside them all throughout the day. There were thirty-two ambulatory men in the whole of the fort. Of these, only thirteen were from his company. Another five had survived from the Seventh, but these men had been severely injured. They would be lucky to return to service. These unfortunates would end up discharged, living on the dole back in the capital and whatever they had accumulated in their pensions.

The company was no more than a shell of what she had been just weeks before. The heart of the Seventh had been thoroughly ripped out. The loss of so many hurt, almost as if it were a physical wound. Stiger understood the company he had come to love would never be the same.

He wasn't even so sure if he would ever be the same. So many good men had perished here that Stiger felt a part of him would forever remain in this place. As he gazed around the parade ground, he was confident Fort Covenant would haunt his dreams for years to come.

"How do you get used to it?" Stiger looked at Tiro.

"Well, sir," Tiro said, "you just smoke some more and keep on smoking. You kind of get used to it."

"That's not what I meant," Stiger said, turning his gaze to the ground.

Tiro was silent a moment. "You never do."

"That's what I was afraid of," Stiger said.

Tiro handed the pipe back to Stiger, who was hesitant to take another puff. He gave in and sucked in a deep breath, almost immediately breaking into an uncontrollable fit of coughing.

"Just a little," Tiro said with a laugh. "At first, you only want to pull in a little. Then, when you're more used to it, you take a bit more."

Stiger cast a doubtful glance at his sergeant and was about to reply when a shout rang out.

"Riders approaching, sir," a sentry called from the top of the keep. "To the east."

Stiger sprang up from his stool, placed the pipe upon it, and started for the eastern wall. Tiro followed a few steps behind. They climbed the rampart and up to the barricade. When they got there, they could see a troop of cavalry riding for the fort, perhaps three hundred yards off. It took Stiger a moment to identify them as legionary cavalry.

"They are ours," Stiger said to Tiro.

"Better for us, then," Tiro said. "I'd hate to have to hold this fort again."

"A stiff wind would overwhelm us," Stiger said.

"Perhaps even a gentle breeze, sir," Tiro said.

"Open the gate," Stiger called and moved over to the platform above the gatehouse to wait for the new arrivals.

Though Stiger had the men busy throughout the day working to organize the dead for funeral pyres, the truth was there were simply too many corpses. They hadn't even begun to start on those of the enemy outside the fort. Heck, it'd taken half a day alone just to shovel the mound of dirt away from the gate that Merritt had ordered thrown up.

The troop rode up to the outer trench and dismounted. Stiger recognized Carbo, but also saw Colonel Aetius. The colonel surveyed the grisly scene before the fort's main gate—the enemy's ram, the bodies, and flocks of birds feasting on the dead. After a few moments, he and Carbo dismounted, handed their reins over, and carefully made their way across the enemy's makeshift bridges.

Stiger met the colonel down at the gate. He offered a salute, which the colonel returned. There was a hard look to Aetius's eyes as he gazed around the interior of the fort.

"Good to see that you made it," the colonel finally said. "It looks like things were somewhat involved here, eh?"

"Yes, sir, just a little," Stiger said. "A lot of good boys were lost holding the fort, and had the enemy not left when they did, we all would have died."

"Did Prefect Merritt survive?"

"Yes, sir, he did," Stiger said. "The prefect was wounded. The surgeon feels that he will recover as long as infection does not set in."

"Well," Aetius said, "that's a good thing. We need more men like him."

"He's a fighter, sir," Stiger said.

"What about Tribune Declin?" Aetius asked. "I understand he remained after he was relieved."

"He went down fighting, sir," Stiger said.

"No more can be asked of a gentleman," Aetius said, "even one in disgrace."

Stiger did not reply to that.

"I would see the prefect," Aetius said, "and hear his report."

"Sergeant," Stiger said, "would you escort the colonel?"

"This way, sir," Tiro said and left Carbo with Stiger.

Carbo silently surveyed the neatly stacked bodies within the fort. Stiger had ordered that the enemy be separated from their own. He glanced back over at Stiger.

"It appears that you held on by only the skin of your teeth," Carbo said.

Stiger simply nodded, but did not trust himself to say anything.

"You did a good thing here," Carbo said, patting Stiger on the shoulder. "It made all the difference."

"What do you mean?"

"Around twenty miles from Fort Covenant, the general made a hard decision," Carbo admitted. "He took the opportunity to maneuver around and get behind the enemy instead of coming straight here."

"That explains why we were not relieved," Stiger said, feeling somewhat betrayed by a man he respected. "We were left here to die then?"

"Oh, no," Carbo said. "The general used Fort Covenant as a diversion. By holding and forcing the enemy to attack, you fixed their attention. It allowed the general to take much of his infantry and swing around behind the enemy a few miles south of Cora'Tol. There was this old road that was on none of the maps. Our enemy didn't even know. It was no more than a path really and mostly overgrown, but it was enough. Can you believe it? A local farmer told the general of it and he took the man at his word. It was a brilliant move and forced the enemy to react."

"Well," Stiger said, still feeling wretched, "I guess it worked. The enemy pulled out something quick."

"There was a battle yesterday in the forest a few miles to the north of here. The general chose good ground around Fort Ida and dug in. The enemy couldn't even deploy their entire army as they came up to our lines. With the trees and us sitting right smack across the road, there just wasn't enough room. Still, they came on confident-like and determined. There was some hard fighting and a few desperate moments." Carbo sucked in a breath. "But in the end, we gave them a real drubbing before they called it quits." Carbo slapped his thigh. "Several thousand prisoners were taken, mostly camp followers and such. Unfortunately, much of their infantry escaped into the forest." Carbo smiled and then chuckled. "They abandoned their baggage and supply train. I bet there will be more than a few hungry bellies tonight."

Stiger thought about what Carbo had said. He had been so sure that the Third was coming to their relief. It was a shock to learn that the general had had other plans. Stiger had unwittingly played his part and contributed to the victory, but that made him still feel somewhat unhappy. He had brought his men to this place and spent their lives in what he had thought was the right thing to do. In a way, the general had done the same. It was certainly something to think on.

"Without your warning," Carbo continued, "we would have never known until it was too late that the enemy was flanking the legions. You made this all possible."

Stiger glanced down to his new boots. He had taken them from Lieutenant Crief. They were made of good-quality material and surprisingly fit quite well. He had also stripped Declin's fine cloak from the tribune's corpse. Neither man now needed them. Stiger's meager funds would not take the hit he had thought they would. He looked back up at Carbo and felt a lightening of his mood.

"Do you smoke?"

"I do," Carbo admitted. "I hope you have some tobacco, for we're so far from civilization that sadly I've long since run out."

"The thing is," Stiger said, "we liberated a bag of what Tiro calls really good stuff."

Stiger and Carbo stood as the colonel walked up to them. Carbo held the pipe. They had been sitting for some time while the colonel spoke with the prefect. Nightfall was coming on quickly.

Aetius waved the two of them back down. The colonel pulled up the third stool and motioned for Carbo to hand over the pipe. Aetius took a long pull and exhaled a stream of smoke.

"This is quite good. I wonder, have you been holding out on us?" Aetius asked Stiger and gestured at the bag of tobacco by his feet.

"No, sir," Stiger said. "Compliments of our enemy, I'm afraid. We liberated it after destroying an enemy company in the Cora'Tol Valley."

"You took out an entire company with eighty-some men?" Colonel Aetius raised an eyebrow and took another pull on the pipe.

"I did, sir," Stiger said.

"I don't have time now," Aetius said, "but when you return to the legion, I want to hear your report on everything that's happened."

"Yes, sir," Stiger said.

"Our enemy has good taste," Aetius said, taking another pull before handing the pipe back to Carbo.

"As I am new to smoking," Stiger said, "I will take your word for it."

"Prefect Merritt thinks highly of you," Aetius said. "He told me you are a fine officer, but I already knew that, Captain, didn't I?"

Stiger felt uncomfortable with the praise, but then what the colonel said registered. "Captain? Sir, I am a lieutenant, acting captain only."

"No, you are now a captain, and it's well-deserved," Aetius said, leaning forward and offering his hand. The colonel grinned. "Congratulations, Captain Stiger."

Still a little shocked, Stiger took the colonel's hand and shook. "Thank you, sir."

"I'm giving you the Twelfth," Aetius said. "They lost their commanding officer in the action this morning."

"What of the Seventh?" Stiger asked, suddenly alarmed. "I don't want to lose them, sir."

"There's not much left of your company, is there?" Aetius asked plainly.

"No, sir," Stiger said. "I've got thirteen effectives, not to mention the two that I sent to the Third with word of the enemy's intentions."

"Your company is essentially ineffective," Aetius said. "It will be disbanded until such time as the legion receives fresh recruits. Your men will be broken up and sent to other companies as replacements. We have a great need for them right now."

"Sir," Stiger said, "I don't want to see the Seventh broken up."

The colonel frowned. "Stiger, there are not enough men available to bring the Seventh back up to strength or anywhere even close to it. The Twelfth is in need of a new commanding officer and you are it. I can't think of a better man for the job."

"I'd like to request that the Seventh remain active, sir," Stiger said. "I've become attached to my men and the company, sir."

Aetius held Stiger's gaze for a long moment. Stiger knew he was going to refuse his request, but then the colonel gave a shrug and stood. Carbo and Stiger got to their feet also.

"Very well," Aetius said. "After this, I think you and your boys have more than earned it. I will see that you get a few men to fill out your ranks so that the Seventh is the equivalent of a light company. I should think that sufficient."

"Thank you, sir," Stiger said, elated that he could keep his company, his home. More important, he would have the chance to rebuild her.

"With the ranger attached to your command," Aetius said, "I am sure that we will find work for you and your boys."

"Ranger? What ranger?"

"The elf," Aetius said. "Seems you impressed him, Captain. That is not an easy thing to do. He requested permission to join your company as an official volunteer from the elven nations. Since the elves have wanted no part of the empire for some time, I have of course accepted his offer of service. Make sure that no harm comes to him, will you?"

Stiger did not know what to say to that.

"An auxiliary cohort is being dispatched to man this fort," Aetius continued. "They will arrive sometime tomorrow morning." Aetius paused and glanced at the dead. "See to your fallen. I expect you to march sometime tomorrow. Meet the legion in the Cora'Tol Valley. I will see you there in two days' time."

"Yes, sir," Stiger said. "I will be there, sir."

Aetius motioned for Carbo to join him and started to turn away.

"Sir, one more request please?" Stiger asked.

"Captain," Aetius said, "I think perhaps you've pushed your luck a bit, don't you?"

"If I'm to command my company," Stiger said, "I need an executive officer."

"We will find you one," Aetius assured him.

"There's one available, sir," Stiger said. "I know he's injured, but I would like to request Lieutenant Hollux for my second."

"I met Hollux when I spoke to the prefect," Aetius said. "An auxiliary and an older man to boot. Why would you want someone like that?"

"I've come to know him, sir. I believe he has the makings of a fine officer," Stiger said. "He's just never gotten a fair shake."

"Very well, he is your headache," Aetius said. "Oh, and take as many of the auxiliaries that are left from Prefect Merritt's command that you like. You see, I've already spoken to the prefect about that. I knew you would want to remain with the Seventh, Stiger. Kindly see that you are at Cora'Tol in two days, will you?"

"I will be there, sir," Stiger said, with a growing smile that the colonel matched.

With that, the colonel strode off for the gate. Carbo delayed a moment.

"Congratulations." Carbo offered his hand, which Stiger took. "See you in Cora'Tol, old man. Make sure you bring some of that good tobacco."

Carbo hurried after the colonel, leaving Stiger alone. He sat down on the stool and took a small puff from the pipe. It didn't burn as much as it had a while before, but he was careful how much he sucked in. He sat there for a time, reflecting upon the battle and his promotion.

Eli strode from the keep and over to him. The elf sat down on a stool and kicked his feet up on the one the colonel had used. Eli seemed rather pleased with himself.

Stiger offered his pipe to Eli, who shook his head. "That stuff will kill you, you know."

"Why do you want to stay with me?" Stiger asked, getting right to the point.

"I miss Tiro's company."

"Seriously?"

Eli let out a sigh. "It's fairly obvious."

The elf fell silent, his unblinking eyes resting heavily upon Stiger.

"Are you planning on telling me?" Stiger leaned forward on his stool, returning the elf's gaze with a flinty one of his own. "Because it's not that obvious to me. What game are you playing at?"

"There's no game," Eli said. "I am here simply as a volunteer. However, it has come to my attention that interesting things seem to happen around you. I like interesting. It makes life … fun."

"Is that so?" Stiger wasn't buying it. He leaned back, contemplating the elf, and took another small pull and puff on his pipe.

"If you'd lived all the years that I have," Eli said with a mischievous grin, "then I think you'd understand why interesting is so important."

Stiger chuckled. An elven ranger wanted to tag along with him. It was an offer that he would be foolish to decline. Even if he did, he wasn't sure that the colonel would allow him to do so, especially considering the state of relations with the elven nations.

"Whatever the reason," Stiger said with a sigh of surrender, "I know Tiro will be happy you're coming with us. And truth be told, my company's a little light at the moment."

Eli seemed pleased with that response. For a while neither said anything, just watched as the shadows of night began to spread across the fort.

"I believe you wanted to know why this place was called Fort Covenant?" Eli asked. "It was here, many long years past, where your empire and my people formed our Covenant, the alliance between our nations and yours."

Stiger had not known that.

"Elves and men once served alongside each other for a higher purpose," Eli continued. "That higher purpose has been forgotten by your people. Worse, in recent years, our alliance has known some difficulty." Eli paused to shoo away a fly. "In a way, I think it fitting that I join your company in this hallowed place, even if I had to spring you from jail just to do it."

Stiger took another pull on the pipe and this time didn't notice the burn. They fell into another long silence.

"Well," Stiger said, looking at the elf after a time, "Tiro thinks we both attract trouble, so I'm sure things are going to be interesting."

The End

Stiger and Eli's adventures will continue...

ADDITIONAL NOTE FROM THE AUTHOR

I hope you enjoyed *Fort Covenant: Tales of the Seventh Part Two* and continue to read my books. Stiger and Eli's adventures will continue. On that, I promise!

A positive review would be awesome and greatly appreciated, as it affords me the opportunity to focus more time and energy on my writing and helps to persuade others to read my work. I read each and every review.

Don't forget to sign up to my newsletter on the website to get the latest news.

Thank you for reading and your patronage,

Marc Alan Edelheit

Coming Soon

Stiger and Eli's Adventures Continue in:

Chronicles of an Imperial Legionary Officer
Book 4
The Tiger's Time

Also Coming Soon

Tales of the Seventh
Part Three
Eli
(A Prequel Novel)

Care to be notified when the next book is released
and receive updates from the author?
Join the newsletter mailing list at Marc's website:

http://www.MAEnovels.com
(Check out the forum)
Facebook: Marc Edelheit Author
Twitter: @MarcEdelheit